GREAT LIVES
Painting

Painting

GREAT
LIVES

Shirley Glubok

Charles Scribner's Sons · New York
Maxwell Macmillan Canada · Toronto
Maxwell Macmillan International
New York · Oxford · Singapore · Sydney

Charles Scribner's Sons Books for Young Readers
Macmillan Publishing Company · 866 Third Avenue · New York, NY 10022

Maxwell Macmillan Canada, Inc.
1200 Eglinton Avenue East, Suite 200 · Don Mills, Ontario M3C 3N1

Macmillan Publishing Company is part of the
Maxwell Communication Group of Companies.

First edition   10 9 8 7 6 5 4 3 2 1
Printed in the United States of America
Cover illustration copyright © 1994 by Stephen Marchesi. All rights reserved.

Library of Congress Cataloging-in-Publication Data
Glubok, Shirley.
    Painting / Shirley Glubok. — 1st ed.
        p.   cm. — (Great lives)   Includes bibliographical references and index.
    Summary: A collection of biographical sketches of European and American painters from
the late fifteenth to the twentieth centuries.
    ISBN 0–684–19052–4
1. Painters—Biography—Juvenile literature.
[1. Artists.   2. Art appreciation.]
I. Title.   II. Series: Great lives (Charles Scribner's Sons)
ND36.G68 1994   759—dc20   [B]   93–8319

My heartfelt thanks to these distinguished scholars for reading sections of my manuscript:

Kevin J. Avery, Assistant Curator, American Paintings and Sculpture, The Metropolitan Museum of Art; Elizabeth Easton, Assistant Curator, Department of European Painting and Sculpture, The Brooklyn Museum; Susan Gallasi; William H. Gerdts, Professor of Art History, The Graduate School and University Center of the City University of New York; Howard S. Greenfeld; Mary-Anne Martin, director of Mary-Anne Martin Fine Art; Richard McLanathan; Lisa Messenger, Assistant Curator, Department of Twentieth Century Art, The Metropolitan Museum of Art; Alan E. Salz, director, Didier Aaron Inc.; Patricia Sands; Charles Scribner III; Daniel Schulman, Assistant Curator, Department of Paintings, Art Institute of Chicago; Suzanne L. Stratton, Director of Fine Arts and Cultural Programs, The Spanish Institute; and Nadia Tscherny, director, Bartow-Pell Mansion Museum.

Contents

Foreword

It was not an easy task to choose a mere twenty-three artists out of all the talented and creative people who have enriched the world through their genius. From the beginning I knew this had to be a purely personal choice. Although the book is about those who were essentially painters, Albrecht Dürer is better known for his prints and drawings and Pablo Picasso is acknowledged as one of the most inventive sculptors of the twentieth century. Michelangelo, perhaps the most famous sculptor of all time, is even better known today for his wall paintings in the Sistine Chapel at the Vatican in Rome. As for Leonardo da Vinci, his creativity revealed itself in scientific experiments as well as in art.

And how does one set time and geographical limits? What about the superb Chinese and Japanese artists or the ancient Greeks and Romans? I quickly saw that it would be necessary to limit my choices to Europeans and Americans. Great painters flourished in the ancient world and in medieval times, but facts about their lives are usually obscure and their work may be inaccessible to young readers. I chose people whose life events were recorded and whose work could be clearly understood. However little is known about the life of Jan Vermeer, his paintings tell such interesting stories that I felt he must be included. In contrast, an abundance of information is available on Vincent van Gogh, Pablo Picasso, and James McNeill Whistler. They wrote hundreds of letters, were often interviewed and photographed, or cooperated with biographers during their own lifetimes.

It is interesting to note that almost all of the artists included were appreciated while they still lived. Most could afford a comfortable life-style; some even grew rich from the sale of their works. An exception, Vincent van Gogh, died unappreciated and penniless.

All people are the products of their times. The places where they live and events they experience shape their lives. In order to tell the story of an artist, I tried to describe his or her geographical and historical setting. Moreover, I attempted to give a picture of the artist's character, personality, and appearance.

Some of the artists included in this book were admirable, others disagreeable, and some had life-styles that were not socially acceptable. Each was interesting, however, and each made a major contribution to the mainstream of art.

Mary Cassatt

1844–1926   An American who settled in Paris and exhibited with the French Impressionists

Mary Stevenson Cassatt spent most of her life in Europe among the outstanding French artists of her day, but always remained an American. She was born in Allegheny City (now part of Pittsburgh), Pennsylvania, on May 22, 1844. Her father, Robert Simpson Cassatt, was a banker of French descent and her mother, Katherine Johnston, was a cultured woman of French and Scottish ancestry. They had five children: Lydia, Alexander, Robert, Mary, and Gardner.

In 1851, when Mary was seven, the family sailed to Europe so that young Robert, who was ill, could get the best medical attention. They stayed for a time in Paris and then went to Germany, first to Heidelberg and then to Darmstadt, so that Alexander could attend an excellent technical school. Cassatt learned to speak French and German fluently and developed a taste for living abroad. Robert died in 1855. Before leaving Europe, the family went to France where the works of Eugène Delacroix and Jean-August-Dominique Ingres were being exhibited at the Universal Exposition, a World's Fair in Paris, and works by Gustave Courbet and other popular artists could be seen in museums and galleries. Then they returned to Pennsylvania, dividing their time between a house in Philadelphia and a country home.

Philadelphia had been the art center of America since colonial days. As soon as Cassatt was sixteen she enrolled in the Pennsylvania Academy of the Fine Arts. She took classes in drawing, sketching from live models and plaster

1

casts of ancient statues. She also heard lectures on human anatomy by professors from the medical school of the University of Pennsylvania and attended art exhibitions in the city. An ambitious student, she worked steadily and with great concentration. Thomas Eakins, one of America's greatest painters, was a student at the same time. Cassatt studied painting on her own and enjoyed going to concerts, plays, and art galleries with her classmates. The Civil War broke out while she was at the Pennsylvania Academy, and it was feared that Philadelphia would be invaded by the Confederates. However, the Union Army stopped them at Gettysburg.

Cassatt dreamed of becoming a successful professional painter. She felt that art was not learned in schools but by studying great pictures. There were no outstanding collections of European paintings by the old masters in America. She wanted to return to Europe to get the best professional training and to show her own works at important exhibitions. Her mother did not object to the idea, but her father did. Young ladies of her social class were expected to stay at home. They might take watercolor classes and paint flowers as a hobby, but they were not supposed to go off by themselves and become professional artists. Cassatt, who was

fiercely independent and determined, won out.

In May 1866, shortly after the end of the Civil War, she sailed for Paris with her mother, who had arranged for her to stay on with friends. Thomas Eakins came to Paris shortly afterward and enrolled in the École des Beaux-Arts, France's national school of fine arts. Since only men were admitted, Cassatt could not attend. She took special women's art classes and private lessons from Jean-Léon Gérôme, a famous teacher at the École des Beaux-Arts, who emphasized the importance of drawing. She also copied the paintings of old masters in the Musée du Louvre, the national museum of France.

Eliza Haldeman, a classmate from the Pennsylvania Academy, was also in Paris. In 1867 she and Cassatt traveled together, going first to Courances and then to Ecouen and Villiers-le-Bel, small art colonies outside Paris that were popular with foreign students. There Cassatt enjoyed life in the countryside with other young Americans and met French artists who chose peasants and childhood scenes as their subjects. Their influence can be seen in her painting of a woman playing a mandolin, which was selected by a jury in 1868 to be shown at the Salon, the official art exhibition held each year in Paris. Cassatt was living in Paris in 1870 when France went to war with Prussia. Mary's parents wanted her to come home. She went to Rome for the summer, then sailed for America.

Mary lived with her parents in Philadelphia and rented a studio. The Cassatt family soon moved to Hollidaysburg, Pennsylvania, where Alexander held an important position with the Pennsylvania Railroad, a company that was rapidly expanding its tracks westward. For Cassatt it was a difficult time. She was unable to get models, and art supplies were limited. Moreover, there were no great pictures to look at. She was further distressed because her paintings were being exhibited at a New York gallery but not selling well. She took some of her works to Chicago in 1871, where they were displayed in a shop window, but unfortunately they were destroyed in the tragic Chicago Fire that burned down the entire city.

At the end of the Franco-Prussian War, Cassatt was eager to return to Europe, but her father insisted that she now pay her own expenses. To earn the money she obtained a commission from the bishop of Pittsburgh to make copies of paintings by the north Italian painter Antonio Correggio in Parma, Italy. She set sail in December 1871 with fellow artist Emily Sartain, daughter of a well-known engraver. In Parma Cassatt copied the Correggios and studied other old masters. She made friends with Carlo Raimondi, director of the Academy of Art, who taught her the fundamentals of printmaking. She painted colorful scenes of local people. *Two Women Throwing Flowers During Carnival* was a great success when it was exhibited at the Academy.

In the fall she went to Spain to enjoy the beautiful scenery and fine museums and to study the works of the Spanish masters Diego de Velázquez and Bartolomé Murillo. In Seville she painted solid, realistic images of bullfighters. This was the only time in her career that she included male subjects in her works, except for little boys and portraits of her father and brothers. *Torero and Young Girl* was accepted for exhibition at the 1873 Paris Salon. Cassatt returned to France, where her mother was visiting, to see it on view. The following year it was shown in New York at the National Academy of Design but did not receive much attention.

In the summer of 1873 Cassatt took a trip to Holland and Belgium with her mother and settled in Antwerp, where Peter Paul Rubens had lived. His works influenced her to make her own paintings more colorful. After a visit to America in 1875, she settled down in Paris where she could set up a studio, associate with other American painters, and pursue a successful career in art.

She lived in elegance, surrounding herself with fine things. Slender and erect, with small feet, Cassatt always looked ladylike, wearing stylish long dresses and hats trimmed with feathers and lace. She was witty, with natural charm, yet strong-willed and stubborn in her views, always expressing her frank opinion. She could be generous, although she was hardheaded about money and would try to acquire paintings from her artist friends at the lowest possible prices. For recreation she read French literature and attended the theater and horse races.

The artists Cassatt admired the most were the avant-garde realists Gustave Courbet and Edouard Manet, not the established artists who painted dark-toned pictures of grand subjects. Manet stressed the importance of light and urged young artists to paint outdoors. For her own subjects, Cassatt chose well-dressed women, reading, sewing, or drinking tea in their comfortable homes. Although these works, painted in pure colors and with broad brush strokes, appear to be spontaneous, Cassatt always made a series of sketches in order to develop her composition. Her pictures sold well and were usually accepted in the Salon, even though her style was often criticized.

A portrait by Cassatt in the Salon of 1874 was admired by Edgar Degas, who said, "There is someone who feels as I do." In turn, Cassatt praised Degas's work, which she first saw in a gallery window. "It changed my life," she said. "I saw art then as I wanted to see it."

Three years later she met Degas, who invited her to join his friends and exhibit her works independently of the official salon. The group, who called themselves Independents but became known as Impressionists, were dedicated to a new realism in which art reflected modern life. Their pictures were painted freely in bright colors.

Cassatt, like the Impressionists, painted outdoors in rich sunlight and was concerned with color and the way light fell upon an object. But her style, like Degas's, was more realistic than the Impressionists. Her lines and structures were firmer and the forms did not dissolve. Cassatt, who was the only American to exhibit with the Impressionists, was included in four of their exhibitions between 1879 and 1886. She later said, "At last I could work with absolute independence without considering the opinion of a jury."

Degas and Cassatt became good friends. No one knows if they were romantically involved because Cassatt made certain that their letters were destroyed. He guided her in her work, influencing her with his lively subject matter and the natural, relaxed poses of

Mary Cassatt painted this self-portrait in 1878 at the age of thirty-four. *The Metropolitan Museum of Art, Bequest of Edith H. Proskauer, 1975.*

Mary Cassatt's 1879 painting *At the Opera. Museum of Fine Arts, Boston. The Hayden Collection.*

his figures. Degas and Camille Pissarro asked Cassatt to produce a series of etchings for a journal they were trying to start, called *Le Jour et la Nuit*.

In 1877 Cassatt's parents and her ailing sister Lydia came to Paris to live with her. They all moved into a large apartment, where they led a gracious life. Cassatt rode horseback and attended theater and opera. When painting, she used members of her family in natural poses as her subjects. Lydia, until she died in 1882, served as her sister's model, posing for the masterpiece *The Cup of Tea*. Cassatt's dogs, Belgian griffons, sometimes appeared in her pictures. When her brother Alexander, by then the wealthy and powerful first vice president of the Pennsylvania Railroad, visited the family in France in 1880, his children posed for their artist-aunt.

Cassatt was a devoted daughter, nursing her mother through a serious illness and coping with her father as he grew quarrelsome with age. The men in her family lost a great deal of money in a financial crash in Paris in 1882, and the art market fell drastically. These setbacks distracted Cassatt from her work. The situation had improved by 1886, although her works did not sell well when they were shown in America. More frequently she chose the mother-child theme for which she became famous,

working in a bold and original style. The subjects were not always actual mothers with their own children, but were often unrelated models carefully chosen by the artist.

In 1890 Cassatt, Degas, and the painter Berthe Morisot attended a major exhibition of colorful Japanese wood-block prints depicting scenes of city life at the École des Beaux-Arts. Influenced by the prints, she adopted flat colors and strong outlines, arranged her compositions slightly off-center, and cut figures off unexpectedly at the edge. A series of ten color prints on a woman's daily life, reflecting her admiration for Japanese prints, were included in her first one-woman show in Paris in 1891, the year her father died. The same gallery again spotlighted Cassatt in 1893, this time including nearly one hundred paintings.

That year Cassatt completed a huge mural for the walls of the Woman's Building at the World's Columbian Exposition, the World's Fair in Chicago. The theme of the mural was modern women and their pursuit of knowledge, science, and the arts. Cassatt was uncooperative with the committee and her mural was not well received.

When her works were exhibited in 1895 at the Durand-Ruel Gallery in New York City, her first important one-woman show in America, she was

Mary Cassatt in 1912, photographed at Arles, France. *Frederick A. Sweet Papers, Archives of American Art, Smithsonian Institution.*

criticized for moving away from the Impressionist style.

In 1893 Cassatt bought a country house called Château de Beaufresne northwest of Paris. There she lovingly tended her garden, feeling pride in her one thousand roses. She continued to entertain at Beaufresne as well as in her Paris apartment. Among her friends were the painters Pierre-Auguste Renoir and Camille Pissarro. After her mother died in 1895, Cassatt was lonely.

When she was nearly sixty she wrote a friend that her life centered on art. "I work and that is the whole secret of anything like content with life, when everything else is gone."

Cassatt went back to America for the first time in more than twenty years in 1898, bringing a little dog with her. After visiting her brothers in Pennsylvania and friends in New England, she returned to France and continued to work on her mother-child theme, using pastel on paper in a plain and direct style. The mothers were simply dressed, stressing character rather than social status. Children from the village near her country home often posed as models.

In her later years Cassatt spent much of her time advising Americans on their art collections. In 1901 she traveled to Italy and Spain with her old friends Louisine and Henry Havemeyer, helping them collect Old Masters as well as modern paintings that would eventually end up in museums in the United States. She wanted the American public to enjoy great masterpieces.

In 1904 Cassatt was named a knight of the Legion of Honor by the French. The same year she took a trip to Chicago to be honored at the Art Institute. An article in a magazine called her "The Most Eminent of All Living American Painters." In 1914 the Pennsylvania Academy of the Fine Arts would award her a gold medal of honor.

Cassatt was again saddened when her brother Alexander died in 1906. In 1910 she joined her brother Gardner and his family on a trip to Egypt where they sailed up the Nile River. Gardner, falling ill during the rigorous expedition, was rushed back to Paris, where he later died.

Cassatt was devastated by the loss of her last remaining sibling. She was old and her eyesight was failing. She grew more and more bitter and expressed a passionate dislike for the new generation of painters such as Henri Matisse and Pablo Picasso. She felt that the people and their paintings were "dreadful."

With the outbreak of World War I, Cassatt's German housekeeper was deported and her chauffeur was drafted. Cassatt herself had to flee from her country home because it was in the war zone, only fifty miles from the battlefront. She went to Grasse in the south of France, and did not return until the war had ended. Meanwhile, the Knoedler Gallery in New York held an exhibition of her work in 1915 to raise money for the suffrage movement to give American women the right to vote. Cassatt supported the movement.

Following the war the elderly Cassatt went out for a drive every day in her 1906 Renault, driven by her chauffeur. When Degas died in 1917 she mourned the loss of her good friend. Cassatt lived on, nearly blind, until June 14, 1926, when she died at her country home at the age of eighty-two, having made a reputation as the most distinguished woman painter of her time. A picture of the artist, wearing a hat trimmed with feathers, is on a United States postage stamp.

Marc Chagall

1887–1985   Russian-Jewish painter-poet, who settled in France

Marc Chagall was born Moishe Segal in the Russian village of Vitebsk on July 7, 1887, when Russia was still under the rule of the czars. His childhood memories served as a theme for his painting throughout his lifetime. Vitebsk, on the Dvina River, was a town of small yellow or gray buildings bordered by wooden fences and dotted with white churches graced with domed towers. The population of Vitebsk was around fifty thousand, half of them Jews. At that time the Russian government required all Jewish people to live within special quarters in certain towns. The Jewish community in Vitebsk was Hasidic, a group devoted to a mystical interpretation of the Bible. Hasidim respect people of all faiths and try to do good work for others. They also respect animals and will not overload them with too heavy a burden.

The atmosphere in the Chagall home was deeply devout. Chagall's father, Zahar, was a shy, gentle man who worked for a dealer who sold herring. Chagall felt close to his father and deeply loved his mother, Feiga, a lively, sociable woman who ran a small grocery store. "Moishe" was the eldest of nine children, seven girls and two boys. Chagall's paternal grandfather had been a religious teacher; his mother's father was a butcher in nearby Lyozmo, where Chagall would spend his holidays. He loved the gentle beasts that were around him, especially the cows and horses, and he enjoyed riding in a horse-drawn cart to neighboring villages to bring back cattle for his grandfather's butcher shop. He had numerous aunts and uncles. One was a fiddler, who entertained the villagers with his violin and taught his nephew to play. Chagall loved music. Violinists often appear in his work.

As a little boy Chagall attended the *heder,* or Jewish elementary school, where he learned to read Hebrew, the language in which prayers are written. He studied biblical history and the Talmud, or Jewish law. At home the family spoke Yiddish, the international language used among Jews so they can understand each other worldwide.

When he was thirteen, Chagall went to a public school where lessons were taught in Russian. His favorite subjects were geometry—with its study of lines, triangles, and other shapes that he would later use in his art—and drawing, for which he already showed talent. He was always a dreamer. He liked to walk about in the town observing people and making drawings which were realistic in style. Chagall was slight, with light, curly hair, a large nose, wide, blue eyes, and pearly teeth shining between thin lips. When he spoke he stuttered slightly, the result of a terrible childhood fright when he was bitten by a mad dog. Even as an adult Chagall admitted that he still had bad dreams now and then.

After finishing school in 1906, he attended the only art school in Vitebsk, which was run by Yehuda Pen. Chagall knew he wanted to be a painter. He said that painting "seemed to me like a window through which I could have taken flight into another world." A career in art was unknown among the Jews of a small eastern European community. Drawing and painting were not practiced because it was considered sinful to depict the human form. According to the Second Commandment, "Thou shalt not make unto thee any graven images."

That winter Chagall received the special permit he needed as a Jew to go to Saint Petersburg, the czarist capital. He left his village with only twenty-seven rubles in his pocket. When he took the entrance examinations for one art school he failed, but then he was admitted to another, the school of the Imperial Society for the Protection of the Fine Arts. In order to stay in Saint Petersburg Chagall needed working papers, so he apprenticed himself to a sign painter. During this time he lived under miserable conditions, often going hungry, until a kindly patron took him into his home.

Every young Russian man was required to do military service for the czar, but Chagall's teacher, Nikolay Roerich, took a special interest in him, gave him a scholarship, and managed to keep him out of the army. While in

Saint Petersburg, the young artist met Russian intellectuals who had advanced ideas about art and literature and inspired him to write poetry. His poems were beautiful. His prose was also poetic, and there is a poetic quality to his painting.

Saint Petersburg had fine museums and churches where Chagall could study European art as well as paintings in the traditional Russian style. He looked at icons, small paintings on wood that were carried in Christian religious processions, and frescoes, which are painted on walls while the plaster is still wet. He watched Russian peasants going to market in their colorful costumes and developed an interest in folk art. Chagall absorbed everything he saw while developing his own original style using scenes of Jewish village life as his theme.

In 1908 the young painter enrolled in a private art school that was in tune with the modern trends that were popular in Paris. His teacher was Léon Bakst, who was involved in the theater and designed sets and costumes for Sergei Diaghilev's brilliant dance company, the Ballets Russes. One of the important new trends in Paris among poets and painters was the Symbolist movement in which symbols are used to stand for reality. Chagall used symbols in his pictures, but he refused to tell people what his paintings meant and objected when people tried to interpret them. At the time he was painting Jewish religious themes that were delicate, poetic, and fresh, always with a touch of fantasy. His figures often float in space or appear topsy-turvy. His choice of figures seems illogical, but they were actually carefully chosen. "Everyone can see them in his own way, interpret what he sees and how he sees it," said the artist.

During this period, Chagall returned to Vitebsk for visits, and in 1909 met and fell in love with Bella Rosenfeld, the attractive, generous, well-educated daughter of a wealthy jeweler. He also met Max Vinaver, a wealthy Saint Petersburg attorney who bought two paintings from him, the first he had ever sold, and encouraged the young artist in his work. After his teacher Bakst left Saint Petersburg in 1910 to join Diaghilev's dance company in Paris, Vinaver generously offered Chagall a monthly allowance so that he, too, could go to Paris.

Chagall found France to be a wonderful place, although he was homesick for Vitebsk and missed Bella. He decided to make France his adopted country. Paris gave him a new joy of life. He strolled happily through the streets, loving the light of the city that was so different from Russia. He also loved the freedom that as a Jew he

The Chagall family in a photograph taken sometime before 1910. The artist is second from the right, standing behind his grandmother. *The New York Public Library Picture Collection.*

could not enjoy in Russia. He attended art classes and visited galleries and museums, especially the Louvre, where he studied the Old Masters. He also spent a good deal of time with the painter Robert Delaunay and his Russian wife.

Paris was filled with excitement over the new art movements. The boldest of these was Cubism, a style in which naturalistic forms are broken up, reduced to geometric shapes, and reconstructed in a composition. Chagall was influenced by the Cubists. He was also attracted to the Fauvists, especially Henri Matisse, who painted in bright, intense colors arranged in balanced surface patterns. And he was affected by the strong, pure colors in paintings by Vincent van Gogh. Although he experimented with the new styles, Chagall continued to work in his own original way, painting from the private world of his mind and from childhood memories. Sometimes he used representational forms in combination with Cubist symbols. One of his best works from this period was *I and the Village*, in which he used diagonal and circular forms along with naturalistic figures in an unexpected arrangement.

In 1911 he exhibited at the Salon des Indépendents for the first time. Early the next year he moved into a modest studio in a building occupied by an international assortment of poets and artists. Among them were Amedeo Modigliani, an Italian, Fernan Léger, a Frenchman, and the Lithuanian Chaim Soutine. His closest friends were poets, including Blaise Cendrars, who spoke Russian, and Guillaume Apollinaire. Both men wrote poetry about Chagall's work.

The artist worked at night, by kerosene lamp. When he could not afford canvas on which to paint he used tablecloths, bed sheets, or even the back of his nightshirt. Although many of his pictures reflected his memories of Russia, he also painted simple fairy tales and biblical scenes. The critics in France at the time did not yet understand Chagall's work; they objected to the fact that it was not logical.

In June 1914 the editor of the German review *Der Sturm* arranged for Chagall's first one-man show. The artist went to Berlin for the opening of the exhibition. It was a huge success and established his fame. While in Berlin he met artists who were painting in the Expressionist manner, a new art that gave complete freedom to imagination and emotions.

On June 15 he went to visit his family in Russia. He intended to stay only a short time, but the First World War broke out, so the borders were closed, and he could not leave. In March 1915 twenty-five of his paintings were exhibited at the Art Salon of Moscow.

On July 25, 1915, Chagall married Bella, whose family, fearing the artist would not be able to make a living, did not altogether approve. After the wedding the newlyweds went to the country and stayed there until September. Like all able young Russian men, Chagall was eligible for military service. He managed to get a desk job in the Office of War Economy, which took him to Petrograd (the name for Saint Petersburg from 1914 until 1924). Forty-five of his works were shown at the Jack of Diamonds exhibition in Moscow that year. In the spring of 1916 a daughter was born to the young couple; they named her Ida.

Chagall loved the theater, an interest he shared with Bella who at one time had hoped to become an actress. In 1917 he designed the sets for two plays by the great nineteenth-century Russian author Nikolai Gogol. That was the year of the October Revolution that overthrew the government of Czar

A self-portrait of Marc Chagall in 1914. *Philadelphia Museum of Art. The Louis E. Stern Collection.*

Nicholas II and led to the establishment of the Soviet Union.

A new cultural policy was adopted by the Soviet government in the summer of 1918, and Chagall was appointed Commissar of Fine Arts for Vitebsk. One of his duties was to design celebrations. On the first anniversary of the Revolution he organized the sign and house painters of Vitebsk to decorate banners with green cows, and horses flying through the air in a style typical of his own work. Triumphal arches were erected and flags were flown on trolley cars and in shop windows. The workers marched in a parade through town carrying flags and torches. Afterward, officials said they did not understand the green cows and flying horses. They thought Chagall should have used a theme that would honor the new Communist party. Later that year an exhibition was held in the Winter Palace in Petrograd in which a special room was devoted to Chagall's work. The government bought twelve of his paintings.

Chagall organized an art school which opened in 1919. He served as director. Among the artists who taught there were El Lissitzky and Kazimir Malevich, who were Constructivists; they painted in a nonobjective style that reduced the subject to geometric forms. Chagall's style was not in tune with avant-garde abstract art. Early in 1920 a dispute erupted with Malevich which led to Chagall's resignation as director.

Now the artist moved to Moscow, where he again turned to theater design, creating stage sets and costumes for the new State Jewish Chamber Theater. He also decorated the walls of the theater with large murals, painted the ceiling, and designed the curtain. The theater's first production, which opened on New Year's Eve, 1921, was three plays by the Yiddish humorist Sholem Aleichem. Unfortunately Chagall's theater work brought him little money and his paintings were not selling, so he taught art in two colonies for war orphans on the outskirts of Moscow. The children loved him. In 1921 he began writing his autobiography, using notes he had been jotting down for a decade. He called it simply *My Life*.

Chagall's work was out of tune with the popular art that was realistic and served as socialist propaganda for Lenin, the Russian Communist leader. He was feeling restless. A friend, writing from Germany, asked him, "Are you alive? They claim you were killed in the war." The letter went on to say that his pictures were selling for high prices and ended with, "Come back; you're famous." In 1921 Chagall left Russia, taking his pictures with him. He went to Lithuania to exhibit his work and then

Chagall with his wife and daughter in his Paris studio in 1923. *The New York Public Library Picture Collection.*

to Berlin to find the pictures he had left behind for the 1914 exhibition. Bella and Ida, now six, joined him. On arriving he learned that all but three of his paintings had sold, but the money coming to him was almost worthless due to inflation.

In October he received an offer to publish his autobiography. To create illustrations for the book he took up etching, a method of printing by which a picture is drawn on a copper plate with a pointed instrument. Chagall made twenty etchings for the project,

but as it turned out, the book was not published until 1931 and then it was illustrated with drawings.

Chagall remained in Berlin with Bella and Ida until the autumn of 1923 when Ambroise Vollard, a publisher in Paris, asked him to illustrate books. The first book he illustrated was *Dead Souls* by Nikolai Gogol, whose plays he had designed scenery for in Moscow. The novel reflected rural life in Czarist Russia in a setting similar to that of Chagall's own youth.

On arriving in Paris in September,

the artist searched for the paintings he had left behind before the war, but they were gone, and there was no money to show for them. He proceeded to reproduce them, working from memory, because he liked to surround himself with his own paintings. Once again he felt at home in Paris. The critics had come to understand him, and he was popular socially, as he was a friendly, charming, and witty person with a lively manner.

A new art movement, called Surrealism, had taken hold. The Surrealists revolted against creating rational images and tried to break through their conscious thoughts in order to free their imaginations. Although Chagall drew upon his imagination and his dreams, mixing fantasy with realism to create paintings having unexpected, supernatural effects, he did not join their group. He was active, pursuing his own personal style. His first retrospective show was held in Paris in 1924, and his first exhibition in America took place two years later.

In 1926 Vollard asked Chagall to illustrate another book, this time the *Fables* of the French poet Jean de La Fontaine. The artist produced more than one hundred gouaches, pictures painted with colors that are ground in water and mixed with a preparation of gum. Many of the fables had animal subjects, which he dearly loved. The il-

lustrations were exhibited in Berlin in 1930; Chagall attended the opening.

The artist also produced a series of gouaches using the circus as his theme. He was fascinated by the circus, and often spent evenings there with Vollard. "It is a timeless dancing game where tears and smiles, the play of arms and legs take the form of great art," he said of the circus.

Chagall always liked being in the country and, while living in Paris, he vacationed with his family in all parts of France—Normandy, Brittany, the Pyrenees and the Riviera in the south of France, which he especially loved. He was inspired by the intense blue of the Mediterranean Sea, the vegetation, and the quality of light. He painted landscapes and compositions of the flowers that surrounded him in his garden and studio. His work from this period reflected his happiness. Eventually he would settle on the Riviera and live there until he died.

From the time he was a child Chagall had loved stories from the Bible. In 1930 Vollard commissioned him to create a series of etchings illustrating the Old Testament, although these, like the pictures for Gogol's *Dead Souls* and La Fontaine's *Fables*, were not published until after World War II. In the spring of 1931 Chagall and his family traveled to Palestine (now Israel) to study biblical history and to Egypt. The beauty of the Holy Land, the wonderful atmosphere, and the quality of light deeply impressed the artist and inspired him to paint a series of gouaches.

In 1932 Chagall designed scenery and costumes for the ballet and continued his travels outside of France. He visited Holland, where his work was exhibited, and studied the Dutch masters, especially Rembrandt, whose paintings he deeply admired. In 1933 he went to Spain where he was impressed with the work of El Greco. While in Vilna, Poland, a leading center of Jewish culture in 1935, he painted the interior of a synagogue and other religious pictures.

Chagall was upset by the anti-Semitism that was on the rise under Nazi influence. Later in 1935 his works were burned in Mannheim, Germany, on the orders of Joseph Goebbels, Adolf Hitler's minister of propaganda. In 1937 the Nazis ordered all of Chagall's works removed from German museums. That same year he became a French citizen.

Among the artist's more pleasant trips was one he took to Italy in the spring of 1937, where he enjoyed the atmosphere and studied works by Titian. In Paris Chagall had cultivated an international group of friends. All the while he was deeply concerned about the economic and political situation in Europe, one that was growing steadily worse. The 1929 stock market crash and the Great Depression that followed affected him financially.

In the summer of 1939, after Hitler invaded Czechoslovakia and war seemed unavoidable, the artist gathered the pictures in his studio and went with his family to stay in a farmhouse in the Loire River Valley. War was declared in September, but still Chagall did not want to leave France. In the spring he moved to the village of Gordes, north of the Mediterranean seaport of Marseilles. Things got worse for him when the government enforced anti-Jewish laws.

At the end of 1940 the Museum of Modern Art in New York City had the Emergency Rescue Committee contact Chagall to invite him to come to America. The artist hesitated, and in April 1941 he and his family were arrested in a hotel in Marseilles. Luckily, the United States consul general in Marseilles, with the aid of the head of the Emergency Rescue Committee, managed their release. Chagall sent his paintings and drawings ahead, and on May 7, 1941, the family sailed to America via Lisbon, Portugal. On June 23, they arrived in the United States, the day after the Germans attacked Russia, bringing Chagall's native country into World War II.

Many of Chagall's French friends had already found refuge in America and were in New York when he arrived. Because he was so well known he easily found a dealer to handle his work. But he felt cut off from his former life and disturbed over the Nazi occupation of France. Pictures from this period reflect his state of mind, especially his paintings showing burning houses. By now Vitebsk had been overrun by the Germans. He was concerned about his old home and his relatives in Russia.

Chagall and Bella lived in New York City, but whenever possible spent time at Cranberry Lake in the Adirondack Mountains in upstate New York, where they enjoyed the landscape. The wooded area, especially when it snowed, reminded the artist of Russia.

Fortunately, work in the ballet came along to raise his morale and give him a chance to deal with people from his native country. Early in 1942 Léonide Massine, a Russian choreographer, invited Chagall to design scenery and costumes for *Aleko,* a new ballet being presented in Mexico City. The artist traveled to Mexico to supervise the production, which was based on *The Gypsies,* a story by the great Russian author Aleksandr Pushkin with music by the brilliant Russian composer Peter Tchaikovsky. The ballet was a triumph and Chagall's stay in Mexico influenced him to use more intense color in his painting. Later the production was performed in New York.

In 1944 Chagall and his wife were at Cranberry Lake when they heard the good news that the Allied troops had entered Paris and liberated it from the Nazis. All during the war they had been longing to return to France, and now it would finally be possible. Then on September 2, 1944, Bella, who had been such a devoted companion, tragically died from a viral infection while they were at Cranberry Lake. It was a dreadful loss. The artist was devastated and unable to do any work for months. When he finally started painting again, his pictures reflected his grief.

In the summer of 1945 he was invited to create scenery and costumes for the New York Ballet Theater's production of the *Firebird.* Once again through work in the ballet, he was able to find distraction. The *Firebird* was performed in the Metropolitan Opera House in New York to the music of Igor Stravinsky. Afterward, the ballet was performed in London, and then once again in New York, with Stravinsky himself conducting the orchestra.

In the spring of the following year, a retrospective of more than forty years of Chagall's work was held at the Museum of Modern Art in New York City and then at the Art Institute of Chicago.

During his years in America he was asked to illustrate *A Thousand and One Nights,* so he took up lithography, a method of printing that reproduces a picture drawn with a greasy crayon on stone.

Lonely without his beloved wife and still longing for Paris, Chagall went to France for a three-month visit in the summer of 1946, returning the following year for an exhibition of his work when the National Museum of Modern Art reopened after the German occupation. An exhibition was also held that year in Amsterdam, and in 1948 his work was shown in London, Zurich, and in the French pavillion at the Venice Biennale, where he received first prize for his graphic art. That August he left America to make his home again in his adopted country, France.

For two years Chagall lived on the outskirts of Paris and spent winters at Saint-Jean-Cap-Ferrat near the city of Nice on the Riviera. Then in 1950 he bought a villa on the edge of Vence where he could see the old walled town with its medieval cathedral from his window. Henri Matisse and Pablo Picasso lived nearby.

In 1951 the artist took a trip to Israel where exhibitions of his work were held. The following year he met and married Valentine Brodsky, whom he called Vava, and they went to Greece together. The same year, he was commissioned to create a series of colored lithographs illustrating the ancient Greek love story *Daphnis and Chloe,* a perfect project for the artist. The story tells of a boy and a girl who are left alone and are nursed by a sheep and a cow. They are found by a shepherd who raises them and they tend the shepherd's flocks. When the boy and girl grow up, they fall in love and marry. As in all of Chagall's lithographs, his figures seem to flow and his colors seem transparent. Two years later the artist again visited Greece and then designed the scenery and costumes for the ballet *Daphnis and Chloe,* performed at the Paris Opera to the music of Maurice Ravel.

The themes of Chagall's works are varied. A series of poetic paintings exhibited in 1954 were devoted to the landmarks of Paris. Also he created new works on the subject of the Bible, an appropriate theme for him because of the spiritual quality of his work.

Near his home there were numerous pottery workshops where he could get ceramics. He began decorating ceramic pots and plaques with paintings and soon learned to model his own vessels. This led to carving sculpture in stone, primarily marble. When he was asked to decorate the baptistry of the Church of Notre Dame de Toute Grâce on the

Plateau d'Assy, he created a ceramic mural consisting of ninety separate plaques to cover the main wall. He chose his subject from the Old Testament—Moses dividing the waters of the Red Sea. At the bottom of the mural, which was completed in 1957, Chagall inscribed the words, "In the name of Freedom of all religions." For the two side windows of the church he experimented with stained glass, an art form that had interested him since he studied the windows in the cathedral of Chartres in 1952. The technique suited him because he enjoyed working with color and admired the light that shone through his glass windows. He continued to design stained-glass windows for churches in Germany and Switzerland and for the synagogue of the Hadassah Hebrew University Medical Center in Jerusalem in 1960. Chagall was proud of being a Jew and he loved decorating this synagogue with sacred subjects. He filled each of the twelve large windows of the synagogue with an illustration of one of the twelve tribes of Israel. When the synagogue was consecrated in 1962, he traveled from Vence to Israel for the celebration.

Chagall's creative genius can also be appreciated at the Paris Opera where, in 1963, he covered the panels of the enormous ceiling with paintings. In 1964 he designed a stained-glass window, "Peace," for the United Nations building in New York. The following year he began work on the scenery and costumes for a production of Mozart's *The Magic Flute*. He also designed two large murals for the Metropolitan Opera House in New York's Lincoln Center. For the Knesset (Parliament) of Israel, he designed an enormous woven wool tapestry thirty-six feet wide with Odysseus, the ancient Greek hero of the Trojan War, as its subject.

Chagall and Vava built a house in a wooded valley, in Saint-Paul de Vence near Nice. In 1966 they donated seventeen paintings with Old Testament themes from the books of Genesis, Exodus, and Song of Songs to the French government for the establishment of the Marc Chagall Museum of the Biblical Message near their home. The completed building was opened to the public in 1973. It was the only national museum in France dedicated to a living artist. Chagall was highly regarded in his old age, and he continued to be active. In 1967, when he turned eighty, he visited New York. That year, retrospective exhibitions were held for him in France, Germany, and Switzerland.

He was always experimenting with new techniques. In 1968 he created a mosaic for the University of Nice, laying small cubes of colored glass and stone closely together to form a picture.

After an absence of half a century, Chagall visited Russia in July of 1973 for an exhibition of his work in Moscow and Leningrad (the name for Saint Petersburg from 1924 until 1991). He was able to see two of his sisters again, but refused to return to Vitebsk. "I would have been too afraid not to recognize my town, and in any case I have carried it forever in my heart," he said.

In 1974 he went to Chicago for the unveiling of a monumental mosaic that he designed, and the city was decked with flags in his honor. When he celebrated his ninetieth birthday in 1977, President Valéry Giscard d'Estaing of the French Republic awarded him the Grand Cross, the highest rank of the Legion of Honor. He was also named an honorary citizen of the City of Jerusalem.

Marc Chagall was a painter-poet who made a lasting contribution to the theater and became the most famous stained-glass artist of his time. Even though he had lived for nearly a century, he was able to work until his last days. He died on March 28, 1985, at the age of ninety-seven in Saint-Paul de Vence and is buried there. His life spanned almost the entire twentieth century, and the experiences of his lifetime went into his pictures.

Frederick E. Church

1826–1900   American landscape painter of the Hudson River school

Frederick Edwin Church was born in Hartford, Connecticut, on May 4, 1826, son of Joseph and Eliza Janes Church. His mother bore two other sons, but they did not survive. When he was sixteen he studied painting with local artists. His father, a successful businessman who was rigid in his thinking, thought that the life of an artist was not a worthy pursuit. He wanted his son to be a doctor. Nevertheless he consented to the choice of a career in art and young Church moved to Catskill, New York, on the banks of the Hudson River to study art with Thomas Cole, America's first landscape painter. Cole had established himself as the leader of a group of New York artists that became known as the Hudson River school of landscape painting. Church was eighteen when he became Cole's pupil in 1844.

Thomas Cole was a deeply religious and poetic man who felt that he experienced the presence of God in nature. He spent summers walking through the beautiful valley of the Hudson River, which flows through New York State, sketching scenery. Church accompanied Cole on his outings, which sometimes took them into wild, untouched places where Church would make observations on the trees, vegetation, moving clouds, and changing sunlight. He learned to paint landscape scenes and also experimented with religious themes.

Church was talented and hard working. Within a year he exhibited his own paintings at the National Academy of Design. Following two years with Cole,

24

he returned in June of 1846 to Hartford, but stayed only a few months. In 1847 he settled in New York City. A tall, handsome man, Church was intelligent and sociable, with a good sense of humor. He soon entered into the social life of the city and was invited to join some clubs. In 1849, when he was only twenty-two he was one of the youngest members ever to be elected to full membership in the National Academy of Design. The American Art Union also showed his work, and prints of his paintings were widely distributed. He began accepting pupils to study with him, but he was not an especially good teacher. Theories about art did not interest him; he simply believed that "an artist should paint what he sees."

Every summer Church sketched outdoors in the countryside of New York and in the Berkshire Mountains of Massachusetts. During the winter he worked in his studio in the city, creating large paintings based on his sketches. His works reflected a new taste in art in America that sprang from an appreciation of the country's natural wonders. Thoughtful essays by Ralph Waldo Emerson and Henry David Thoreau about living in unspoiled nature enjoyed great popularity. Church painted the beauty of the untouched wilderness in the same way that these authors wrote about it.

Beginning in 1851 the artist traveled farther afield in summertime to sketch the scenery of Kentucky, Virginia, Vermont, and Maine. His approach to the outdoors was not only artistic but poetic as he expressed the relationship between people and nature. His landscapes also revealed careful scientific observation that reflected his interest in botany, geology, and meteorology. Most young American artists wanted to travel in Europe to study the old masters, but Church found inspiration in the untouched wilderness of the New World. He was deeply influenced by Alexander von Humboldt, a German naturalist and explorer who traveled to Central and South America and wrote about wilderness areas of incredible beauty. Von Humboldt's descriptions of exotic tropical scenery inspired Church to see these marvels firsthand and to develop a more scientific approach to nature.

In 1853 he took an extended trip to New Granada (now Colombia) and Ecuador with his friend the merchant Cyrus Field, who later laid the first telegraph cable across the Atlantic Ocean. No American artist had ever explored South America before. It was an arduous journey involving travel high in the Andes Mountains by foot and on the backs of burros and mules. Church studied and sketched every detail of the exotic surroundings, including luxurious, unknown jungle plants, the foliage of trees, the stems of plants, and towering waterfalls. Back in his New York studio, he used his sketches to paint majestic canvases. His South American paintings received high praise.

Church's first outstanding success was a monumental painting of a scenic wonder closer to home: Niagara Falls. He visited the falls in 1856, and the following year painted *Niagara,* an awesome work that captured the majestic reality of the world's most spectacular waterfall. *Niagara* expressed the spirit of America and the country's optimism in the period before the Civil War. This was the artist's first so-called Great Picture, a huge landscape that people paid to see in a gallery where it was exhibited by itself in a specially designed frame and they could imagine they were looking at it through a window. People viewing *Niagara* had the sensation of being at the water's edge, seeing it close up, almost feeling the drops of spray. The painting was exhibited in London, and its success made Church internationally famous.

In 1857 he made a second visit to Ecuador and spent nine weeks sketching the Andean scenery and intensively studying a volcano that von Humboldt had enthusiastically described. Whenever Church traveled, the public waited eagerly for more paintings. They were curious about the vast, unexplored wilderness. Americans were especially eager to see the colossal mountains and towering waterfalls of his South American scenes and the clearly detailed renderings of exotic plants and brightly colored birds from a tropical climate so different from their own. Admirers stood in front of his canvases with binoculars for a close-up view, and let their eyes wander over his paintings. Any figures shown in Church's enormous landscapes were tiny, stressing man's place amid the marvels of nature. Viewing his huge landscapes was like stepping into another world, one with spiritual meaning.

Heart of the Andes, Church's great South American picture of 1859, stood five-and-a-half feet tall and ten feet wide and combined vast space with minute detail. It was shown in New York and then went on tour to several American cities: Mark Twain saw it in Saint Louis, Missouri. Viewing it through opera glasses, he wrote to his brother describing its beauty and saying, "You may count the very leaves on the trees." It was later shown in London, England, and Edinburgh, Scotland. The picture was so inspiring that essays and poems were written about it.

Church explored the Arctic as well as the tropics. He became interested in the polar region when he read an

Church's *The Heart of the Andes. The Metropolitan Museum of Art, Bequest of Mrs. David Dows, 1909.*

American explorer's account of vain attempts to find an English expedition that had disappeared. In June 1859 he journeyed north with his friend the Reverend Louis L. Noble, an Episcopal clergyman. The two men hired a boat to cruise off the coast of Labrador in search of icebergs. The artist sat on the deck in rolling seas, drawing and painting the scenery, while Noble took notes for a book. The icebergs they saw seemed strange and supernatural. Noble's book, *After Icebergs with a Painter*, was illustrated with six of Church's drawings and gave a full account of the trip. The artist's name became so closely connected with the Arctic that an explorer later named a

mountain on the coast of Labrador Church's Peak.

The following year Church visited Mount Desert Island in Maine where he liked to spend summers. There he made further observations of northern waters for a great painting of icebergs. Back in his New York studio he took four months to complete his work. The painting was exhibited in a New York art gallery in April 1861. The Civil War had just broken out, so he named it *The North*, which stood for both the polar region and the Union. The exhibition fees that were collected were donated to a fund to support needy dependents of Union soldiers.

The work, renamed *The Icebergs,*

Frederick Church's home, Olana. *New York State Office of Parks, Recreation, and Historic Preservation, Taconic Region, Olana State Historic Site. Photograph by Ted Spiegel.*

went on view in England. (See reproduction in the color section of this book.) It was bought by a wealthy man who hung it in his mansion, Rose Hill. After the owner's death Rose Hill was turned into a home for delinquent boys, and Church's painting of gigantic icebergs hung on the wall of the staircase. The painting's whereabouts were forgotten by the world for more than a hundred years, although the work itself was known from colored lithographs. Then in 1979, when American landscape paintings had become popular again, *The Icebergs* was discovered at

Rose Hill. It was brought back to New York and sold for a sum that was the highest price paid for any American painting sold at auction up to that time.

Meanwhile in 1860 Church married Isabel Carnes of Dayton, Ohio, and the couple moved into a cottage in Hudson, New York. They had two children, who tragically died of diphtheria in March 1865. To recover from the loss the artist went to Jamaica to immerse himself in nature. While in the Caribbean, he made studies of the mountains, coastline, and tropical vegetation. *Rainy Season in the Tropics*, painted in 1866, was the result of the trip. Later that year, Isabel gave birth to another child and three others were to follow. In 1867 the artist purchased three hundred acres on a wooded hill, five hundred feet above the river in Hudson, New York, with a superb view of the main range of the Catskill Mountains.

Church won a gold medal when his work was exhibited at the International Exposition in Paris in 1867. That November, on his first voyage to the Old World, he sailed for France, accompanied by family and friends. The party traveled abroad for a year and a half, touring London, Paris, Rome, Greece, Italy, and the Middle East. The group sailed through the Black Sea and up the Danube River to the Alps, before returning to London. There Church studied the works of Joseph M. W. Turner, an English artist who based his landscapes on the study of nature and painted in a new manner.

Greece and the Middle East impressed the artist, as is reflected in landscapes he later created from sketches made on the trip. He especially admired the architecture he had seen in the Islamic countries. Back in America in 1869 he began work on his property in Hudson, and had a house built that ended up looking something like a Moorish castle. He named it Olana, a word that refers to a place in

Frederick Church in 1893. *The New York Public Library Picture Collection.*

Persia, and said that it was the Center of the World. He furnished the house with exotic objects acquired on his travels and spent a good deal of time on its landscaping.

Church had become the leading landscape artist in America, but his style was losing popularity. Since the Civil War the American public had become less idealistic and more materialistic. People were interested in fashionable European styles and more modern trends in art. Nevertheless, when America celebrated its one hundredth anniversary of independence in

A view of the court hall at Olana. *New York State Office of Parks, Recreation, and Historic Preservation, Taconic Region, Olana State Historic Site. Photograph by Robert and Emily de Forest.*

1876, Church showed two paintings at the Centennial Exposition in Philadelphia, and in 1878 his work was again shown at the International Exposition in Paris. Eight of his paintings were exhibited in New York's Metropolitan Museum of Art, which had elected him an officer when the institution was founded in 1870.

Church created only a few paintings during his last years. Ailing from in-

flammatory rheumatism in the late 1870s, he found it difficult to paint. When his right arm and hand were crippled he learned to paint with his left until that arm troubled him, too. He started spending winters in Mexico where the weather was warm. His wife, Isabel, passed away in 1899. After that he spent one more winter in Mexico and went from there to New York, where he died April 7, 1900. He was buried in Hartford, Connecticut, where he had been born nearly seventy-four years earlier. Six weeks later a memorial exhibition of fourteen of his paintings was held at The Metropolitan Museum.

Hundreds of oil studies and sketches lay in the attic in Olana for years after his death. His youngest son Louis Church lived in the house until he died, and Louis's widow Sallie remained there until her death in 1964. Olana was then tightly shut and fell into disrepair until the house and its furnishings were rescued from destruction by a preservation group. Now it is restored and can be visited by the public.

Many paintings by Church are displayed in museums throughout the country. Viewing them will help make us sensitive to the wondrous beauties of nature.

Jacques-Louis David

1748–1825   Painter of the French Revolution

Jacques-Louis David's career as an artist was so closely tied to his activities in the French Revolution that it has been said he mixed paint and politics. At the same time, he created a new style of painting that in itself was revolutionary and changed the course of French art.

David was born in Paris on August 30, 1748, the only child of Louis Maurice David, a wholesale iron merchant, and Marie Geneviève Buron. When he was nine his father was killed in a duel, so the boy was brought up by two uncles on his mother's side who were master masons and architects. He attended classes at the Collège de Beauvais and then at the Collège des Quatre Nations.

His family wanted him to become an architect, but he had a talent for drawing and, after taking some lessons, was determined to become a painter. François Boucher, a distant relative who was a prominent artist, introduced him to Joseph-Marie Vien, a famous history painter and respected teacher. In 1766, when David was eighteen, he became Vien's pupil and apprentice and was enrolled in the Royal Academy of Painting, where Vien was a professor.

Every year talented, young pupils from the Academy competed for the Grand Prix de Rome, a fellowship to study in Italy. It was an important prize because winners got the chance to get ahead quickly when they returned to France. Rome was a great artistic center with its wealth of sixteenth- and seventeenth-century Italian paintings. Ancient buildings and statues were everywhere and could be studied first-hand. David tried for the Prix de Rome twice between 1770 and 1772, without success. His failure depressed him so deeply that he locked himself in a room without food, determined to starve to death, but he was rescued by his godfather, in whose home he was living. Finally, on his fourth attempt for the fellowship in 1774, he succeeded, fainting when he heard the good news. The experience of having failed three times made him bitter, however, and he carried a grudge against the Academy.

In the meantime the artist Jean-Honoré Fragonard was painting a series of wall decorations for the new home of a famous actress and asked David to finish them. The young artist was grateful for the favor and later, when he was in a position of power, he awarded a government position to Fragonard, who was by then an old man.

In October 1775, at the age of twenty-seven, David went to Italy with his teacher Vien, who was now director of the French Academy in Rome, and two other pupils. Vien placed his students on a rigorous routine starting early each morning. They drew from live models to learn anatomy. They also studied perspective, the handling of space on the picture plane. David was a superb draftsman, always reaching for perfection. He quickly filled his note-books with beautiful drawings of different parts of the human body and careful sketches of ancient statues and buildings.

In 1779 the artist took a trip to Naples; he also visited Pompeii and Herculaneum, ancient cities that had been covered by lava and volcanic ash when Mount Vesuvius erupted in A.D. 79. They had been rediscovered in the eighteenth century buried underneath the ashes but perfectly preserved. Archaeologists were digging there, and the finds inspired an interest in classical art. The ideal beauty expressed in classical art appealed to David, who liked to read ancient Greek and Roman literature and use the themes as subjects for his work. An art style known as Neo-Classical, based on the art and architecture of ancient Greece and Rome, was developing in France with David in the forefront. The Neo-Classical style was very different from the sweet, delicate Rococo style of François Boucher and Jean-Honoré Fragonard that had been popular. David's compositions are dramatic, with only essential elements included, in scenes that have a sense of heroic grandeur. The solid, muscular figures, clearly painted with firm outlines, look like statues.

In 1780 David returned to France after five years in Rome, stopping for a while in Florence. Back in Paris, he

A portrait of Jacques-Louis David. *Lauros-Giraudon/Art Resource/Musée des Beaux-Arts, Paris.*

continued to paint subjects based on ancient Greece and Rome. His works usually contained a moral message, teaching lessons about duty, sacrifice, and courage. The following year his paintings were received favorably at the Salon, the official exhibition in France, named for the salon of the Louvre Palace where it was first held. Young painters gathered around David, and people were eager to acquire his pictures.

Early in 1782 King Louis XVI gave David a studio in the Louvre Palace, and a special bed alcove was designed for him. On May 16 the artist married Marguerite Charlotte Pécoul, daughter of the king's superintendent of construction at the palace. The bride was seventeen; David was twice her age. She was not a pretty woman, but she had a fine character and would prove to be a good wife and mother.

David had a speech defect and his face, although handsome, was twisted: A cheek wound from a fencing match had grown into a benign tumor that distorted his mouth. As for his character, he was quick to seize an opportunity to further his own interests and was not always understanding of other people. He could be melancholy or become emotional and act without reason.

At the Salon of 1783 the artist exhibited a work based on *The Iliad*, the epic by the ancient Greek poet Homer that tells the story of the fall of Troy. The painting represents Andromache mourning the death of her husband Hector, a Trojan hero who had been killed in battle by Achilles, a Greek. It was a brilliant success. When David was recognized by admirers at the Salon exhibition, they lifted him from the ground and held him in the air. He was elected a full member of the Royal Academy in 1783.

The Davids's first son, Charles-Louis-Jules, was born in 1783 and their second son, Eugène, the next year. Twin daughters, Félicité-Emilie and Pauline-Jeanne, were to follow in 1786.

In 1784 David received a royal commission from the king to create a painting based on ancient Roman history. The picture, *The Oath of the Horatii*, would prove to be his most memorable accomplishment. (See reproduction in the color section of this book.) The subject was based on the story of three brothers who received swords from their father to go into battle for their kingdom. The brothers pledged an oath to return to Rome victorious, although they would have to sacrifice the lives of their brothers-in-law. The story illustrates the idea of duty to one's country over love for one's family.

David formed the idea for the painting after seeing a play that impressed

David's studio as depicted in a painting by Mathieu Cochereau. *The Bettman Archive/The Louvre, Paris.*

him deeply. He said that he wanted to reproduce in painting what he had seen on the stage. The artist enjoyed the theater and was a friend of many playwrights, actors, singers, and dancers. He designed costumes for the stage, basing them on classical paintings and statues discovered by archaeologists. He often had actors pose for paintings in costumes he had designed himself. The influence of the theater can be seen in many of David's pictures where his figures gesture like actors on the stage.

The artist started *The Oath of the Horatii* in Paris. Then he returned to Rome for inspiration in 1784; there he continued working on the painting. When it was completed he invited people to see it in his studio in Rome. It was highly praised. One critic wrote, "The figures exist outside the canvas.

We can almost see the blood circulate in their veins."

David returned to France in 1785 and exhibited the painting in Paris. At first it was not given a favorable place in the exhibition, but it received so much attention that it was rehung as the focal point of the show. A witness wrote, "For days it was just as though a procession were in progress. Princes and princesses, cardinals and bishops, priests, citizens, and workmen all hurried to see it." Some people saw a message in the painting that could be understood in terms of political events that were developing in France.

Another heroic picture with a classical setting, *The Death of Socrates*, followed in 1787. It centered on the Greek philosopher who lived in the fifth century B.C. Socrates spent his life in search of truth and wisdom but was treated unjustly. He drank a cup of poisonous hemlock, sacrificing his life for his ideals. That same year David painted *The Lictors Carrying the Bodies of the Sons of Brutus*, which was exhibited in 1789. The subject was taken from ancient Roman history. The central figure, Lucius Brutus Junius, was said to have freed the Romans of an evil king. Brutus was so patriotic that he condemned his own sons to death for treason. David's painting was seen as a symbol for all Frenchmen who would make personal sacrifices to protect French liberty. Because the theme reflected the political turmoil that led up to the French Revolution, it alarmed royal authorities, who tried to prevent its exhibition. Brutus was also the subject of a play by Voltaire that was performed in the same month at the National Theater. The last line in the play, spoken by Brutus, was "Gods! Give us death rather than slavery." On the second night of the performance David's painting was acted out on stage.

France was ruled by the Bourbon family with Louis XVI on the throne. Many French citizens were poor and hungry, and they strongly objected to the luxurious life-style of the royal family and their lack of concern for the people. David opposed the old régime even though the king had been his patron. David was a member of the third estate, a group that declared itself to be the voice of the nation. On June 20, 1789, the group met to form a constitution but were locked out of the meeting hall by royal troops. They met on an indoor tennis court, declared themselves a National Assembly, and swore to work together until a new constitution was established that limited the power of the king. The meeting set the stage for the French Revolution.

On July 14 a group of citizens, David among them, marched on the Bastille, a great fortress, looking for ammunition, and they freed the prisoners being held there. The storming of the Bastille was the beginning of the French Revolution.

David became a political figure, supporting Maximilien de Robespierre, the leader of the third estate. In 1791 members of the society of revolutionary leaders known as the Jacobin Society of Friends of the Constitution asked David to illustrate the tennis court oath, but he never completed more than a large preparatory sketch. The following year he was elected a deputy of the National Convention of Jacobins and was made a member of the commission of monuments and artistic advisor to the new régime. His duties involved organizing revolutionary festivals, including enormous outdoor pageants and funerals. He also designed furniture for the backgrounds of his classical paintings and posed the female figures in natural, white robes based on classical Roman fashion. His models were copied by stylish people, and a Neo-Classical style in dress and decoration became popular. Under David's leadership the Royal Academy was abolished in 1793 and the National Museum of the Arts was established.

King Louis XVI attempted to flee the country in June 1791 but was brought back to Paris and imprisoned in a tower with his family. He was deposed, France was declared a Republic, and the monarchy was abolished in 1792. When the Jacobins met to determine the king's fate David voted for his death. Louis was executed at the guillotine in January 1793. David's wife, whose father remained a supporter of the king, divorced him in 1794 and moved to her parents' home with the twin girls. The two boys remained with their father.

With France in the midst of a revolution and at war with Austria, Prussia, England, and Spain, the Reign of Terror began. While Robespierre dominated the government, thousands of victims were arrested and executed. David signed orders for the arrest of a number of people, including artists who were his friends.

During this period the revolutionary leader Jean-Paul Marat, a scientist turned politician, published a journal attacking supporters of the king. A young woman named Charlotte Corday wrote him a letter asking to see him, then murdered him in his bath. In a now famous painting, David portrayed the incident, showing Marat in the tub reading the letter from Miss Corday.

Robespierre fell from power in 1794 and was arrested and guillotined. David was imprisoned. From a window in his cell in Luxembourg Palace, which was serving as a prison, he could see his own children at play in the gardens. The pleasant view inspired him to paint his only landscape, with materials that his friends had brought him. He was released in December 1794 but arrested again five months later. He was finally freed in October 1795. His wife returned to him during his time of trouble and worked for his release. They were remarried in 1796.

While he was in prison David got the idea for another picture based on a classical theme, *Battle of the Romans and the Sabines.* The story involved two brothers who were reconciled, suggesting that all Frenchmen restore harmony after the Revolution. He finished the picture in 1795, placed advertisements in the newspaper, and exhibited it in his studio. Visitors who paid admission were provided with a booklet he had written explaining the plot. Napoléon Bonaparte, an army officer who was making a name for himself as a great military leader, went to see the picture and admired it.

In 1797 Napoléon commissioned the artist to paint his portrait astride a horse. Two years later, Bonaparte rose to a position of power as first consul, and the country began to prosper. David supported Napoléon politically and was made a knight of the Legion of Honor in 1803. In 1804 Napoléon de-

clared himself emperor, and France was a monarchy once more. He commissioned David to paint a huge scene of his coronation in Notre Dame Cathedral. David was considered the most important painter and greatest teacher in France. His pupil, François Gérard, became the official painter to the Empress Josephine.

The emperor's good fortune did not last. He suffered a series of military defeats and was forced to abdicate in 1814. He was exiled to the island of Elba, and the Bourbon dynasty was restored to the throne.

The following year Napoléon managed to return to France with six hundred loyal soldiers, entering Paris and seizing power. David, a faithful follower, signed a pledge of loyalty to Napoléon, but the new reign lasted only one hundred days. Bonaparte was decisively defeated by allied forces at the Battle of Waterloo in June 1815, ending the wars that had been fought over a period of twenty years. He was forced once more to abdicate, and he spent the rest of his life on the island of Saint Helena in the South Atlantic.

Now with the Bourbon monarchy again restored to the throne, David fled to Brussels, Belgium, in January 1816. He lived a comfortable life in exile, receiving visitors and continuing to paint. His last great picture, *Mars Disarmed by Venus*, based on a classical love story, was finished in 1824. David died December 29, 1825, at the age of seventy-seven, having redirected the course of French art as France emerged as the art center of the world. Jean-August-Dominique Ingres, David's greatest student, became the head of the Neo-Classical movement after David's death. The influence of the movement continues to this day.

Edgar Degas

1834–1917   French artist best known for his paintings of ballet
dancers

Hilaire-Germain-Edgar Degas, best known for his scenes of ballet dancers and racehorses, was born in Paris on July 19, 1834. Although he traveled extensively, he lived in that city all of his long life. Degas's paternal grandfather, René-Hilaire De Gas, had to leave France after the French Revolution in 1789 when the common people came to power, overthrowing the royalists and beheading the King and Queen. He settled in Naples, Italy. There De Gas married a woman from an upper-class family and established a bank. When their son Auguste (Degas's father) grew up he was sent to Paris to work in the family banking business.

Degas's mother, Célestine Musson, was born in New Orleans. Her family had emigrated to America from France and ended up in the cotton business in Louisiana. There, Célestine's father married a woman who was also of French descent and the family moved to Paris, where Célestine met and married Auguste De Gas. Two years later their son Edgar was born; two brothers and two sisters were to follow. (The family had been spelling their name "De Gas," but when Edgar grew up he changed it to "Degas" which had been the original spelling.)

When Degas was eleven, he was enrolled in school at the Lycée Louis-le-Grand, where he learned Latin and Greek, as well as French literature. He studied music and took classes in drawing, where his talent became apparent. Degas was brilliant and witty and made some lasting friendships, but he was not

41

A self-portrait (etching) of Edgar Degas at the age of twenty-one. *The New York Public Library Picture Collection.*

generally popular with the other boys because he had a sharp tongue. When he was only thirteen his mother died; he was deeply affected by the loss.

Degas's father enjoyed music and art and often took the boy to concerts and to the Louvre, the great art museum in Paris. He also took him to the homes of friends who had their own private collections of paintings and sculptures. Au-

guste could see how beautifully his son drew and allowed him to set up a studio in the family's home when he was in his last year of school. After graduation in 1853, Degas enrolled in law school to conform with the wishes of his father, who wanted him to become a banker. But his heart was not in it; he preferred to spend his time at the Louvre, studying works of art and copying his favorite paintings. After only a few months he dropped out of law school to become an artist.

Degas greatly admired Jean-Auguste-Dominique Ingres, whose paintings stressed beautifully drawn lines and clear forms. When a friend introduced him to Ingres, the great master advised Degas to practice his art by drawing lines, both from life and from memory. The young artist was admitted to the École des Beaux-Arts in 1855, and he worked for a time in the studio of Louis Lamothe, a pupil of Ingres. The Beaux-Arts was France's official academy of fine art. There students drew from live models and from plaster casts.

In 1856 Degas set off for Italy to visit his relatives in Naples and Florence and to study and copy ancient Roman sculpture and High Renaissance paintings. By now he was a skillful draftsman and painter himself. His portraits, usually of his family and friends, displayed a deep understanding of human nature and psychological insight. He captured the individual personalities of his sitters by arranging them in unexpected poses and surrounding them with objects that revealed their interests and important events in their lives. Degas's own portrait of himself as a young man reveals an aristocratic appearance with a melancholy nature underneath.

Following a second trip to Italy, Degas settled down in Paris in 1859, at the age of twenty-six. He attended the opera and theater. He also liked to go to the racetrack where he sketched the jockeys in their colorful silks, mounted on elegant, high-strung thoroughbreds.

For the annual exhibition of the official Paris Salon, Degas created large paintings, choosing traditional historical and biblical subjects, but his approach was highly original. He continued to experiment with his materials for the rest of his life.

By the mid-nineteenth century Paris had become the art center of the world. The Exposition Universelle, a world's fair held in 1855, introduced Japanese art into France. The air was filled with excitement over Japanese woodblock prints with their bold simplified forms, flat colors, and fresh, lively subject matter. The Japanese artists liked to choose a surprising, chance view of a subject, showing it from an unusual angle. They composed their pictures with figures that were off-center and sometimes abruptly cut off by the frame. Degas collected these wood-block prints and was strongly influenced by them in his work.

The newly invented art of photography was also becoming popular. Degas was impressed with the way a fleeting moment could be captured in a photograph with the subject unaware of the camera. Also objects could be shown close up in sharp detail or at a distance with a blurred background. Degas was so interested in photography that he eventually bought a camera. Some of the pictures he took were used as aids to his paintings.

A new generation of artists and writers was active in Paris by the late 1860s. They regularly gathered at a café to talk about art and literature. The leader of the group, Edouard Manet, became a friend of Degas and drew him into the circle, which included Claude Monet, Pierre-Auguste Renoir and Paul Cézanne. Manet also invited Degas to musical evenings at the home of his mother and introduced him to the Morisot family. Berthe Morisot, a talented young artist, was married to Manet's brother.

The group led by Manet called themselves the Société Anonyme des Artistes. Moving against the establishment, they became the center of a

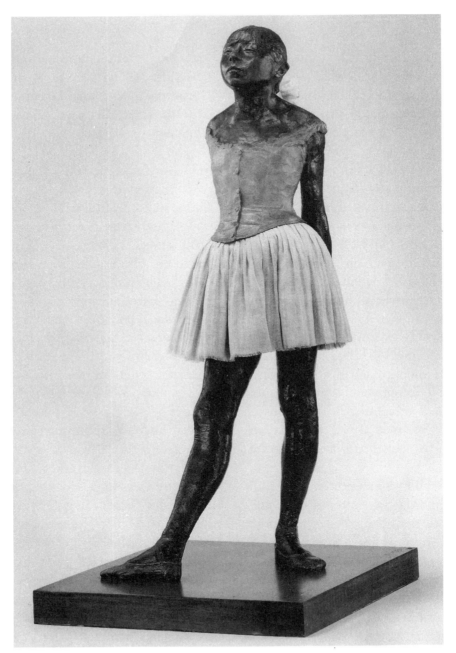

Ballet Girl, a sculpture in bronze by Degas, executed between 1880 and 1881. *The Metropolitan Museum of Art, Bequest of Mrs. H. O. Havemeyer, 1929. The H. O. Havemeyer Collection.* (29.100.370)

movement that would revolutionize the world of art. They focused on modern themes and new methods of applying paint to canvas. Degas, who was already enjoying some success as an artist, gave up his traditional subject matter and presented his fleeting impressions of Parisian life in a daring new way. At the same time, he held on to the basic techniques of drawing that he had learned by copying the Old Masters.

The country in the meantime was in serious political turmoil, and in 1870 France declared war on Prussia. Many young artists chose to leave Paris at the onset of the Franco-Prussian War, but Degas and Edouard Manet stayed on, serving in the artillery. The Prussians bombarded Paris and occupied the city. Conditions were extremely difficult, and Degas suffered a bad chill that affected his eyesight. Unfortunately, his sight grew progressively worse during the course of his lifetime.

In the midst of the war Degas renewed his acquaintance with Henri Rouart, a former schoolmate at the Lycée who had become an engineer and was an amateur artist and collector. The men formed a lifelong friendship. Rouart and his family were always hospitable to Degas, who remained a bachelor all his life, and often invited him to their country home.

The French were defeated in the war, and Paris was left in ruins by the Prussians. To recover from the ordeal Degas planned a trip to New Orleans with his brother René to visit their American relatives. Traveling first to England, the brothers took a steamship across the Atlantic to New York. From there they proceeded to Louisiana, where they stayed for five months. One of Degas's finest paintings was created on this trip. It shows a scene inside his uncle's office in the Cotton Exchange and features fifteen figures of men, among them his brothers Achille and René, an uncle, and some cousins.

Degas's works were receiving praise from the critics, and on his return from America in 1873 the prominent art dealer Paul Durand-Ruel arranged to sell his paintings. The following year his father died in Italy and it was discovered that his bank was in serious financial difficulty. Degas, as the eldest son, felt honor-bound to assume responsibility for his father's business debts. He moved to modest quarters and sold his art collection.

When a group of his artist friends, who called themselves independents, had their first exhibition, L'Exposition des Indépendents, in 1874, Degas's works were included. Most of the members of the revolutionary group were landscape artists who worked outdoors, flooding their pictures with sunlight and applying the paint in patches of rich colors that dissolved forms and blurred outlines, thus giving the effect of an unfinished sketch. People were shocked by these new paintings, so different from the traditional works accepted by the Academy, and the critics cried out in opposition. One critic named the group the Impressionists after a painting by Claude Monet called *Impression: Sunrise.*

Degas himself was not interested in painting the outdoors, in capturing the effects of light, or in blurred images. He preferred to shape his forms with firm outlines and to experiment with figures in motion, viewing them from unexpected angles. He often went backstage during theater rehearsals to observe the movements of dancers practicing or at rest and to study the musicians in the orchestra pit, or even the laundresses pressing the ballerinas' costumes. He also liked to observe people in cafés. Sometimes he used pastels, powdered pigments molded into sticks, which gave him greater freedom.

Degas made sketches on the spot, noting his subjects' every movement. His ballet dancers might be strained in action or be caught off guard, relaxing before or after rehearsal. The actual paintings were done in his studio, where he reused the same sketches in different works. Although his composi-

tions seemed entirely spontaneous, they were meticulously thought out in advance. A perfectionist, Degas never stopped reworking a painting. He often managed to get a picture back after it had been sold, and he would proceed to change it. Never fully satisfied with the way it looked, he would be unwilling to return it to the owner.

Although Degas showed his work in seven of the eight Impressionist exhibitions that were held over a period of twelve years, he did not want to be called an Impressionist. Mary Cassatt, who was born in Pennsylvania, but lived in Paris, and who was the only American to be included in the Impressionist exhibition, became a good friend of Degas and sometimes posed for him. She admired his work and encouraged her family and friends in America to collect his paintings. By the 1880s Degas's pictures were selling well, and he could afford to form his own collection of works by other artists. He enjoyed an active social life in Paris and took trips to Spain and Switzerland. In 1892 he had his first one-man show.

As time went on, however, his disposition became increasingly difficult. He quarreled with his artist friends. Because of his bad temper, Degas often found himself alone. He grew lonely and his eyesight worsened, so he felt all the more isolated. Forced to give up

Degas's pastel *At the Milliner's* depicts Mary Cassatt. *The Metropolitan Museum of Art, Bequest of Mrs. H. O. Havemeyer, 1929. The H. O. Havemeyer Collection.* (29.100.38)

painting he turned to modeling wax or clay figures of dancers and horses and sketching with pastels on paper. He drew large figures, concentrating on movement, omitting details, and reworking the same subject over and over.

In 1912 the artist was deeply saddened by the death of his good friend Henri Rouart, who had formed the most important collection in France of Degas's work. When Rouart's collection was auctioned, a Degas painting brought one hundred thousand dollars, an extremely high price for the time. Two years later a private collection that included works by Degas was acquired by the Musée du Louvre for all French people to enjoy.

In spite of his success, Degas was miserable. He was forced to move from his comfortable home because the

Degas's painting *The Racetrack. Giraudon/Art Resource/The Louvre, Paris.*

house was being torn down, and he never got used to his new home.

The outbreak of the First World War made things worse. The aging artist wandered alone through the streets of wartime Paris, or he sat in a public park, unable to see what was going on around him. Finally, on September 27, 1917, he died at the age of eighty-three in the city he loved.

The war was still on, and Degas's paintings in the Durand-Ruel Gallery narrowly escaped destruction by a German bomb that exploded just on the other side of the street. In late March 1918, with the Germans still advancing on Paris, his pictures were auctioned in a sale that brought two million francs. Seventy years later, when enormous exhibitions of his works were held in museums on both sides of the Atlantic, thousands of people traveled hundreds of miles to stand in long lines to see his works. His enchanting ballerinas continue to serve as inspiration for little girls who like to dance.

Albrecht Dürer

1471–1528   German artist famous for his prints; credited with introducing the Italian Renaissance to the North

The greatest German artist of all time was Albrecht Dürer the younger. His father, Albrecht Dürer the elder, who was born in the Kingdom of Hungary, was a goldsmith, like his father before him. His mother, Barbara Holper, was the daughter of a goldsmith in Nuremberg, Germany. Albrecht the younger, born May 21, 1471, was the third of eighteen children. Unfortunately almost all of them died young. Albrecht and two younger brothers were the only children to survive.

Nuremberg was a free imperial city, part of the Holy Roman Empire. It was the center of European trade routes and a thriving manufacturing town. As a little boy Dürer could see objects of beauty all about him. He spent a lot of time in church, with his mother, where he could admire the religious paintings and other works of art. As a child he attended a grammar school near his house and learned how to read and write. After about three years his father took him out of school to train him as a goldsmith in his shop. The boy studied there for two years, learning to draw and engrave designs on metal. He was already a master of the art of drawing by the time he was thirteen years old, as revealed in a remarkable self-portrait. He drew with a sure hand, recording accurately what he saw. Years later he inscribed the portrait, "This I drew of myself in a mirror, the year 1484, when I was still a child, Albrecht Dürer."

His father expected him to become a goldsmith, yet permitted him to enter the workshop of the artist Michael Wol-

Dürer's self-portrait at age thirteen. *Albertina Museum, Vienna.*

gemut who lived just a few doors away. By now Dürer was fifteen, older than the other apprentices, who sometimes teased him. He was hardworking and eager to learn. He quickly mastered the technique of designing woodcuts, blocks of wood that are carved and inked for use in printing, and learned the art of painting on panels of wood.

After he finished his apprenticeship in April 1490 his father sent him on the traditional young workman's journey to see the world and receive further training. He traveled for about two years before reaching Colmar, in what is now France, where he expected to study with the great engraver Martin Schöngauer. Unfortunately the master had died a few months earlier, but Schöngauer's brothers did all they could to help the young visitor. They took him into their studio and put him to work on engravings, which are made by pressing the image onto a metal plate with a sharp tool. Afterward the plate would be inked for printing. From Colmar the young Dürer went to Basel, an important center for printing books, where he worked in a shop making drawings for woodcuts.

In 1494 Dürer was back in Nuremberg. His parents had arranged for him to marry Agnes Frey, daughter of a master craftsman who worked in metal. The couple never had any children.

That autumn Dürer went off by himself to Venice in northern Italy to study Italian art. As he traveled across the Alps he made watercolor drawings of the towns and landscapes around him.

Venice, built on a system of canals at the edge of the Adriatic Sea, was the wealthiest city in Europe. Carpets, silks, and spices came by boat from the Orient and were transported throughout Europe. Dürer, always observing the world around him, was fascinated by the wide variety of foreigners from distant countries. Intensely interested in nature, he was fascinated by marine life, which he had never seen before, as Nuremberg is so far from the sea. Now for the first time he could make scientific drawings of live crabs and lobsters, giving close attention to every detail.

The following spring he was back in Nuremberg where in 1497 he established his own workshop. Dürer had become well known as a painter and was especially skilled at drawing. His work was in demand. It was his engravings and woodcuts that made him famous; they could be reproduced in great numbers and distributed all over Europe. A series of woodcuts based on the Apocalypse, a book of the New Testament that forecasts a sudden, violent end of the world in the year 1500, was finished in 1498 and became his best known work from this period.

By now Dürer was serious about making scientific studies on the theory of perspective, the way of representing objects on a flat surface as they actually appear. He also made studies to determine the ideal proportions of the human figure, based on a system of mathematical measurements. He constructed figures with the aid of a compass and ruler.

Frederick the Wise, elector of Saxony, one of the princes who elected the Holy Roman emperor, admired Dürer's work and asked him to paint his portrait. Frederick also ordered religious pictures from the artist. In 1502 the elector sponsored a young painter, another Frederick, to serve the artist as an apprentice. Three other young men, including Dürer's brother Hans, were apprentices in his workshop learning to become masters. His other surviving brother, Endres, became a goldsmith like their father.

Dürer always got along well with his workers. Self-portraits from this time show him in elegant dress with curly blond, shoulder-length hair, mustache, and short beard. He was lean, with a handsome face, an aqualine nose, and eyes that stared as if they saw everything. It is said that one of his self-portraits was so lifelike that, after he finished it and put it outdoors to dry, his dog wagged its tail at the portrait and rubbed its nose on its master's face, making a mark on the wet paint.

Dürer met socially with a group of learned scholars who liked to discuss scientific and religious subjects. His best friend was Willibald Pirckheimer, an educated, aristocratic gentleman who had a fine private library and knew Greek, Latin, and Italian. The learned people they met with were humanists, men interested in the studies that enrich people's lives: philosophy, history, and poetry. Dürer is considered a humanist: His interests were wide and he had great curiosity, always desiring to learn more. He liked to write poetry, although he had little talent for it. He was religious and was tolerant of other people's religions. He was also humble. He once said, "The genius of the artist comes from God."

Dürer was well-read and had a pleasant way of talking and a concern for justice. Letters he wrote show that he was witty and had a good sense of humor. Pirckheimer often invited the artist to his house when friends gathered in the evening, while Agnes Dürer stayed at home. She and Pirckheimer disliked each other intensely. Pirckheimer encouraged Dürer in his work and they remained lifelong friends.

In 1502 Albrecht Dürer the elder died and Albrecht the younger took his brother Hans into his home. Two years later his mother also came to live with him and he took care of her for the rest of her life. In 1504 the artist made an engraving of Adam and Eve, attempting to create the ideal male and female human figure in perfect proportion, based on mathematical measurements. He used a drawing of an ancient statue of the Greek god Apollo as a guide.

The following year, after an epidemic of the plague broke out in Nuremberg, Dürer set out again for Venice. He left a small allowance for Agnes and his mother to run the household and instructed them on handling the sale of his works while he was away. His talent as an artist was highly respected in Italy, and he was welcomed by princes, nobles, and scholars.

However, the local artists were jealous of Dürer and they were unfriendly, except for the great painter Giovanni Bellini, who was an old man by now. Bellini praised the visitor from Germany. He went to see him and wanted to buy one of his works. Dürer presented him with a painting, *Christ in the Temple*. (See reproduction in the color section of this book.) Bellini asked Dürer for one of his brushes, thinking it would be special because the German artist's work was so fine, and was surprised to learn that it was an ordinary brush like that of any other artist.

A group of German merchants lived in Venice, where they were active in international trade, buying loads of goods that came in by boat and shipping them overland for sale. The German merchants commissioned Dürer to create a painting for their church, San Bartolomeo. The work, entitled *The Feast of the Rose Garlands,* would take five months to complete. While he was in Venice Dürer also had many commissions to make drawings and prints.

In 1506 the artist visited Bologna where he hoped to meet a man who would teach him the secrets of the art of perspective. He was back in Nuremberg in February 1507 after an absence of a year and a half. At this time he produced a life-size painting of Adam and Eve, based on his earlier engraving, and was asked to paint a large altarpiece for a church in Frankfurt on the Maim. In 1509 he bought a fine house where he installed a printing press and could publish his own works.

That year the Greater Council of Nuremberg made Dürer a member and asked him to paint portraits of the emperors Charlemagne and Sigismund dressed for their coronations. In 1512 the Holy Roman emperor, Maximilian I, arrived in Nuremberg for an official visit and saw the portraits. Maximilian was so impressed with them that he commanded Dürer to work on projects to glorify himself. Dürer designed a series of woodcuts, *The Triumphal Arch of Maximilian I,* that showed the emperor's heroic deeds and scenes from his life and the lives of his ancestors. Seven hundred prints of the woodcuts were sent to all parts of the empire. A second series, *The Triumphal Procession of Maximilian I,* showed his military victories with the emperor riding in a fancy chariot drawn by elegant horses.

Maximilian, a brave soldier who loved the tournament, a mock battle in which knights tried to knock one another off their horses, also had the artist design a suit of parade armor. In 1515 the emperor granted Dürer a pension to be paid yearly by the city, but the artist had a hard time collecting it.

During this period Dürer produced the masterpieces of engraving *Melancholia I* and *Saint Jerome in His Study.* A third engraving, *Knight, Death and the Devil,* reflects studies that the artist made on the ideal proportions of a horse.

In 1518 Dürer went to Augsburg with two friends to attend an important assembly of the Holy Roman Empire. He hoped to meet Martin Luther, a prominent German preacher and leader of a movement that broke away from the Roman Catholic Church and would lead to the Protestant Reformation. Luther's writings and teachings were of great interest to the artist. He admired

the religious leader and wanted to paint his portrait but never even managed to meet him. However, he did go to Maximilian's palace where the emperor sat for his portrait. The artist transformed the image into a woodcut, to be distributed throughout Europe.

Maximilian died in 1519 and the following year Dürer set out for the Netherlands, which was under Spanish rule. He wanted to attend the coronation of Maximilian's grandson Charles I, king of Spain, who succeeded him to the throne as Holy Roman emperor Charles V. He also wanted to arrange to have his pension renewed. This time he took his wife and a maidservant. They traveled by boat on the Rhine River and overland by horseback. The artist kept a detailed diary, carefully recording his travel experiences as well as his expenses. He drew constantly, filling his sketchbook with fascinating studies drawn in great detail. On the way they stopped in Cologne to visit a cousin. In the Netherlands Dürer studied great Flemish art by the Old Masters Jan van Eyck, Rogier van der Weyden, and Hugo van der Goes. They made Antwerp their headquarters. Dürer was entertained by princes and was well received by other artists. In Antwerp the Painters Guild and the city council gave a banquet in his honor to welcome him to town. Agnes and the maid went with

IMAGO · ALBERTI · DVRERI ·
ÆTATIS · SVÆ · 32 · 1503 ·

A self-portrait of Dürer in later life. *Giraudon/Art Resource.*

him. Their hosts bowed to the visitors to show their respect. They were served a delicious meal and presented with gifts. Afterward their hosts saw them home with torchlights.

At the end of August the artist went to Brussels. In the royal palace he saw a display of Aztec gold and silver from America. These treasures had been sent to the king of Spain by Hernán Cortés, the conquistador who had defeated the Aztec emperor Montezuma and claimed the land that is now Mexico in the name of the Spanish Crown. These were the first works of pre-Columbian art ever seen by Europeans. Dürer was spellbound by the craftsmanship of the works. He said, "All the days of my life I have seen nothing that has gladdened my heart so much as these things, for I saw amongst them wonderful works of art."

Behind the palace was an animal park with wild beasts brought from distant lands over new trade routes that were being established. Dürer was fascinated by the animals and he sketched them. In Brussels he dined with Desiderius Erasmus, the great Dutch priest and scholar, and drew his portrait. Dürer's portraits are simple, revealing the subject's character in a direct and penetrating manner.

Next the artist went to Aachen in Germany to witness the coronation ceremonies when the king of Spain was crowned Holy Roman emperor Charles V. Dürer traveled there on horseback with a group of wealthy citizens of Nuremberg, leaving Agnes behind in Antwerp. After the coronation he wrote, "There I saw all manner of lordly splendor, the like of which no man now alive has ever seen." He also went to Cologne for the grand ball and coronation banquet. There he stayed with his cousin's family again and waited to hear about his pension from the new emperor. In Cologne he did the usual sight-seeing, drew more portraits, and designed a family's coat of arms.

The imperial order renewing the artist's pension was finally signed by Charles V on November 12. After receiving the good news Dürer took a riverboat back to Antwerp. When he arrived he learned that while he was away a pickpocket had stolen his wife's purse containing her money and some keys. In the meantime, news had spread that during a storm in the North Sea an enormous whale had washed up on a beach in Zeeland, not too far away. He set out by boat to see it. He then had to ride horseback to the beach where the whale was stranded, but by the time he arrived the creature had been carried back to sea by the tides. Dürer did see a walrus; he made a drawing of it in his sketchbook and wrote a description of it. The weather was so dreadful that he suffered a chill and caught a fever from which he would never recover.

Before returning to Antwerp he bought a present for Agnes. He spent that winter in Antwerp and in the spring took a trip to Bruges and Ghent where he saw great works of art in churches. He also saw a lion that was kept in a cage and he made sketches of it. Dürer's wildlife sketches are among his finest works. He was honored by painters and goldsmiths in both cities.

Back in Antwerp the artist was preparing to return home when Christian II, king of Denmark, brother-in-law of Charles V, arrived in the Netherlands. He sent for Dürer, asked him to draw his portrait, and invited him to a banquet in honor of the emperor Charles V.

In July Dürer and Agnes left the Netherlands and were back in Nuremberg by the end of the month, having been gone a little more than a year.

Soon the artist was placed in charge of a project to decorate the great room in the Town Hall with paintings; he also designed a chandelier in the shape of a dragon for another room. Dürer no longer did much painting. He spent most of his time writing about measurements and the theory of human proportion for future generations of artists. War had broken out between France and Germany, which inspired him to write about fortifications as well.

By now the artist was a wealthy man, but he suffered from ill health, resulting from the chill he had caught in the Netherlands. He died on April 6, 1528, at the age of fifty-seven. His death was deeply mourned and he was highly praised by friends and famous people. Three centuries later, beginning in 1815, an annual Albrecht Dürer day was announced in Germany. Although the day is no longer observed as a holiday, the artist is a world figure of long-lasting fame.

Thomas Gainsborough

1727–1788   English portrait painter of eighteenth-century aristocracy

Thomas Gainsborough made countless portraits of the British royal family and leading members of the nobility and aristocracy, yet he is best known for his painting of an ordinary boy with a handsome face wearing a fancy, blue suit. In fact that picture, known as *The Blue Boy,* has become one of the most popular portraits in the world, and numerous legends have grown up around it. (See reproduction in the color section of this book.)

Gainsborough was born in Sudbury, in Suffolk County, England, and he never traveled outside his country. He was one of nine children of John Gainsborough, a textile manufacturer whose family was well established in the area. His mother, the former Mary Burroughs, was skilled at painting flowers and she encouraged her son to draw. The exact date of Gainsborough's birth is not known, but records show that he was baptized May 14, 1727. He attended the Sudbury Grammar School but preferred being outdoors in the countryside to sitting in class. By the time he was ten years old, he was drawing and painting scenes from nature. And he copied Dutch landscapes, which were highly admired in England, to gain skill in his technique.

When he was only thirteen Gainsborough persuaded his parents to let him go to London to study art. There he lived in the home of a family friend who was a silversmith. During his early years in London he modeled numerous little clay figures of horses, cows, and dogs, which he would use in landscape compositions. He took instruction in drawing from the artists Hubert Gravelot and Francis Hayman, and probably served the former as an apprentice. Gravelot liked to dress up dolls in costumes to use as models when he taught figure drawing, a practice that Gainsborough adopted for himself. Gainsborough did not like to read books and did not choose to be around people who did, but he had a passion for music and could play several instruments, primarily by ear. He was a sociable man, known to be generous, and kind-hearted, but, having left home so young, he had picked up coarse habits and could behave crudely.

Around 1745 Gainsborough set up his own studio. The following year he married a beautiful young woman named Margaret Burr, who had run away from her home in Sudbury to marry the nineteen-year-old artist. Margaret had a private income that helped the young couple meet their expenses. Gainsborough was reckless with money, while his wife Margaret was thrifty. They had two daughters, both of whom seemed to have suffered from a mental illness.

After his father died in 1748 Gainsborough returned to Sudbury. By then he was an independent painter who specialized in landscapes, but they were not exact views of nature. He would

A portrait of Thomas Gainsborough. *International Portrait Gallery/Gale Research Company.*

make figure studies and drawings outdoors in preparation for his compositions and gather branches, sticks, weeds, broccoli, clay, moss, dried herbs, stones, and lumps of coal. Then he composed his landscapes indoors on a worktable in his studio, setting up the materials that he had collected in the fields, adding dolls in costumes and his modeled animals to the scenes. Because his works were not true to nature, spring, summer, and autumn foliage might appear in the same picture.

The artist was able to sell some of his

A mezzotint of Gainsborough's portrait of his wife, Margaret. *Culver Pictures.*

landscapes to people in Suffolk who hung them over fireplace mantels in their homes. But it was not possible to make a living painting landscapes, so Gainsborough had to paint portraits, even though he did not like this work. His early attempts were timid and stiff, but through experimentation and practice, with himself and his family as subjects, he improved, gaining freedom and ease in his technique. He developed an informal style of portraiture that was both fashionable and appealing while maintaining a close resemblance to the sitter. Sometimes he combined his portraits with landscape backgrounds, merging the sitter with nature.

After two years Gainsborough moved to Ipswich, a larger town where some prosperous families lived. There he was able to establish a fairly good portrait practice for a time, even though he did not like the aristocratic people whom he painted. When he exhausted his source of subjects he traveled around Suffolk County seeking commissions.

In October 1759 Gainsborough settled in Bath, where wealthy people liked to go to relax and take the famous mineral waters. For the first time he had a chance to visit people living in great houses and see their private collections of paintings by the Old Masters. He especially admired the seventeenth-century Flemish portrait painter Sir Anthony Van Dyck who had spent much of his life in England. Gainsborough's own elegant, refined portrait style became similar to that of Van Dyck. He also admired Peter Paul Rubens and Jacob van Ruisdael. Their influence can be seen in his landscapes.

Many well-known musicians came to Bath to perform, and Gainsborough attended their concerts and made friends with them. Clients wanting portraits painted soon started coming to his studio, and he was able to raise his prices, but he had less time to paint landscapes. A nephew, Gainsborough Dupont, came to live with the family in Bath when he was a young child. The lad became an apprentice to his uncle in 1772, when he was seventeen, and later became his assistant. He seems to have been Gainsborough's only pupil.

In 1761 Gainsborough first exhibited in London with the Society of Artists. He sent full-length portraits and a few landscapes to annual exhibitions and made yearly visits to London, where he was able to arrange some portrait commissions. He had become adept at showing the play of reflected light in the silk and satin clothing worn by his fashionable subjects, and his pictures seemed to come to life. He continued exhibiting with the Society of Artists until 1768.

In 1769 he sent his works to the first exhibition of the Royal Academy of Arts in London. The Academy, a society of artists sponsored by King George III and headed by Sir Joshua Reynolds, had invited him to become one of its original members. Reynolds, who taught the students at the Academy's art school, was England's most distinguished portrait painter. He admired Gainsborough's work, but some jealousy existed between them.

In the second exhibition of the Royal Academy, Gainsborough displayed *The Blue Boy*. It is said that he was challenged to paint this portrait by Reynolds, who claimed it was not possible to produce a fine picture with blue as the predominant color.

The youth who posed for the portrait, Jonathan Buttall, was the son of a successful hardware merchant. The boy's father had died, and he and the artist became friends.

Gainsborough had wanted his work to be in the style of Van Dyck, so he had Jonathan pose in an antique costume. The costume, a brilliant blue suit with lace at the collar and cuffs, included blue silk stockings, and slippers with bows. The artist slung a cloak over Jonathan's arm and placed a large hat with a feathered plume in his hand. The youth made several visits to the studio to sit for the portrait. First the artist made a pencil sketch of his model. Then he made the final, life-size work with oils on a six-foot-tall canvas, adding an outdoor landscape as a background for the solid, graceful figure. The portrait of Jonathan Buttall won high praise in the 1770 Royal Academy exhibition. It was appreciated for its charm and its simple, lively style.

When Gainsborough's paintings were exhibited at the Royal Academy, he objected to the way they were shown. He felt they were not hung at the proper height for a viewer to see them to their best advantage. He began quarreling with the Academy and for four years he refused to send them his pictures.

In 1774 the artist settled in London, where he lived in a grand house and was able to pursue his interest in music. In 1780 King George III commissioned him to paint portraits of the royal family, including Queen Charlotte and the young princes and princesses. He also painted portraits of some of the English officers who had fought in the American War of Independence that was going on at the time.

In 1781 Gainsborough toured the Lake District in Cumberland, to sketch outdoors. He had begun painting seascapes as a way of experimenting with a new direction in his work. He also took an interest in experiments in lighting and in theatrical scene paintings, which were transparent and lit from behind. This interest led to designing the Show-Box, a box of wooden construction containing a magnifying lens that displayed painted scenes on glass. A colored screen was placed behind the glass. When candles were lit behind the screen, the flickering effects of the light gave the scene a lifelike, almost mysterious, three-dimensional quality. His friends would come by in the evening to enjoy exhibitions of the Show-Boxes.

Gainsborough's landscapes, influenced by Dutch painting, seemed to take on a more poetic quality. His scenes, representing a return to nature, recalled the rustic, wooded river valleys of his childhood, but they were actually ideal settings representing no real places. The simple people who inhabited them were ideal figures as well. Many artists in London were painting serious scenes of historical subjects, but Gainsborough avoided history painting.

Now he was taking a greater interest in studying the Old Masters and was especially influenced by the Spaniard Bartolomé Murillo, whose works he copied. In 1781 he began making what were called Fancy Pictures. They showed simple peasant children in ideal settings who seemed suddenly to have come to life to sit for their portraits. These figures in their rustic surroundings—a shepherd boy, a peasant with a donkey, or a girl with a pony—were made large to give them more importance than the landscape. Gainsborough made direct studies from nature for these pictures. He actually brought some piglets into his studio for a picture of a girl with pigs. He also used groups of dogs as subjects and would place a pet dog in a portrait with its master to add an air of informality and a sense of the subject's private life. A critic once remarked that many of the dogs in the paintings were more memorable than their masters.

Gainsborough's portrait of his daughters. *Roger-Viollet/National Gallery of Art, London.*

Gainsborough had his final quarrel with the Royal Academy in 1784, over the hanging of his pictures, and never exhibited with them again. From then on he conducted private exhibitions in his own studio that became a regular event until he died. His late works were more serious and often included groups of ordinary people in a setting that conveyed a moral lesson.

It seems that the artist was just reaching his full stride in the breadth and depth of his work when his life ended. On his deathbed, he said he was sorry to leave life just as he was beginning to do something with his art. He also worried that his daughters would not be provided for, but his wife then revealed that she had been secretly saving money for years.

Gainsborough died on August 2, 1788, at sixty-one and was buried in Kew Churchyard in London, having a private funeral as he had requested. The following year an exhibition for the sale of his own pictures that had remained in his possession as well as his collection of Old Masters was held at a London gallery. After his death he was remembered more for his Fancy Pictures and landscapes than for his portraits. The young landscape painter John Constable admired these works, which turned out to be in harmony with the romantic tone set by the poet William Wordsworth in the period that was to follow.

Gainsborough's portraits did not receive much attention until the twentieth century, when interest in them was revived by an art dealer who managed to sell *The Blue Boy* for what was reported to be the highest price paid for any painting ever sold up to that time. The portrait of Jonathan had remained in the Buttall family for a time and then passed into the possession of various people in England, including the prominent painter John Hoppner and the Duke of Westminster. Through the years, the owners lent the work to various exhibitions, where it was listed as *Portrait of a Young Gentleman* and *Portrait of Master Buttall* before its nickname *The Blue Boy* won out. When it was bought from the duke by American railroad magnate Henry E. Huntington in 1921, it was considered to be something of a national treasure by the British. It was exhibited in London one last time before leaving England. Then it was secretly packed in a triple waterproof case, and quietly put on a ship that left port in the middle of the night, and sailed across the ocean. No one on the ship knew that the boy in the fancy blue suit, whom all would have recognized, was aboard.

The picture was exhibited in New York before traveling across the United

States by train, chaperoned by the dealer who had arranged the transaction. When it arrived in San Marino, California, at the Huntington estate, it was hung in the English-style dining room at a height that showed it to its best advantage. Surely, this would have pleased the artist. That home is now open to the public as the Huntington Library and Art Gallery and *The Blue Boy* is available for all to see.

Paul Gauguin

1848–1903   French painter; best known for his pictures of Tahiti

The colorful life of Eugène-Henri-Paul Gauguin reads like a geography lesson. He was born in Paris, spent his earliest youth in Peru, traveled all over the world as a seaman, worked in Panama, tried living on the island of Martinique, stayed for a time in Denmark, settled in Tahiti, and died in the Marquesas Islands. His serene paintings of the South Pacific create the image of an ideal world on an island paradise. Yet his own life was filled with torment, poverty, ill health, and pain.

He was born on June 7, 1848, the year after the birth of his sister, Maria. His father, Clovis, whose own father was a well-to-do grocer in Orléans, was a journalist who wrote for a liberal newspaper. His mother, Aline Chazal, came from a noble Spanish family that had settled in Peru. His grandmother, Flora Tristan, was a feminist and social reformer who wrote and traveled across France, making speeches to try to improve conditions for the working class.

After the 1848 revolution in France and Louis-Napoléon Bonaparte's election as president, political conditions were unfavorable for Clovis Gauguin and his newspaper. In 1849 he set out for Peru with his family. Tragically, he had a heart attack at sea and died, leaving Aline to go on to Lima alone with the children. Aline's wealthy uncle took them in, and they spent four years in the sunny South American country.

In 1855 they returned to France and moved into the Gauguin family house in Orléans. Paul was enrolled in a day school and, when he was eleven, in a boarding school run by local priests. In 1861 Aline went to Paris to set up a dressmaking shop, taking Maria with her. Paul joined them the following year and went to school in Paris. He was always dreaming of faraway places, and in 1865 when he was seventeen, he entered the merchant marine and traveled the world on a sailing ship. He saw further sea duty in the Imperial Navy of Napoléon III, serving until 1871. While he was at sea, during the summer of 1867, his mother died, leaving her children a modest inheritance that included her house. Unfortunately, after the Franco-Prussian War broke out in 1870, the Prussians burned the house down.

Aline had appointed Gustave Arosa, a financier, art collector, and photographer, as guardian of her children. In 1872 Arosa helped Gauguin get a job in a stockbroker's office in Paris. A young man named Émile Schuffenecker who worked in the same office encouraged Paul's interest in art, and the two would go to a studio in the evening to draw. Arosa's daughter, Marguerite, was an artist; she gave Gauguin lessons and took him out painting on Sundays. In the meantime Gauguin met Mette Gaad, a Danish woman who was intelligent but not tender, and the two married in 1873. The following year a son, Emil, was born.

While Gauguin was working hard and doing well in business, he was growing increasingly interested in art. Around 1875 he met the well-known artist Camille Pissarro, who encouraged him, and gave him advice. Sometimes they painted together. Gauguin's early works were like Pissarro's, done in the Impressionist style, using subjects from nature, and applying the paint with loose brush strokes, breaking up the forms. In 1876 one of his pictures, a landscape, was accepted at the Salon, the official exhibition of France.

The sculptor Jules Bouillot was another important influence. He taught Gauguin to carve, a technique that he practiced for the rest of his life. Bouillot became Gauguin's landlord in 1877, the year his daughter Aline was born. In time three more children would follow, all boys. Gauguin spent increasingly more time on his art, using his family as models for his paintings, and on forming a collection of Impressionist works.

When the Impressionists held their fourth exhibition in 1879, he loaned some of his works by Pissarro, and a marble bust of his son Emil to be included in the show. Gauguin was then spending evenings at a café in the company of Edouard Manet, Edgar Degas, Pierre-Auguste Renoir, and Pissarro. Sometimes in summer he painted with Pissarro at his home in Pontoise, France. There he met Paul Cézanne, an important figure in the development of modern art. Cézanne's style of painting, simplifying forms and applying the colors in flat areas surrounded by definite outlines, had an influence on Gauguin's style.

At the fifth Impressionist exhibition in 1880, seven of Gauguin's paintings were included. In 1881 he showed in the sixth exhibition, and an important art dealer bought three of his paintings. He continued to show with the Impressionists through their eighth and last exhibition in 1886.

A financial crisis hit France when the stock market crashed in January 1882, and Gauguin was badly affected. In 1883, at thirty-five, he gave up his job and devoted himself to painting full-time. He took his family to Normandy in January 1884 and rented a house in Rouen, where it was cheaper to live than in Paris. He thought he could sell his paintings in Rouen but was unsuccessful, and after a few months, all of his savings were gone. Turning to her family for help, Mette went to Denmark with two of the children, leaving the three others in Rouen with their father and the maid. In November Gauguin followed her, taking a job as an agent for a manufacturer in Copenhagen, but that only lasted six months.

Gauguin was unhappy in Denmark. His wife's family treated him coldly, and an exhibition of his art in Copenhagen was a total failure. To make ends meet, Mette taught French and did translations. Soon, she began selling the pictures her husband had collected.

Hoping for a better life in France, Gauguin returned to Paris in June 1885, taking his young son Clovis along and leaving him with his sister. Then he spent two months in Dieppe, Normandy, where a number of artists, including Edgar Degas, painted during the summer.

In October Clovis joined Gauguin in Paris, and they took a small apartment. The artist looked for work, but could only find a job pasting up posters for five francs a day. The weather was cold, Clovis came down with smallpox, and they were too poor to pay for heat. Although they were suffering, Gauguin considered himself a great artist, and he was willing to endure the hardships in order to proceed with his painting. That spring he met Ernest Chaplet, who ran a ceramic studio with a kiln for firing pottery. Chaplet sparked Gauguin's interest in creating works out of terracotta, or baked clay.

In July 1886, with Clovis in boarding school, Gauguin moved to Pont-Aven, a resort in Brittany. He enjoyed the atmosphere and especially admired the primitive quality of peasant life. Pont-Aven was a popular place for painters.

A self-portrait of Paul Gauguin, painted around 1894. *Giraudon/Art Resource/The Louvre, Paris.*

He met other artists, including Charles Laval, Émile Bernard, and Vincent van Gogh. During this time Gauguin painted country scenes in a style that he was developing on his own. He felt that lines and colors have emotional power which can convey a mood to the viewer. Colors and forms became symbols of ideas in his imagination. He would create strong designs, enclosing large, flat areas of color with sharp outlines in a balanced pattern.

When he returned to Paris he was unable to sell his Brittany paintings so he modeled sculpture in terra-cotta in Chaplet's ceramic studio. In April 1887 Mette came to Paris to pick up Clovis and to take some of her husband's paintings back to Denmark. Alone and ill, Gauguin yearned to leave France and fulfill his dream of living "like a savage." His sister was living in Panama where her South American husband was in business. Gauguin convinced Charles Laval to travel there with him, stopping in Guadaloupe and Martinique.

In Panama he took a job as a laborer on the great canal that was being built; but after two weeks his work was suspended, so he and Laval returned to Martinique. There they slept on a plantation in a native hut amid palm and banana trees, living on fish and fruit. Under brilliant tropical skies they made paintings of the natives in clear colors. Then Laval was stricken with fever and Gauguin fell ill with dysentery and malaria. Gauguin managed to work his way back to France on a sailing vessel and was home by November.

In Paris he stayed in the home of his old friend Émile Schuffenecker, who had also given up his job to become an artist. Gauguin's paintings and ceramics were shown at a gallery run by Vincent van Gogh's brother Théo. Unfortunately sales did not bring enough money to live on, and Gauguin was in poor health. In February 1888 he returned to his favorite inn at Pont-Aven where he was joined by Laval, Schuffenecker, and Émile Bernard. Vincent van Gogh, who was staying at Arles in Provence and was depressed and desperately lonely, wanted Gauguin to join him and help him start a studio where poor artists could find refuge and encourage each other in their work. Gauguin was so deeply in debt that he could not go until Théo agreed to give him a sum of money every month in exchange for producing a painting. He finally joined Vincent in October.

Van Gogh had eagerly awaited Gauguin's arrival and had decorated a room for him in "The Yellow House" that was his home and studio. The two men lived and painted together, each making portraits of the other. Gauguin was a strong subject for a portrait: He had a powerful figure, with a short neck and high forehead, heavy eyelids, thin eyebrows, and beaked nose. His skin was tanned, his hair dark, and he wore a short beard and mustache. Gauguin helped van Gogh to get organized, but he was an arrogant person and could be quite cruel. He dominated van Gogh, who was good-natured, and forced his ideas on him.

Van Gogh showed Gauguin around Arles, and in the evenings, they went to a café. One night they quarreled and van Gogh threw a glass of absinthe liqueur at Gauguin. Two nights before Christmas he tried to attack his guest with a razor. Gauguin fled to a hotel where he stayed overnight, and sent a telegram to Théo telling him to come. On Christmas night Gauguin and Théo went back to Paris together.

It was midwinter, and the artist was homeless. Luckily Schuffenecker took him in again, even though he was a rude guest. Gauguin was so arrogant and egotistical that he acted like the master of the house. He took over his host's studio, locking the door in his face. Even so, Schuffenecker would continue to let Gauguin stay with his family off and on in the coming years and would also give him money. Finally the situation grew unbearable, and Gauguin was asked to leave and not return.

The children of Paul Gauguin. © *Le Musée Départmental du Prieuré, Saint-Germain-en-Laye, France.*

In 1889 a world's fair, the Universal Exposition, was being held in Paris. The Javanese set up a model native village with live dancers, and Gauguin, who continued to dream of a savage life in a faraway place, spent time admiring the tropical setting. A group of painters exhibited their works in a café on the grounds of the world's fair. Gauguin was among them, exhibiting his lithographs. (Lithography is a method of printing a picture that has been drawn with ink on a flat stone.) The artist had also begun to write, as his father had done, and his article on the Universal Exhibition was published in a journal.

That June he went back to Pont-Aven, where he painted pictures of the peasants working in the fields. From there he traveled back and forth to the fishing village of Le Pouldu on the coast. Meyer de Haan, a well-to-do Dutchman who admired Gauguin, worked with him that summer and fall and gave him money to live on. The two men decorated the walls and painted the ceiling of the inn where they were staying. Gauguin enjoyed painting windows in rooms where he lived. He even painted his own wooden shoes that he carved himself. He liked to wear the typical Breton shoes with an embroidered fisherman's blue jersey and a blue beret even when he was in Paris.

The artist associated with writers as well as painters. He made friends with the Symbolist poet Stéphane Mallarmé. Symbolism was a revolutionary movement of authors, painters, and musicians who objected to changes in society brought about by the increasing use of machinery. They wanted their work to express a message instead of reproducing reality. Gauguin's work was shown with other Symbolist painters in Brussels at the Salon des XX.

For some time the artist had been thinking about escaping to a place that was warmer and cheaper than France, and where he could find new subjects for his paintings. He once wrote, "May the day come when I shall go fleeing to the woods of some island of Oceania and live there on ecstasy, quiet and art . . . far from this European struggle for money." Later, in a letter to a friend, he said of the French colony of Tahiti, "Under a winterless sky, on a wonderfully fertile land the Tahitian only has to stretch an arm to pick his food."

To raise money for a trip to the South Pacific, an auction of his works was held in Paris in February 1891. Edgar Degas bought one of the paintings. Almost ten thousand francs was raised in all. The following month Gauguin made a quick visit to Copenhagen to see his wife and children for what would be the last time. Back in Paris his friends held a banquet in his honor and later they would have a theater benefit performance to raise money for him. Although his model and mistress Juliette Huet was pregnant, he left her behind in Paris and sailed for Tahiti.

Traveling by way of Australia he arrived in the Tahitian capital of Papeete on June 9. He was disappointed to find that Papeete, ever since it had been colonized by the French, had the same European atmosphere that he was trying to escape. The French colonials did not approve of the long hair Gauguin had grown, so he cut it off, bought a white suit like those worn by Frenchmen in the community, and became a member of the officers' club. He moved into a hut and tried to learn the native language without success.

Gauguin had not found the unspoiled jungle paradise he yearned for, so in August he moved to Mataiéa on the south coast of the island and chose a young woman named Teha'ana to be his mistress. Together they lived the life of the natives around them, in a bamboo hut with no furniture and only a thick layer of dried grass on the mud floor. Gauguin wore a colored loincloth and sandals, let his hair grow long again, and ate mostly roots and fish. He was known to the natives as Koké. Although suffering from ill health, he painted beautiful scenes of Tahitian women in their magnificent natural setting. When he ran out of canvas, he chiseled blocks of wood from the trees and carved them into statuettes.

Gauguin was eager to learn about the Polynesian culture, and he was especially interested in stories of their gods. However, little remained of Tahitian religion and mythology after the French missionaries changed the beliefs of the people. Most of what he learned came from a book written by Jacques Antoine Moerenhout that was published half a century earlier. Although European culture had already taken over, the book

became the basis for Gauguin's own book on ancient Maori religion, which he began writing at the time. He also wrote essays that were later published in the book *Noa Noa,* which includes letters and notes that express his ideas about art. He said, for instance, that he was not a painter after nature, but that everything sprang from his "mad imagination." Some of the works he created at the time represent the traditional culture of the Polynesians, while others used Tahitian subjects to illustrate Christian themes.

Gauguin was living the life he had wished for, but he was ill, and he could now see that it was impossible to exist without money, even in Tahiti. His works were not selling well in France, but luckily exhibitions arranged by Mette in Copenhagen were successful. She sent him money to pay his debts, and he was able to sail home. On his arrival in France on August 30, 1893, he had only four francs in his pocket.

Back in Paris a friend gave him money so he could rent a studio. Eleven of his Tahitian pictures sold at an exhibition late that year, and he inherited some money from his uncle in Orléans, so he was able to rent an apartment and improve his standard of living. He began giving weekly receptions that were attended by prominent artists and authors, including August Strindberg, the

A woodcut executed by Gauguin for his book, *Noa Noa.* © 1993 *The Art Institute of Chicago. Clarence Buckingham Collection.* (*1948.255. recto*)

brilliant Swedish playwright, and the French artist Aristide Maillol. When he went about Paris his clothes attracted attention: He wore a blue cloak with mother-of-pearl buttons, a gray felt hat with a blue ribbon, and carried a carved walking stick inlaid with a large pearl.

Never wanting to be without a woman, Gauguin took into his home a thirteen-year-old from Ceylon known as Annah the Javanese. When he went to Britanny he took her and her pet monkey with him. Eager to have *Noa Noa* published, he made woodcuts, which could be inked to print illustrations. He also painted simplified compositions of peasant life in Brittany in the same style he had developed in Tahiti.

On May 25, 1894, while he and Annah were walking with friends in a seaside village near Pont-Aven, some local boys began throwing stones. The incident led to a fight with the father of one of the boys and his companions. In the midst of the brawl Gauguin fell and broke his right ankle. The ankle never healed properly, and for the rest of his life, he suffered from intense pain, which he tried to relieve with morphine. While he was recuperating from his fall, Annah returned to Paris, ransacked his studio, and then disappeared. When the artist returned, there was nothing left but his paintings.

Gauguin was alone, his ankle hurt badly, and the sale of his works was not bringing in enough money. Even worse, he had contracted syphilis. The ugly effects of the disease, which included spitting up blood and developing hideous sores on his legs, would grow steadily worse over the remaining years of his life. Once again he dreamed of a real paradise on earth and thought of returning to the South Seas. He sailed on July 3, 1895, passing through the Suez Canal and going on to Australia, where he waited more than three weeks for another boat. He arrived in Papeete September 8, to find that the capital had become even more European than it had been when he left. Now there were electric lights and a merry-go-round.

In November he left Papeete to settle in Punoauia eight miles away on the west coast. There he leased land and built a hut out of bamboo canes, and he thatched its roof with palm leaves. Then he sent for Teha'ana. When she saw him she was frightened by the sores on his legs, and she left him even though he gave her presents of beautiful beads and shiny jewelry. He soon found another young woman, however, who moved into his hut on New Year's Day 1896. Before long he spent all of his money and had to borrow from the bank. He was ill, hungry, and suffering from the leg sores and the pain from his broken ankle, but he could not afford hospital care.

Later that year Gauguin felt a little better, and in late December he received some money from France from the sale of his pictures. Then in April 1897 he received an angry letter from his wife telling him that his nineteen-year-old daughter, Aline, who had been named after his mother and was his favorite child, had died of pneumonia. He was stunned, and wrote a harsh letter to Mette in August 1897. After that he never heard from his wife again.

In the midst of his grief Gauguin was suffering from an eye disease and had nothing to eat except tropical fruit. He had no canvas to paint on; nevertheless he was able to create a great work on a large piece of coarse material used for making sacks. He called it *D'où venons-nous? Que sommes-nous? Où allons-nous?* (Where do we come from? What are we? Where are we going?).

Early the next year he was so desperate he went into the mountains and tried to commit suicide by taking arsenic. The following morning he found himself alive, sick, and exhausted. After many hours of lying alone in misery, he managed to drag himself back to town. There was nothing left to do but get up his courage and swallow his pride. He begged the governor for work and got a civil service job as a draftsman in Papeete for six francs a day. It was enough for his bare necessities, but he had no time to paint.

In late January 1899 he returned to his home in Punoauia to find that rats and termites had destroyed his hut and his paintings. His current mistress

Paul Gauguin's *Tahitian Women. Musée d'Orsay, Paris.*

Pahura, who was about to have a baby, had stolen some of his belongings. Too discouraged to paint and with no canvas to paint on, he did some writing for a monthly magazine and then started his own publication. His articles defending the natives, whom he felt were mistreated by the French bureaucrats, led to quarrels with the authorities. His situation was pathetic. He was still poor, and so ill that he had to spend time in the hospital. His son Clovis died in May 1900, but Gauguin never knew it. A

year later, his book *Noa Noa* was published. Discovering that the world was reading about her husband's decadent life made Mette all the more bitter.

Gauguin said that he thought of himself as a savage who needed a truly savage society. He decided that if he moved to the Marquesas Islands to the northeast he could get away from colonial officials and live more cheaply. On September 16, 1901, he bought land in the center of the village of Atuona on the island of Hiva Oa and built a hut surrounded by tropical plants. He called it *La Maison du Jouir* (The House of Pleasure). He was finally getting monthly payments from an art dealer in Paris, but managed to spend it all on his own pleasure. In spite of his poor health he was able to paint, using canvas that arrived from France. He continued to write, too, working on his diary, which he called *Avant et Après* (Before and After).

Gauguin soon realized that the native culture was also dead in Hiva Oa and that the European way of life had taken hold. He quarreled with authorities as he had in Tahiti. He refused to pay the high taxes and complained about the administrators' treatment of the natives, whom he felt should not be taxed nor forced to send their children to the mission school. His quarrels led to a charge of libel, and he was fined and sentenced to three months in prison. Before he could appeal the sentence, he had a fatal heart attack.

Gauguin died alone and bitter in the South Pacific on May 8, 1903, and was buried in a local Catholic cemetery without a funeral ceremony. He failed to find the earthly paradise he had sought, but his paintings of Tahiti made him a legend even during his lifetime. After his death, exhibitions were held in Paris for the world to see his original and imaginative works of art. Today, he is recognized as one of the great figures of Post-Impressionism and a pioneer of modern art.

El Greco (Doménikos Theotokópoulos)

1541–1614   Greek painter who lived in Spain and captured the Spanish spirit in his art

Only a few facts are known about the life of El Greco, the Greek painter with an original style who worked in Spain. Most of what is known had to be pieced together from a small number of documents and records. *El Greco,* Spanish for "the Greek," was the nickname given to the artist after he moved to Spain. El Greco was born Doménikos Theotokópoulos in 1541 in Candia, capital of the Greek island of Crete. His father's name was Jorghi, and he had a brother named Manoussos. His family, who owned land and were probably well-to-do, sent him to school where he received a good education. He was also trained in the art of painting, probably by monks working in local monasteries. The traditional paintings in Crete were icons: small, formal images from the

New Testament that had been popular in the Greek Orthodox church since the Middle Ages. Icons were painted in flat, bright colors on small wooden panels.

At the time, Crete was a possession of the Venetian Republic, which controlled a vast territory. Venice, on the Italian peninsula, was a thriving center of trade and also an important center for art. A large colony of Greeks lived there and Greek artists were respected. Sometime around 1560 El Greco went to Venice to learn to paint in the Italian Renaissance manner.

The leading artist in Venice was Titian, who was then in his seventies. It is not known whether the young Greek ever knew the great master, but he was certainly inspired by him. He was also impressed with Jacopo Tintoretto, and got ideas from works by Paolo Veronese and Jacopo Bassano. El Greco studied their paintings closely in order to learn their styles. He improved his technique of composing pictures, using the rich colors of Venetian paintings, but his figures looked awkward. His New Testament scene *Purification of the Temple* combines the small size and the materials and brush strokes of an icon with the composition and rich colors of an Italian Renaissance picture.

El Greco left Venice for Rome in the autumn of 1570, passing through Parma, where he was impressed with Antonio Correggio's paintings in the dome of the cathedral there. In Rome he made contact with Giulio Clovio, a painter of miniatures who was employed by the wealthy and powerful Cardinal Alessandro Farnese. Alessandro, a patron of the arts, included a number of artists within his circle of friends. Clovio asked him to let El Greco stay for a time in the Farnese palace, and work as an assistant on the decoration of his magnificent villa. In the summer of 1572 El Greco was admitted to membership in the Painters Guild of Rome, the Academy of Saint Luke, which enabled him to open a workshop and have his own pupils.

The great artist Michelangelo, who lived in Rome had died eight years before, but El Greco knew of his work. It is said that Pope Paul V objected to the nude figures in Michelangelo's wall painting of the Last Judgement. El Greco offered to repaint the figures. He criticized the wall painting, especially the great master's use of color, but because Michelangelo was considered "divine" with no one to equal him, the Greek painter was considered arrogant, and he became unpopular in Rome. He did, however, admire Michelangelo's sculpture. He also admired his drawings, even though he thought that color was much more important than drawing. During this peroid El Greco improved his technique of painting.

Cardinal Farnese had a wonderful library in his palace. The librarian, Fulvio Orsini, was a respected scholar and generous patron of the arts who collected rare books and paintings by the Italian masters. The young Greek, who was interested in learning, was allowed to use Orsini's library and study his paintings, which influenced his own work. A drawing by Michelangelo in Orsini's collection would serve as a model for some of El Greco's later paintings. While El Greco was in Rome Orsini acquired seven of his paintings, four of them miniatures.

Orsini's friends were scholars, priests, writers, and artists. El Greco enjoyed their company and made friends with them. One of the scholars, Don Luis de

Castilla, was a visitor from Spain whose brother Don Diego was dean of the Toledo Cathedral. At that time Spain controlled the largest empire the world had ever known, stretching from Europe to America, and the king of Spain, Philip II, was the richest and most powerful ruler in Europe. King Philip was completing the building of El Escorial, a monastery and palace thirty miles north of Madrid, and needed painters to decorate the interior. El Greco, with hopes of becoming a court painter by gaining favor with the king, left for Spain.

He first stopped in Madrid, then went on to Toledo arriving in the summer of 1577. Toledo, where he would spend the rest of his life, was a walled city with narrow streets on a high promontory forty miles south of Madrid. It was the religious center for the Catholic Church in Spain. The high tower of the great cathedral in the center of the city rose above the houses, and there were a great many other churches as well. Toledo had a fine university that attracted writers and men of learning. Toledo was also known for its famous steel sword blades, which were exported throughout Europe. It was a time of prosperity for the local merchant class who profited from a thriving manufacturing business in fine silks and linens. The Spanish royal family resided in the city until Philip II transferred the court to Madrid.

Shortly after his arrival in Spain, El Greco began living with Doña Jerónima de las Cuevas, the beautiful woman who became his lifelong companion. Her lovely face can be recognized in some of his paintings. A son, Jorge Manuel Theotokópoulos, was born in 1578, and the three of them had a happy home life.

The artist's first commissions in Toledo came from Don Diego de Castilla, who was supervising the construction and decoration of the convent church of Santo Domingo el Antiguo, where he wanted to be buried. El Greco was commissioned to paint a series of pictures for the main altar, with the largest picture, the *Assumption of the Virgin,* as the centerpiece. The project was completed in 1579, and it established his reputation as a first-rate artist. As always he signed his work Doménikos Theotokópoulos in Greek in block letters.

That same year he finished another religious picture, the *Disrobing of Christ,* for a room in the cathedral of Toledo. El Greco was proud of the high quality of his work and felt he should be well paid. He had received partial payment in advance, but it was necessary for appraisers to put a value on the painting before he could be paid in full.

Portrait of a Man, believed to be a self-portrait of El Greco. *The Metropolitan Museum of Art, Joseph Pulitzer Fund, 1924.*

When the appraisers said he was asking too much, he would not accept the price they offered him. Moreover, there was criticism of some of the figures in the painting, which did not fit with the teachings of the Church: The head of one, for instance, stood above that of Christ, and a group of three female figures were not in keeping with the New Testament text. El Greco was asked to change the painting, but he boldly refused to do so until a satisfactory price had been agreed on. The argument continued for three years. Finally he delivered the picture at a lower price than he expected, but he did not remove the three female figures. The *Disrobing of Christ* was highly admired, but the officials of the cathedral never commissioned El Greco to do another painting. He did, however, receive a contract to make the large wooden frame decorated with sculpture for the painting.

At the time, the Catholic Church was reacting to the Reformation, the movement that resulted in the formation of the Protestant Church. The Catholic leaders of the Counter-Reformation demanded that paintings be very clear in the story they told and the religious message they carried. They wanted saints to be painted in such a way as to inspire prayer. Most of the pictures that satisfied these requirements were bor-

ing. El Greco worked in the Italian mannerist style, elongating and exaggerating his figures and placing them in elegant poses. His designs and compositions were complex and artificial, with upward-sweeping forms and figures that seemed to move.

In 1580 El Greco got the opportunity he had been waiting for—a chance to gain favor at court. King Philip granted him a royal commission to paint an altarpiece for a chapel in El Escorial. It took more than two years to complete the work, *The Martyrdom of Saint Maurice*. The artist personally delivered the picture to El Escorial in November 1582, but it failed to please the king who ordered another painting from an Italian artist to replace it. This was a terrible disappointment to El Greco. He knew he would not be invited to do further work, either for the court or for the cathedral. He had many important friends and admirers, however, who would bring him customers.

El Greco, a learned man, was accepted in the scholarly community as an intellectual. He read the Old and New Testaments and works on ancient Greek philosophy. His personal library contained books by Church leaders, as well as Giorgio Vasari's *Lives of the Painters* and *On Architecture* by the ancient Roman architect Marcus Vitruvius. He studied these books carefully and wrote

El Greco is believed to have painted his own face (*third from right*) into *The Martyrdom of Saint Maurice*. © *Alinari/Art Resource.*

his own works on art and architecture. El Greco was intelligent, witty, bold, and daring, and he had an independent spirit. He painted numerous portraits, but never one of himself, so we do not know just what he looked like. Certain bearded faces in some of his paintings, however, are thought to be self-portraits.

Without cathedral or royal commissions, El Greco worked independently, receiving commissions from churchmen, merchants, and noblemen. In 1585 he leased three apartments in a rambling palace owned by the Marquis of Villena and set up a well-organized workshop. A chief assistant often acted as his business agent. Prospective customers were invited to come and see samples of his work. Churches commissioned him to create altarpieces, which included the picture, the wooden frame, and painted sculpture. The construction of an altarpiece required skill in architectural design as well as in painting and sculpture. El Greco's business did well and he had a good income, but the overhead on his workshop was high. When times were good he lived like a prince, dining while musicians played his favorite songs. During bad times he was forced to move out of the palace temporarily.

In 1586 he was commissioned to paint a religious work for the Chapel of Santo Tomé where Don Gonzalo de Ruiz, a generous and charitable nobleman, had been buried a century and a half earlier. According to tradition, a miracle had occurred at the nobleman's funeral. As his body was being prepared for burial Saint Augustine and Saint Stephen descended from the heavens to place him in his tomb. El Greco's monumental fifteen-foot-high painting, known as *The Burial of the Count of Orgaz,* became his most famous picture. (See reproduction in the color section of this book.)

In the painting the body of the count, wearing his finest armor, is being lowered into his tomb by the Saints, in the presence of a priest, while his soul, in the form of a baby, is being carried to heaven by an angel. The work blends the heavenly world and the earthly world: divine figures, elongated and twisted, miraculously appear among the group of mourners attending the funeral, dressed in sixteenth-century fashion. The artist used men that were living in Toledo as models. A boy in the foreground, looking out from the painting, is probably the artist's son Jorge Manuel.

Because El Greco's work had an original style, he was successful in attracting patrons from Toledo, as well as from churches, towns, and villages around the city. One of the contracts he re-

El Greco's home in Toledo, Spain. © *Roger-Viollet*.

ceived was for an altarpiece in the college of Doña María de Aragón, a seminary in Madrid, which he finished in 1600. In 1597 he was commissioned to produce three altarpieces for a private chapel in Toledo that was dedicated to Saint Joseph. One of these, *Saint Martin and the Beggar*, is among the artist's finest works. It portrays the rich young Martin in his fine armor, riding a white horse, just after he divided his cloak with a sword. He is giving the splendid cloth to a poor beggar who is suffering from the cold.

Around 1600 El Greco's son Jorge Manuel, whom he had trained in painting and architecture, joined his father as a partner in his workshop. He soon became chief assistant. The business thrived, but again overhead costs were high, and El Greco's brother Manoussos was now living with them. The artist owed money and had to borrow from friends to pay the rent. His health was failing, but he continued to create new paintings. Because his work was in such demand, he kept small samples in his studio of his best-known pictures so people could buy copies for themselves. He was so highly admired that someone said of him, "Doménikos Greco is held to be one of the most outstanding practitioners of art in this or any other kingdom." He started his last important altarpiece, for the chapel of the Hospital of Saint John the Baptist in Toledo, in 1608, but did not complete it. After his death, it was finished by his son Jorge Manuel.

El Greco died in Toledo on April 7, 1614, and was buried in Santo Domingo el Antiguo. He left few possessions, but the paintings he created enriched the world. He was almost forgotten for a long time. His pictures, which were all in Spain, were practically unknown outside of that country except to a few travelers. Those people who did see them thought they looked strange. When French armies occupied Spain in the early nineteenth century some of El Greco's paintings were taken to France. People who saw them for the first time thought he must have been mad. Then later in the century his work began to get attention. People considered him a bold and unusual artistic genius. A group of French painters who experimented with new ideas admired his work which served as an inspiration for modern art. Today many people feel that the paintings of this Greek artist, who adopted Spain as his country, capture the essence of the Spanish spirit.

Winslow Homer

1836–1910   American painter known for his seascapes

All of his life, Winslow Homer had a deep love of the outdoors and that was the setting for his paintings. The Homers, who were descended from generations of native New Englanders, were living in Boston, Massachusetts, when he was born on February 24, 1836. His father, Charles Savage Homer, was in the hardware business and his mother, Maria Benson, was an amateur artist who painted beautiful watercolors of flowers.

When Homer was six years old, his family moved to Cambridge, just outside Boston, and he attended the local school. Cambridge was a village with lovely homes and extensive fields and woods, and young Homer was able to enjoy nature. He ran in the meadows and fished in the ponds. He had two

brothers: Charles, Jr., who was two years older and remained a good friend throughout his life; and Arthur, who was five years younger, and settled in Texas.

Homer's life changed when his father sold his business after gold was discovered in California and went west to join the gold rush of 1849. Like many others he expected to make his fortune but instead returned home broke.

Homer showed a love for drawing when he was young, and both his parents encouraged him in his art. When he was eighteen he went to work in Boston as an apprentice in a shop specializing in lithography, a method of printing from an image drawn on stone. His job was to copy pictures to illustrate sheet music for popular songs. He showed talent, but found the work dull, and he did not like being tied down to a full-time job. He was so eager to be outdoors that he sometimes got up in the middle of the night so he could go fishing before work.

In 1857 when his two-year apprenticeship ended, Homer left the shop, rented a studio in the Ballou Publishing House Building, and began working on his own. This suited his independent spirit, although it did not please his father. He began drawing illustrations for the magazine *Ballou's Pictorial Drawing Room Companion. Ballou's* used the printing method called wood engraving, which involved drawing on a smooth wooden block that would be carved and inked for reproduction. Homer's drawings, centering on everyday scenes in American life, had a feeling of movement and energy, and the editor of *Ballou's* was pleased with his work. By 1859 the young artist was also making drawings for *Harper's Weekly,* whose offices were in New York City. His assignments covered life at Harvard University and other places near Boston. Because New York had become the art and publishing center of America, Homer moved there in 1859. He would continue to return to New England for visits and eventually to live.

In New York Homer could have had a full-time job as a staff illustrator at *Harper's Weekly,* but he did not want to go to an office every day, preferring to continue working as a free-lance artist. He stayed for a time in a boardinghouse where he rented a room and ate meals with the other boarders. After two years he moved into the New York University Building where other artists had studios, including Eastman Johnson, who is known for his fine portraits and his paintings of daily life in America. He took a few evening classes at the National Academy of Design and briefly studied painting with a French artist, but he was almost entirely self-taught.

When Abraham Lincoln became president in 1861 Homer made drawings of his inauguration for *Harper's Weekly.* After the Civil War broke out, he traveled with the Union troops, making drawings mostly of army life in the soldiers' camps. As an artist-reporter he learned to observe carefully and to record accurately what he saw. The photographer Mathew Brady and his assistants were in the battlefield covering the war with the newly invented camera. Their photographs influenced Homer's art.

Around 1863 the artist began exhibiting paintings in oil, using the war as his subject. He was able to sell his works, but many years later he learned that his older brother, Charles, had secretly bought two of his pictures to encourage

In the only photograph of Winslow Homer working in his studio, he is shown painting *The Gulf Stream* in 1898. (See reproduction in color section of this book.) *Bowdoin College Museum of Art. Elizabeth McLaren Stovel, Anne McLaren Griffin, and Donald McLaren in memory of their parents, Thayer McLaren and Madeleine Skinner McLaren.*

him. The National Academy of Design exhibited one of his army paintings, *Prisoners from the Front,* and it brought him recognition. The Academy elected him an associate member in 1864 and a full member in 1866.

That fall Homer went to Europe for the first time and stayed in France, so he was in Paris the following year when *Prisoners from the Front* was exhibited at the Universal Exposition, a world's fair. He enjoyed life in France. He did a little work in a studio that he shared with a friend from Massachusetts and sent some drawings back to the United States for publication in *Harper's Weekly.* Many talented artists were working in France at the time, and Homer must have seen some of the paintings that were being produced, but it is hard to say how much they affected his style. He felt an artist must reproduce what he sees and should not look at the works of other artists. He once

Winslow Homer's *The Fog Warning*, painted in 1885. © *1993 Museum of Fine Arts, Boston. Otis Norcross Fund.*

said, "When I have selected the thing carefully, I paint it exactly as it appears."

Returning to America he continued to spend summers painting, hunting, and fishing in the countryside of either New York State or New England. Country life became the subject of his works. His fresh paintings of the games and pastimes of children give a true picture of rural life in America in the late nineteenth century. Summer seaside resorts also became the settings for his paintings at that time. His solid compositions of fashionable ladies on vacation are among his best-known works. In the wintertime the artist continued to live in New York City. In 1872 he moved to the Tenth Street Studio Building where other artists were living and working.

Short and lean with a mustache that curled up at the ends, Homer was attractive and always well dressed. He had some friends and enjoyed socializing, but not much is really known about his private life. He would not let visitors into his studio and he hated publicity, refusing to meet with reporters or to answer personal questions, even for his biography. It has been said that he was in love with a young woman whom he had hoped to marry, but the relationship did not work out and he remained a bachelor all his life.

In the summer of 1873 the artist went to Gloucester, Massachusetts, and there he began using watercolors. With that medium he could work outdoors, creating his figures quickly and freely in color. When he began exhibiting these works the following winter, they met with success. Homer's watercolors are now considered to be among the finest in the history of American art. By 1874 he was selling enough of his pictures at high enough prices to be able to give up magazine illustration. When the United States Centennial Exhibition was held in Philadelphia in 1876, and thousands of people came to celebrate the hundredth anniversary of the nation, Homer's work was well represented.

In the spring of 1881 he went abroad again, this time sailing to England. He landed in Liverpool, took a train to London for a short stay, and then proceeded northeast to Tynemouth, a fishing village on the North Sea. He settled down by himself in a rented cottage, producing watercolors, some sketches, and a few oil paintings. The subjects concerned the hazardous life of fishermen at sea and the activities of the women who waited for them. While he was in England he exhibited several pictures at the Royal Academy. Returning to New York in November 1882

he stayed in the city all winter and spring.

Homer's family spent summers vacationing in Prout's Neck, an isolated spot on the rugged coast of Maine. His younger brother, Arthur, who had settled in Texas with his wife and two children, built a summer home there while Homer was in England, and his older brother, Charles, built a house there soon after. In the summer of 1883, Homer joined his brothers in Prout's Neck, taking over Charles's stable to use as a year-round studio and home. The following winter he exhibited fifty-one of his English watercolors in Boston, and he continued to exhibit his works in New York as well. Art critics and collectors were pleased with his work. When his mother died in 1884 his father came to Prout's Neck to be with him for a time. Even though their father was a difficult man, Homer and Charles took care of him as long as he lived.

The artist was friendly with his neighbors in Prout's Neck, although he was not friendly to visitors. He had a fox terrier named Sam for company, and he enjoyed working in his garden and taking nature walks. He loved the sea in all its moods. He was fascinated with its power and with the people who had to live by struggling against the dangers of the ocean. Many of Homer's most powerful pictures are oil paintings of the

Winslow Homer with his father and his dog Sam at Prout's Neck. *Bowdoin College Museum of Art. Gift of the Homer family.*

fierce sea, some with New England fishermen in action, others with no people in them at all. He felt that living alone on a rocky cliff overlooking the Atlantic was the best atmosphere for him to create these works.

Sometimes in early autumn or late spring he went fishing and hunting in the remote wilderness of the north woods with Charles. Quebec became one of their favorite places to visit. They also loved the Adirondacks. Sometimes they went together; at other times Homer went alone and stayed at a private club. His interest in the men of the outdoors, the lives they led, and their relationship to nature is reflected in his

paintings. Maine winters are severe, so in cold weather Homer usually traveled south to the Bahamas, Florida, Cuba, or Bermuda. There he painted the tropical sea with its intense sunlight and brilliant colors. Many of these works are watercolors of tropical storms.

When the World's Columbian Exposition was held in 1893 fifteen of Homer's paintings were exhibited. He went to Chicago for the fair. In the Paris Exposition of 1900 his pictures received honors. They were praised as "native to America." As always, Homer was indifferent to the fame and his awards. His work was again represented in the Louisiana Purchase Exposition, another world's fair held in Saint Louis, Missouri, in 1904.

Two years later he fell ill and did not work again until 1908; soon after, he had a stroke. He died in Prout's Neck, Maine, on September 29, 1910, at the age of seventy-four and was buried in Cambridge, Massachusetts, where he had spent his boyhood and learned to enjoy the nature he loved to paint.

Leonardo da Vinci

1452–1519   Italian painter, sculptor, architect, and scientist

Leonardo da Vinci was an extraordinary person: He was a superb artist, a brilliant scientist, and a fine musician. Even during his own time, people called him "marvelous" and "divine" and said that his genius was the gift of God. He was born on April 15, 1452, in Vinci, a little town in the hills twenty miles from Florence, Italy. His father, Ser Piero da Vinci, was a public official and his mother, Caterina, a country girl whose last name is not known. They were never married.

As an infant Leonardo lived with his mother until she married a man named Accattabriga and went with him to live on his family's farm. Leonardo's father had married a young woman from a wealthy family and spent almost all of his time in Florence. Leonardo was left to be brought up by his father's parents and his young uncle Francesco on the small family estate in Vinci.

Leonardo was a handsome child, graceful, wiry, and strong, who was generous and kind to everyone He liked to collect small creatures, such as lizards, bats, butterflies, and grasshoppers and bring them to his room to study them. He loved wild creatures. To avoid harming a living thing he would not eat meat. When he saw songbirds in cages in the marketplace, he bought them so he could set them free. He learned all about horses, which he loved, and became an excellent rider. When he grew up, he kept horses and other animals, which he trained with great patience and affection.

The young Leonardo observed the

winds and watched birds in flight, dreaming of creating a machine so people would be able to fly. He was good at drawing and could write and draw with either hand, but he preferred using the left. In a notebook that he carried in his pocket, he kept a record of interesting things he thought about or saw around him. He did not, however, record anything personal about his own feelings or activities, so facts about his life are vague. He wrote backward with his left hand, from right to left, so the writing could be read only in a mirror.

After his grandfather died in 1468 Leonardo went to live with his father in Florence. Ser Piero could see that his son had a talent for drawing and showed one of his sketches to his artist friend Andrea del Verrocchio. Andrea was amazed and told Ser Piero that Leonardo should study art. The lad entered Verrocchio's studio and went to the master's home to live. Verrocchio, who worked in sculpture as well as painting, was an active artist, and he also kept busy as a goldsmith. Furthermore, he had engineering skills. As an apprentice Leonardo practiced drawing from nature and learned the arts of painting, modeling with clay, and casting, or forming, statues in bronze. He prepared paints by grinding colored minerals and mixing them with egg yolks or linseed oil, and he prepared

wooden panels that would be used for painting by covering them with fine plaster. He learned geometry and how to make instruments for navigation, which were very much in demand. This was a great age of exploration when adventurous men were setting out on sea voyages to seek new routes to distant lands.

Another of the young artists in Verrocchio's studio was Lorenzo di Credi. The group of apprentices enjoyed lively parties, and they amused themselves by playing musical instruments and singing. Leonardo had a fine voice and would accompany his songs on the lyre. He made an impressive figure, with his naturally curly hair, wearing short, rose-colored robes and tights. Leonardo liked to play tricks and practical jokes. He was even tempered, and had a reputation for being somewhat reserved.

In 1472 Leonardo became a master of his trade, joining the painters' guild of Saint Luke. He served as Verrocchio's chief assistant, managing his studio and working on the master's paintings. He also worked on banners for elaborate celebrations and pageants for weddings and feast days. Jousts fought on horseback in the public square were especially colorful. In the course of his activities he often saw Lorenzo de' Medici, known as the Magnificient, the head of the leading family of Florence.

When Verrocchio painted the religious scene *The Baptism of Christ* in 1472, Leonardo was responsible for adding the figure of an angel. It is said that after the master saw the young artist's addition he realized at once that Leonardo was a better painter than he. Verrocchio decided that he would never touch colors again and would devote himself to sculpture, at which he was a leading master.

Leonardo's work was delicate, with curved lines that gave it a sense of rhythm. He liked to use tones of olive green and gray. He aimed for perfection in his figures, and yet they look natural. One of his paintings is a biblical work, the *Annunciation,* in which the Archangel Gabriel delivers a message to the Virgin Mary that she will have a son. First Leonardo made dozens of sketches, carefully planning each detail. He studied botany so that he could show many different species of flowers and plants accurately in the painting. The actual wings of a bird were used as a model for the wings of the Archangel Gabriel. Leonardo also studied anatomy and mathematics to aid him in his painting. He felt that mathematics was the foundation of art, and he established a formula for the perfect proportions of an ideal human body.

Around 1474 Leonardo painted a portrait of Ginevra de' Benci, the daughter of a wealthy Florentine merchant Amerigo de' Benci and the sister of one of his friends. The portrait is remarkable for the manner in which the figure of the young woman and the landscape enhance each other. It captured her likeness so well that someone said that "it seemed not a portrait but Ginevra herself."

In 1478 Leonardo, now working on his own, received his first important commission: to paint an altarpiece for the Chapel of Saint Bernard in the Palazzo Vecchio, the City Hall. Before he could start it, the commission was transferred to someone else.

The same year Lorenzo de' Medici's younger brother, Giuliano, was assassinated by members of a rival clan. Leonardo made a drawing of one of the convicted murderers hanging by his neck.

Soon afterward Leonardo started work on a great altarpiece for a monastery at San Donato on the biblical subject The Adoration of the Magi, but he never finished it. Throughout his life he would start projects that he would not finish.

At the time Milan, in northern Italy, was under the control of Ludovico Sforza, Duke of Bari. He was a patron of the arts, interested in improving his city and making it more beautiful. Milan was a great fortified city, enclosed by high walls, surrounded by a moat, and guarded by towers. The city was an important center for the manufacture of arms and armor. In 1482 Leonardo, now a famous painter and a recognized musician, traveled to Milan with a friend who was a well-known musician. Music was important in the Sforza's court, and Leonardo brought the duke the gift of a lyre from Lorenzo de' Medici. The instrument was made of silver in the form of a horse's head.

At the time, wars were raging up and down the Italian peninsula and Milan was threatened by war with Venice and other states. Leonardo wrote a letter to the duke, offering his services as an architect and military engineer to design powerful machines of war.

In Milan Leonardo lived with a family of artists and did some paintings for churches. In 1483 he was commissioned by a monastery to paint the *Madonna of the Rocks,* a beautiful picture with fragile, natural-looking figures of the Virgin, seated at the entrance to a cave, presenting her infant son to the youthful Saint John. The painting gives the viewer a feeling of endless time.

Although an epidemic of the plague was killing thousands of people in Milan, Leonardo continued to work. He painted a wonderful portrait of the duke's youthful mistress, Cecilia Gallerani, holding an ermine. In 1485,

when there was a total eclipse of the sun, he designed a device to study it without damaging the eye. His interest in architecture included town planning. Wanting to replan parts of the city of Milan, he designed a model city with two levels of streets and underground canals, but the plans were never carried out. For one of his designs, the cupola of the Milan Cathedral, he made a wooden model.

As time went on the artist gradually won the confidence of Ludovico Sforza and was appointed as his engineer. He was given his own workshop and living quarters in the palace. Also he owned several horses. His duties included designing sets and costumes for lavish weddings, festivals, and planning court plays, musical performances, and tournaments. Leonardo seems to have enjoyed the luxury of the Sforza court, and he fit easily into the life-style. The duke was impressed with Leonardo's conversation, and people in the court were entertained by his songs. The artist had a quiet, mysterious manner and always dressed to perfection. He made friends with nobleman Girolamo Melzi, who lived in a large house surrounded by a garden. Melzi had two sons whom Leonardo liked very much and the artist enjoyed a kind of life with the family that he had missed as a child.

Leonardo had several young pupils in

Milan. One of them, ten-year-old Giacomo Salai, came to live with him in 1490. The boy also acted as his servant. Salai was handsome and graceful, but he was a rascal and caused a lot of trouble. Even so, the artist was fond of him and spoiled him, giving him expensive presents, such as a cloak of silver brocade trimmed with green velvet. Salai stayed with Leonardo for twenty-five years.

Ludovico Sforza asked Leonardo to create a colossal bronze statue of a mounted horseman as a memorial to his father, Francesco, and the artist set to work on this project around 1483. As models he used horses in the duke's stable of five hundred prize steeds. He even measured some of them to get the proportions for a perfect horse. He filled his sketchbook with drawings of the animals, complete with notes, in the hope of writing a book on the anatomy of the horse. Also, he made small wax models to try out different poses.

Leonardo designed the colossal statue for the duke and made a full-scale clay model of the horse twenty-two feet high, which he exhibited in the courtyard of the ducal castle in 1493 as part of the wedding festivities for the marriage of Lodovico's niece, Bianca Maria Sforza, to the Holy Roman emperor Maximilian I. Leonardo invented a special method for casting the immense sculpture in bronze by doing it in parts, but the project was never completed. There were threats of war and the duke sent all of the bronze that had been collected for the horse to be made into cannon in the defense of Milan.

In 1495 Ludovico commissioned Leonardo to paint a mural in the monks' dining hall at the monastery of Santa Maria delle Grazie. The wide mural would include thirteen figures as his subject was the Last Supper of Christ, the final meal that Jesus took with his disciples. The artist planned the composition by making a series of drawings. It was his practice to wander through the streets of Milan, studying people's faces and their expressions, sketching figures, and writing descriptions of them in his notebook.

Before starting to paint he erected a scaffold. He would usually climb up on it early in the morning and work until sunset. He often concentrated so hard that he forgot to eat or drink. At other times he would just look at the wall, apply one or two brush strokes, and depart. He welcomed those who wished to watch him and express an opinion of the work. The mural, which was nearly finished in autumn 1497, is amazingly dramatic and lifelike, with the figures arranged in graceful groupings in an interesting variety of gestures. Hailed as a masterpiece, the *Last Supper* was famous from the time it was painted. (See reproduction in the color section of this book.)

Leonardo's notebooks describe his theories of painting and how he solved certain problems with his art. He began writing a work called *Divine Proportion* in 1497, collaborating with a mathematician. Meanwhile he continued to decorate Ludovico's castle, and the duke gave the artist a house and a vineyard just outside the city.

Leonardo's works during this period were remarkable for strong contrasts of light and shade in the figures, rather than clear tones and firm outlines. One of his religious pictures, created for a monastery, was on the subject of the Virgin and Saint Anne with the infant Christ. People of all ages came to see it, marveling at the simplicity and beauty of the Virgin's face.

In October 1499 French armies invaded Milan and Ludovico was distracted by military matters. He managed to escape from the French by hiding, but was later taken prisoner and sent to France under guard. Leonardo's best friend, the architect Andrea da Ferrara, was hanged. A group of French archers destroyed Leonardo's model of the gigantic horse by using it for target practice, even though their king, Louis XII admired it when he saw it.

Meanwhile Leonardo worked at geometry and anatomy and conducted mathematical and flying experiments. At one point he invented a flying machine that he planned to try out by jumping from a rooftop at the ducal palace, but luckily he gave up that idea.

In December 1499 the artist left Milan for Mantua, bringing a lyre he had designed as a gift for the duchess Isabella d'Este, who was a great patron of the arts. A portrait in profile that he drew of the duchess pleased her. From Mantua Leonardo went to Venice, arriving early in 1500. There his skills as a military engineer and an artist were highly admired by Venetian artists. Masters such as Giorgione were influenced by his style of modeling his figures with delicacy and with his use of deep shadows. By April the artist was back in Florence; he had been gone for almost twenty years. He was welcomed by admirers and by his father, who was living with his fourth wife and eleven children.

In late spring 1502 the artist went off to Urbino and other towns in central Italy, where he served as chief military engineer in the service of Cesare Borgia, a cruel and deceitful prince who was the illegitimate son of Pope Alexander VI. As Leonardo traveled about he drew plans to fortify towns, drain marshes, and build canals to divert the

Leonardo's *The Virgin, the Infant, and Saint Anne. The Louvre, Paris.*

Arno River. While in Cesare's service, he met Niccolò Machiavelli, a brilliant statesman who was secretary of the Republic of Florence and author of *The Prince,* a book about Cesare Borgia. Leonardo left Urbino early in 1503 as a result of Cesare's cruel acts including his having Leonardo's artist friend Vitellozzo Vitelli strangled.

The artist returned to Florence early in 1503. Prominent people, including princesses and kings, were begging him to paint their portraits but he turned them down. That year he did paint a portrait of a shy young woman who was probably the wife of a Florentine merchant. This became his most famous work, the *Mona Lisa.* It is said that while the woman posed, Leonardo amused her with musicians and jesters, trying to keep her merry so she would not look sad in the picture. He showed her in an easy pose with her hands crossed, against a rocky background of fantastic mountain peaks. Her sweet, slightly mysterious smile seems to reflect her inner life. The artist and biographer Giorgio Vasari called the painting "an extraordinary example of how art can imitate nature." He added, "To look closely at her throat you might imagine that the pulse was beating." Leonardo kept the painting until the king of France managed to acquire it for himself.

The artist continued to make studies of birds in flight, thinking that man, too, should be able to fly, and he wrote a short book *On the Flight of Birds.* He made anatomical drawings, and in order to learn about muscles and joints, studied the human body by dissecting the corpses of criminals in a morgue. His notes and drawings were copied and circulated among medical schools.

The government of Florence commissioned Leonardo to paint a great mural in the Council Chamber of the Palazzo Vecchio on the subject of a famous battle in which the Florentine cavalry was victorious. Michelangelo, a rising star and Leonardo's archrival, was asked to paint a different battle scene in the same room. Leonardo proceeded to make drawings for the enormous composition and also small wax models of figures, arranging them on a table set up as a battlefield. In 1503 he began a cartoon, a full-scale preparatory drawing, of men and horses in violent motion, but his work advanced slowly. It was not until 1505 that Leonardo finished the cartoon of the battle scene and began painting the wall. As the work progressed it was highly admired, especially for the representations of horses. Artists came from all over Europe to make copies. In the meantime his father died in 1504.

On May 30, 1506, Leonardo was

Leonardo's *La Gioconda* (The Mona Lisa). *The Louvre, Paris.*

called to Milan by the French royal governor Charles d'Amboise, Lord of Chaumont. The artist got permission to leave Florence even though the wall painting was not finished. Nor had he completed a religious picture for which he had received a large sum of money.

Charles d'Amboise succeeded in keeping Leonardo in Milan until March 1507. Then the artist returned to Florence to settle a lawsuit with his stepbrothers regarding his inheritance. In late July he was back in Milan at d'Amboise's request.

A year later, when King Louis XII arrived in Milan, the monarch was enchanted with one of Leonardo's paintings of the Madonna and so impressed with the *Last Supper* that he tried to find a way for his engineers to remove it from the wall and ship it to France. Louis XII appointed the artist painter and engineer to the king and granted him a salary. Leonardo also served the French royal governor as court painter, engineer, and artistic advisor. His architectural plans included designs for a town house and miniature palace. His position gave him the freedom to travel, so he took trips to the mountains to study nature. He was interested in the movement of water from melting snow, in fossils and rocks, and in flowers and plants. The vast landscape in the background of his religious work of 1508–1510, *Virgin and Child with Saint Anne,* reflects these interests.

One of the leading French generals, Gian Giacomo Trivulzio, asked Leonardo to create a funeral monument for his family chapel that would be surmounted by a life-size bronze statue of a man on horseback. Once again the artist turned to drawing and observing horses. He continued his studies in anatomy, with a special interest in the muscles and the action of the heart and arteries.

In September 1513, at the invitation of Giuliano de' Medici, Leonardo left Milan and headed for Rome, stopping in Florence on the way. Giuliano, whose brother had just become Pope Leo X, was commander in chief of the papal troops. He was keenly interested in art and science and invited the artist to live in the Belvedere Palace in the Vatican with any servants and pupils he had brought with him. In Rome Leonardo was surrounded by leading artists, including Michelangelo, who was influenced by the expression in Leonardo's subjects and the grace and movement of his figures.

Leonardo was not happy in Rome. He was used to a quiet life, and the activity of Rome and the competitive atmosphere depressed him. He withdrew into himself and resumed his experiments in the science of optics. He

Leonardo's self-portrait. *Roger-Viollet/Palais Royal de Turin.*

wanted to learn more about the action of light striking a surface and about the way in which the human eye sees things. Leonardo's interest in light and shade is reflected in his paintings. Also, he did strange experiments such as creating a dragon by adding wings, a horn, and big eyes to a large lizard which he tamed and kept in a box. He used the creature to frighten people so they would run away screaming. His unhappiness in Rome was intensified by the spying of his servants and gossip of craftsmen in his service. Also the pope's craftsmen assisted him in his workshop, designing machinery for the textile industry and mirrors for an enormous reflector to view the stars, caused him trouble, and also spread gossip. And there were problems with the pope, who was annoyed by Leonardo's habit of leaving projects unfinished. At the time the artist had disturbing visions of the destruction of the world and he made dark drawings with violent, swirling lines.

After Giuliano de' Medici died in March 1516, Leonardo returned to Milan and was living quietly on his estate when he received an invitation from King Francis I to come to France. Leonardo accepted and set out early in 1517 with all of his possessions in a horse-drawn wagon. He left Salai behind, giving him permission to build a house on his land, and took a new servant and a pupil, Francesco Melzi, with him. The king invited them to live in the manor house of Cloux, a peaceful spot on the Loire River near Amboise. An underground tunnel connected the house with the Royal Palace. King Francis and Leonardo met everyday for discussions. The monarch admired Leonardo's gift for brilliant conversation. He believed the artist knew more about science, painting, and architecture than anyone in the world. Leonardo was chief painter, engineer, and architect to the king and collected a good salary. He continued his experiments and his designs for court festivals and he planned a palace for the king, a model town, and a canal system with locks and gates. However, he did not follow through on many of his projects.

Leonardo had grown old, and his right side was partly paralyzed. He had never considered himself religious, but seeing that death was near, he returned to the Catholic Church. With the help of a servant and friends he rose from bed to receive the last rites and pray. In April 1519 he made out his will and planned his own funeral, naming the exact number of candles to be carried at the service. On May 2 he died at age 67, at Cloux, and was buried quietly in a church at Amboise.

The artist's fame lived on. He is thought of as the ideal universal man of the Renaissance, the period in which he lived. The sculptor Benvenuto Cellini said of him, "No greater man than he, I believe, has been born into the world."

Today we know that technology drawn from Leonardo's imagination foreshadowed the airplane, helicopter, parachute, submarine, and bicycle centuries before they were invented. His painting the *Mona Lisa* is perhaps the best-known portrait in the world. During World War II the monastery of Santa Maria delle Grazie in Milan, where Leonardo had painted the *Last Supper*, was destroyed by a bomb in an air raid, but the wall bearing the painting miraculously was spared. As Giorgio Vasari wrote of him, "His name and fame will never be extinguished."

Michelangelo (Buonarroti)

1475–1564   A superb Italian Renaissance sculptor who is best known for his paintings in the Sistine Chapel, Rome

Michelangelo claimed that painting was not his profession; yet he was one of the greatest painters who ever lived. He was also a sculptor, architect, and poet. During his lifetime, at the height of the Italian Renaissance, he was considered a wonder and was called "the divine master." Many people still think of him as the greatest artistic genius of all time.

Michelangelo di Lodovico Buonarroti Simoni was born on March 6, 1475, in Caprese, Italy, a tiny village in the Apennine Mountains about forty miles from Florence. His father, Lodovico, who was descended from a very old family, was serving a short term there as mayor. Lodovico had five sons, one older than Michelangelo and three younger. A month after Michelangelo's birth the family returned home to Flor-ence. His mother, Francesca di Neri, was sickly, so she put the baby in the care of a wet nurse in a tiny village nearby where the family owned a farm. The wet nurse's father and husband were both stonecutters. Michelangelo would later say that he was destined to become a sculptor in stone.

By 1481 the boy was living with his parents in Florence, where he attended grammar school. Lodovico wanted his son to have a literary life or go into government service, but on April 1, 1488, when Michelangelo was thirteen, he entered the busy workshop of the painters Domenico and David del Ghirlandaio. Other apprentices paid tuition, but Michelangelo was given a salary. As an apprentice he learned to prepare colors and the backgrounds for the paintings, and he also learned drawing and the technique of fresco, or painting on wet plaster. He drew with strong lines and his works showed great power and originality. It is said that his master once remarked, "That one, in truth, knows more about drawing than I do." The term of Michelangelo's apprenticeship was three years, but he left after only a year.

In 1489 the wealthy and educated nobleman Lorenzo de' Medici allowed Michelangelo and his good friend Francesco Granacci to study his collection of sculpture in the Medici Gardens. Lorenzo, known as the Magnificent, owned some wonderful ancient statues which he allowed a select group of young artists to study. Michelangelo probably learned the technique of sculpture from the elderly Bertoldo di Giovanni, who looked after the collection for Lorenzo. When Michelangelo carved his first marble figure, the head of a fawn, it was so beautiful that Lorenzo invited him to live in his palace as if he were a son. He gave the artist a purple cloak and an allowance, and granted his father an official position in the customs office.

Michelangelo now lived in beautiful surroundings and had the chance to talk about poetry, art, philosophy, and politics with the learned men who gathered around Lorenzo. After dinner they would compose poems and recite them to the accompaniment of a lute. The young artist drew from frescoes in churches and from ancient statues, using the same pen that he wrote with, perfecting his handwriting as well as his drawing.

The quality of Michelangelo's stone carvings was astonishing for a teenager, and he showed great skill in creating interesting compositions with the figures in his works. Most young sculptors admired his talent, but some were jealous of him. One day when he was making copies of wall paintings by the great master Masaccio, a fellow student started a fight with him. He punched Michelangelo in the face, breaking his nose, which remained flattened forever. Michelangelo had a rather large head, with flat ears and thin lips. His hair was black and curly. He was of medium height, thin and wiry, and had broad shoulders. As he worked in stone his wrists and forearms became powerful from wielding heavy hammers. He apparently could use his left hand as well as his right.

Lorenzo de' Medici died in 1492 and Michelangelo returned home to live with his father. His mother had died and Lodovico had remarried. The artist loved his family and was proud of his noble heritage. Throughout his lifetime he worked hard and sacrificed so that he could give them money, even though his father was mean to him, and Buonarroto, the brother whom he helped the most, was unworthy.

Michelangelo found great pleasure in carving stone. He bought a large block of marble and carved a statue of Hercules. A hospital connected with the monastery of Santo Spirito had a morgue where Michelangelo was allowed to dissect corpses in order to study every muscle, vein, and nerve so that he could understand human anatomy. He had to work at night because the practice was illegal. He made a wooden crucifix for the monastery in gratitude to the abbot.

Lorenzo de' Medici's son Piero, known as the Unfortunate because he lacked good judgment, invited Michelangelo back to the palace in 1494. There had been a heavy snowfall, and Piero wanted the artist to construct a giant snowman in the palace courtyard. Michelangelo stayed in the palace in his old room. Piero de' Medici was an unpopular leader and Italy had fallen into a state of unrest. Enemy troops from France, under Charles VII, were advancing toward Florence. Michelangelo fled to Venice with two friends in October 1494. They remained there until his money ran out and then he started back toward Florence. He stopped in Bologna, where he was invited to live in the home of a nobleman. In Bologna he studied Italian literature and carved some small marble figures for a church. After the French armies retreated in 1495, the artist returned to Florence. At this time he carved a marble cupid for his own amusement. It looked so much like an ancient statue that it fooled experts.

At the end of June 1496 Michelangelo went to Rome, a city filled with art. Ancient marble sculpture, great Roman architecture, and beautiful paintings were all around him. While there he carved two life-sized marble statues for the garden of a rich art collector, Jacopo Galli. He did not have enough money and he missed his family, but there were important opportunities in Rome.

A French cardinal commissioned the artist to carve a large marble statue of the Virgin Mary holding the dead Christ, a type of composition called a Pietà. To get the best block of marble, he went to a quarry in Carrara in northern Italy. When Michelangelo carved marble he imagined that inside the block of stone a figure was imprisoned and that he was freeing the form by chipping away at the stone. When he finished the *Pietà,* around 1500, people said it was the most beautiful work in marble existing in Rome. The limbs of the dead Christ are beautiful, with muscles and veins that look real. The cloaks on the figures, although carved from hard stone, fall in folds like real cloth. The *Pietà* made the young artist instantly famous.

In the summer of 1501 Michelangelo was back in Florence, where he was commissioned to carve a colossal marble statue of the young biblical hero David, who had killed the giant Goliath, an enemy of his people, with a stone from his slingshot. The block of marble Michelangelo used was eighteen feet high and weighed several tons. It had been damaged and therefore discarded by another sculptor thirty-five years earlier. Before carving the stone Michelangelo made a wax model of the figure. He modeled the statue in beautiful proportions, in a graceful pose, free and natural. Three years after it was begun it was set up in front of the Palazzo Vecchio, the city hall. The young hero David served as a symbol of liberty and of strength and courage for the people of Florence. The artist also created a statue of David out of bronze for a French patron.

In 1505 Michelangelo started work on a large fresco, a painting on wet plaster, for the wall of a new council chamber in the Palazzo Vecchio. The subject was a battle that was important in the history of Florence. Leonardo da Vinci, the most popular artist in Italy at this time and a rival of Michelangelo, was commissioned to paint another battle scene in the same room. Neither work was ever finished. However, Michelangelo did complete the cartoon, the drawing made to exact size, that would be laid against the plaster wall and from which the artist would trace the outlines of the figures on the surface. Michelangelo's cartoons were much admired for their mastery of figures in action, in every possible position. He analyzed the anatomy of the human form and showed it in a variety of movements. He tried for perfection, yet always felt that he failed to achieve it.

Pope Julius II was impressed with the artist's work and called him to Rome in 1505, giving him one hundred ducats for his traveling expenses. The pope wanted him to design and build a three-story tomb that would have more than forty marble statues, many of them larger than life-size, to be finished in five years. In April the artist went to Carrara for the stone, staying in the mountains with two workmen and a horse, and a little food. Thirty-four wagonloads of marble were quarried and shipped by barge to Rome. Later, Michelangelo would order sixty more wagonloads for the same project. The artist returned to Rome in December and set up a workshop.

The marble from Carrara had to be paid for, so the artist paid the cost him-

Portrait of Michelangelo. © *Alinari/Art Resource/Palazzo della Cancelleria, Venice.*

self. When he went to the pope for the money, Julius refused to see him. Angry and upset, Michelangelo fled to Florence in April 1506. He attempted to finish his work on the tomb off and on for more than forty years, at great hardship to himself. As an old man he said, "I have wasted all my youth chained to this tomb." In the end its design would be completely changed.

Pope Julius II sent five couriers after Michelangelo to bring him back to Rome, but the artist dismissed them and stayed in Florence. Soon afterward the pope went off to Bologna on a military mission. He summoned Michelangelo to join him there in November 1506. Michelangelo felt like a captive, saying that he went to Bologna "with the rope around my neck." Pope Julius wanted a huge bronze statue of himself to be set over the main door of the cathedral in Bologna, and he commissioned the artist to create it. Michelangelo did not ask for enough money to cover his expenses, so he had to work under difficult conditions. He had trouble with the men who worked for him, and had to live in the same room and share a bed with three assistants. The weather was unbearably hot, and an epidemic of the plague broke out.

When the statue was finished in 1508 the artist returned to Florence and rented a house, but he was not home

long before the pope called him back to Rome to paint the ceiling of the Sistine Chapel in the Vatican, where papal ceremonies were held. He refused to take the job because he considered himself a sculptor, not a painter. Moreover, he wanted to finish the tomb, but when the pope grew angry at his refusal, he accepted. He set to work in 1508, designing a scaffold from which he would work, arranging for the surface of the ceiling to be plastered, and hiring assistants. He prepared sketches for the design and ordered colors.

He began painting late in 1508. It was a tremendous task and one of great physical labor. He expected to have the help of other artists, but he sent them away because he was not satisfied with their work. He had to cover an enormous space and work on the high scaffold with his head turned upward. Paint dripped down onto his face. He worked constantly and did not even have time to eat properly, taking only a piece of bread up the scaffold with him or eating what little food might be sent up. He descended only to sleep, and then he would not even remove his clothes. He kept his boots on for such a long time that when he finally did remove them, his skin peeled off with his socks. "I strain more than any man who ever lived," he said. Any visitor who tried to watch him work was turned away, except for Pope Julius, whom the artist would help ascend the scaffold on a stepladder. When the pope would get impatient and ask him when he would finish, the artist would reply, "When I can."

Michelangelo was deeply religious and lived modestly, devoting himself to his work and saving his earnings to send to his father and brothers. He once said, "Rich though I have become, yet I have always lived as a poor man." Michelangelo's personality is revealed in his art. He was bursting with inner tension and was quick-tempered, yet he was gentle with his friends.

While working on the ceiling, he wrote to his brother Buonarroto, "I am living here in a state of great anxiety and of the greatest physical fatigue; I have no friends and want none." All the while, the artist had to deal with troubles his father and brother were having in Florence. He was trying to buy a business for them. He sent his brother, Lodovico, most of the money he had received as first payment for the ceiling, although Lodovico never appreciated the sacrifices that Michelangelo made for him. In the meantime, the pope was off fighting a war against the French and was not paying the artist for his work.

The ceiling of the Sistine Chapel was first shown to the public on August 4, 1511, when Mass was celebrated by Julius II. The center of the ceiling is filled with nine scenes from the Book of Genesis, the first book of the Bible. Around them, the figures of biblical prophets and sibyls (ancient female prophets) sit on great thrones. Michelangelo painted more than three hundred figures altogether, relating the early history of the world and mankind, according to the Old Testament. The manner in which they are arranged and the way they look when viewed from below are remarkable. The framework, painted to look like architecture, and the sheer beauty of the entire ceiling led Giorgio Vasari to write, "There is no other work to compare with this for excellence, nor could there be." People came from everywhere to see the ceiling and poems were written to praise it. (See reproduction in the color section of this book.)

Pope Julius II died in 1513, leaving money to complete his tomb. Continuing his work, Michelangelo carved statues of two slaves and a seated Moses with a beautiful face and a soft, glossy beard. The muscles of the arms and legs are amazing. In the end, these works were not used in the final design for Julius's tomb.

The new pope, Leo X, was a son of Lorenzo de' Medici. He had known Michelangelo when they were young men living in the palace. Leo X honored Michelangelo in 1515, conferring the title of Counts of Palatine on the family. Two years later he asked the artist to design a facade, or front, for San Lorenzo, the family church of the Medici in Florence, which had never been finished.

The artist bought a house in Florence, and now he began work on the facade of San Lorenzo, drawing designs and supervising a clay model, then a wooden model with sculptured figures. The project met with difficulties. The pope insisted that Michelangelo get his marble from new quarries in the mountains of Pietrasanta. This led to serious problems because new crews had to be trained and a road had to be built through the mountains to transport the stone.

Cardinal Giulio de' Medici, who was later elected Pope Clement VII, put Michelangelo to work on the architecture and sculpture for the funerary chapel in the Medici Church in 1519. The following year the contract for his work on the facade of San Lorenzo was suddenly canceled. The artist was bitter, complaining that he had lost three years. He proceeded with designs for the tombs of Giuliano and Lorenzo in the Medici Chapel, which would have a seated statue representing each of the men. At their feet, would be reclining

figures of Day and Night and Dawn and Dusk.

In 1523 Michelangelo went to Rome for an audience with the new pope, Clement VII, and they talked about designs for a library to be attached to the Medici Chapel in Florence. The artist's work was interrupted once again when Pope Clement VII met with political misfortune after the Holy Roman emperor Charles V started an uprising and imperial troops marched through Italy. In 1527 Rome was invaded, her defendants were tortured, and the city was looted. The pope was captured and imprisoned in the Castel Sant' Angelo, then escaped and fled the city to live in exile.

Florence was also in danger of military attack and in need of defense. Michelangelo was appointed Governor General with the task of designing fortifications and supervising their construction. Knowing Florence was certain to be besieged, he set out with two pupils for Venice in September 1529. All of their money was hidden inside their clothing. Michelangelo returned to Florence in November. The brave citizens of the city had been defeated, and an order had been issued to find and assassinate Michelangelo, who was considered to be a traitor. The artist hid out in the house of a friend.

Imperial troops, who had joined

forces with Pope Clement VII, entered Florence in August 1530. Michelangelo was forgiven by the pope, and he resumed his work on the Medici Library and Chapel.

The artist's father died in 1531, the same year Alessandro de' Medici came to Florence as duke, his rule enforced by a Papal army. Alessandro hated Michelangelo and the artist, no longer feeling comfortable in Florence, went to Rome. There he met a handsome young Roman nobleman, Tommaso de'-Cavalieri, and the two became good friends. Michelangelo wrote poetry to him and presented him with drawings on subjects from Greek mythology.

In 1533 Pope Clement VII decided to have the artist paint the end wall of the Sistine Chapel, but he died in September 1534 just as Michelangelo was ready to begin work. The following year the newly elected pope, Paul III, paid a visit to the artist and issued a decree declaring him the chief architect, sculptor, and painter to the Vatican Palace and granting him a lifetime income of twelve hundred gold ducats a year.

Michelangelo began painting the altar wall, as previously planned, in 1536. The work was extremely difficult, and he often became ill from the strain. In 1541 he fell from the scaffold and injured his leg, putting him in great pain. He refused treatment, but a doctor who admired him went to his house and took care of him. On All Saints Day in 1541 Pope Paul III said High Mass as the wall was unveiled. It was a superb work representing the Last Judgment, the day when all men stand before God to be judged. Christ appears in glory on a cloud, considering the words and deeds of each person before separating those who should be rewarded for leading good lives from those who should be punished. The powerful figures are in violent motion, with angels driving sinners out of heaven. Every human emotion is expressed, and each part of the work fits together to form a whole.

While he was working on the wall in the Sistine Chapel Michelangelo made friends with a noblewoman named Vittoria Colonna and became very much attached to her. She was a wise and deeply religious widow, a gifted poet, who lived in a convent. Michelangelo loved her deeply. They often met on Sundays at a church on a hill that had a beautiful view of Rome. He wrote some of his finest sonnets to her and made beautiful drawings that he gave her as gifts. He was overwhelmed with grief when she died in 1547.

In 1542 the artist once again climbed a scaffold to paint frescoes for Pope Paul III on the walls of the pope's private chapel in the Vatican. The project, based on the subjects of Saint Peter and

Saint Paul, would take eight years to complete. Two years after starting it, the artist, who was now nearly seventy, became ill and nearly died. A friend took care of him until he recovered, and in gratitude, Michelangelo gave his friend two statues of slaves that he had made.

In 1545 Michelangelo's statues for the tomb of Julius II, were finally installed. The tomb which turned out to be quite different from his original design was unveiled in 1547, forty-two years after it was begun. Although the artist was old and ill, he was still very active. In 1546 he was appointed architect in chief by Pope Paul III and assigned to direct the building of the new Saint Peter's in Rome. He began making drawings and a clay model of his design for the dome and drum, the base on which the dome rests. This was followed by a large wooden model that he started the following year. He built most of the drum himself, but the dome was not built until long after his death.

The artist began carving a Pietà, which he wanted to use for his own tomb. As he progressed he was not satisfied with it. He would have smashed it to pieces if his pupils had not stopped him.

Meanwhile Michelangelo was appointed to redesign the Capitoline Hill, the seat of government in ancient

The elderly Michelangelo surveys the work being done on Saint Peter's Basilica. *Roger-Viollet/Albertina Museum, Vienna.*

Rome, and to direct the construction of a bridge over the Tiber River. And Pope Paul IV asked for his help with fortifications in Rome, as the French army was approaching the city.

Michelangelo's faithful servant, Urbino, who had cared for him for twenty-five years, died late in 1555. The artist was grief-stricken and fled to the mountains to stay with hermits, hoping to find inner peace. In a letter to a friend, he said, "One cannot find peace except in the woods."

Upon returning to Rome, he continued working on the model for Saint Peter's in spite of his advanced age. He would still be working on the drum and dome when he died. He now hoped for his own death; he was nearly ninety and had been working for seventy-five years. He felt disappointed because he had wanted to reach perfection in his work. He even burned many of his drawings because he did not want people to see any of his works that he felt were less than perfect.

In 1564 he dictated a will, leaving "my soul to God, my body to the earth and my belongings to my nearest relatives." He was ill, but refused to go to bed. Going outdoors in the rain, he told someone who saw him on the street, "I am ill and can find no rest." Two days later, as he lay in bed, he spoke these words: "I regret that I am dying just as I am beginning to learn the alphabet of my profession."

Michelangelo died in his home in Rome on February 18, 1564, in the presence of his dear friend Tommaso de'Cavalieri, his friend and pupil Daniele da Volterra, a servant, and two physicians. His body was taken to a church, where he lay in state. His friends and all of the artists in Rome came to pay their respects. The pope planned to erect a special memorial to Michelangelo in Saint Peter's, but Duke Cosimo de' Medici wanted to honor him in Florence, which the artist had considered his home and where he wished to be buried. Michelangelo's nephew had the body secretly taken away and shipped to Florence by wrapping it as an ordinary package.

When the body arrived Georgio Vasari received it, and it was prepared for burial by members of the Academy, who had elected Michelangelo "head, father and teacher of everyone." The coffin was carried to the Church of Santa Croce, where other members of Michelangelo's family were buried. Every artist in the Academy followed the coffin. When it was inside the church it was opened so that all could see the body. It is said that he seemed to be resting sweetly, as if asleep, and his body looked perfect. There was no foul odor, even though he had been dead for more than three weeks. When each member of the Academy went up to the coffin and touched the artist's face the flesh felt soft and lifelike. It is also said that his body still looked perfect when the coffin was opened one hundred and fifty years later. Some believed that this was a divine sign and that Michelangelo's body was still fresh because he was saintly . . . the Divine Michelangelo!

Claude Monet

1840–1926   French Impressionist painter whose work gave the movement its name

Impressionism, the important development in nineteenth-century art that gave us a fresh way of seeing the world, got its name from a work by Claude Monet, *Impression: Sunrise*. Oscar-Claude Monet was born in Paris, France, on November 14, 1840. His father, Adolphe, and his mother, Louise-Justine, lived above their grocery store. When Monet was five years old he moved with his mother, father, and older brother Léon to Le Havre, a busy French seaport on the English Channel in the province of Normandy. His father went into business with his brother-in-law Jacques Lacadre, who was a wholesale grocer supplying provisions for the ships that docked in the harbor.

Monet attended a small private school until he was eleven and then went to the local high school, where he learned to draw from François-Charles Ochard. He was bored with school and spent his time drawing caricatures of his teachers, cartoons that exaggerated their features. After school he would escape to the seaside where he loved to spend time on the cliffs and beaches and watch the boats sailing in the harbor. He was always sure of himself and clever about money. By the time he was fifteen he was selling caricatures of local people, charging twenty francs each and giving the money to his Aunt Sophie for safekeeping. An amateur painter, she had a studio in her attic where she allowed her nephew to work.

The art supply shop in Le Havre exhibited his drawings in the window, along with paintings by the artist Eugène Boudin, from nearby Honfleur, who specialized in views of the seashore. Boudin was impressed with the boy's talent and invited him to work with him to learn to paint landscapes. At this time most artists worked inside in their studios creating still lifes, pictures with subjects from everyday life. When they did paint landscapes they would sketch outdoors and finish the works in their studios. Boudin, however, painted his landscapes outdoors. He said, "Everything that is painted directly on the spot has always a strength, a power, a vividness of touch that one doesn't find again in the studio." Monet often joined Boudin when he set up his easel outdoors. By the time Monet was seventeen, one of his landscape paintings was accepted for an exhibition in Le Havre.

Monet's mother died early in 1857, and the following year his uncle Jacques died also. The father moved with his sons into his sister Sophie's home. In May 1859, when he was eighteen, Monet left Le Havre and went to Paris, the capital of France and the art center of the world. At first his father, who was not a wealthy man, gave him a small allowance while he applied for a fellowship for the youth so he could support himself as an art student. When the fellowship did not come through, Monet's father wanted him to come home and go into the grocery business, but the young man was stubborn and insisted on staying in Paris. He rented a room in an artists' section of the city and lived off the money he had saved from his caricatures. He hoped to make a living drawing caricatures for a newspaper, but sold only one.

Monet's family wanted him to learn to draw correctly and to study with the painter Thomas Couture. Monet, however, considered Couture's methods old-fashioned and preferred to attend the Académie Suisse, which was free and had no formal classes. At the Académie Suisse he drew from live models who were paid by collecting a small fee from each artist. Monet met Camille Pissarro there.

Paris was an exciting adventure for the young artist. He liked to pass time at the Brasserie des Martyrs, the café where Gustave Courbet, a well-known realist painter, met with other artists and writers. Later Courbet and Monet became friends. At the café the men might do some sketching and they would have long conversations, discussing their ideas and the problems of their art. Monet liked to sit around and talk, but he never really cared for intellectual discussions.

Young Frenchmen were required by law to register for military service. Names of those called for active duty

Marc Chagall. *Couple above Saint-Paul.* Art Resource/Private Collection, Saint-Paul de Vence.

El Greco. *Burial of the Count Orgaz.* Giraudon/Art Resource/Church of Santo Tome, Toledo.

Leonardo da Vinci. *Last Supper.* Scala/Art Resource/S. Maria delle Grazie, Milan.

Rembrandt van Rijn. *The Nightwatch.* Scala/Art Resource/The Rijksmuseum, Amsterdam.

Diego Velázquez. *Las Meniñas*. Art Resource/Prado, Madrid. Photograph by Erich Lessing.

Jacques-Louis David. *The Oath of the Horatii.* Giraudon/Art Resource/The Louvre, Paris.

Albrecht Dürer. *Christ in the Temple.* Scala/Art Resource/Collection Thyssen Bornemisza, Lugano.

Titian. *La Bella.* Scala/Art Resource/Pitti Palace, Florence.

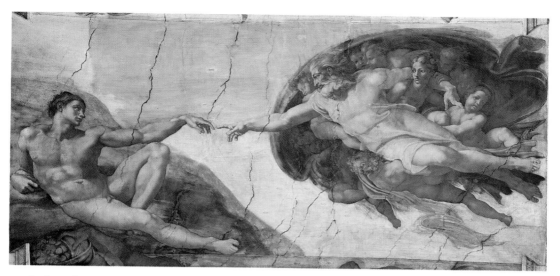

Michelangelo Buonarroti. *The Creation of Adam.* Scala/Art Resource/Detail from the ceiling of the Sistine Chapel, The Vatican.

Peter Paul Rubens. *Garden of Love.* Scala/Art Resource/Prado, Madrid.

Winslow Homer. *The Gulf Stream.* The Metropolitan Museum of Art, Wolfe Fund, 1906. Catherine Lorillard Wolfe Collection. (06.1234)

Frederick Edwin Church. *The Icebergs.* Dallas Museum of Art, anonymous gift.

Thomas Gainsborough. *The Blue Boy*. Bridgeman/Art Resource/Huntington Library and Art Gallery, San Marino, California.

Pablo Picasso. *Family of Saltimbanques.* National Gallery of Art, Washington, D.C. Chester Dale Collection.

Georgia O'Keeffe. *The Red Poppy*. Art Resource/Private Collection.

Diego Rivera. *Man, Controller of the Universe*. Art Resource/Museo del Palacio de Bellas Artes, Mexico City, México, D.F.

Vincent van Gogh. *Irises.* The Metropolitan Museum of Art, Gift of Adele R. Levy, 1958. (58.187)

Paul Gauguin. *Breton Girls Dancing, Pont-Aven.* National Gallery of Art, Washington, D.C. Collection of Mr. and Mrs. Paul Mellon.

Edgar Degas. *The Dance Class*. Art Resource/Musée d'Orsay, Paris. Photograph by Erich Lessing.

Mary Cassatt. *Young Girl Sewing in a Garden.* Art Resource/Musée d'Orsay, Paris. Photograph by Erich Lessing.

Jan Vermeer. *View of Delft, Netherlands, after the Fire.* Art Resource/Mauritshuis, The Hague. Photograph by Erich Lessing.

Claude Monet. *Poppies.* Art Resource/Musée d'Orsay, Paris. Photograph by Erich Lessing.

James McNeill Whistler. *The White Girl (Symphony in White, No. 1)*. National Gallery of Art, Washington, D.C. Harris Whittemore Collection.

were chosen by lottery. Monet drew an unlucky number, and in 1860 he signed up to serve with a regiment in the French colony of Algeria. He loved the bright sunlight and desert landscape of North Africa, but after serving a little more than a year, he contracted typhoid fever and was sent home on sick leave. He stayed at his aunt Sophie's summer house at the seaside in Sainte-Adresse, a suburb of Le Havre. That summer he painted on the coast with Boudin and with the Dutch painter Johan Jongkind.

Monet still had five years of military service ahead of him, but his aunt Sophie arranged for his release by paying someone else to serve in his place. His father offered him an allowance to go to Paris if he would attend a proper art school. In the autumn of 1862 he was back in Paris and entered the studio of the Swiss artist Charles Gleyre. There he learned to draw from live models, but he was only interested in painting landscapes and did not like Gleyre's classes. Monet did not stay at the studio for long. He made friends with Pierre-Auguste Renoir, Alfred Sisley, and Jean-Frédéric Bazille, and in the spring of 1863 they all took a trip to the village of Chailly-en-Bière in the forest of Fontainebleau. These artists were interested in everyday subject matter and liked to experiment, painting outdoors directly from nature. Monet returned to

the same area the following spring and then went to the Normandy coast, where he stayed at a country inn that was popular with artists. Bazille and Jongkind joined him. That fall Monet exhibited a still life at an exhibition in nearby Rouen; it was bought by a Le Havre shipowner.

All the while, Monet's father and aunt were distressed because he was not earning any money, and they thought he was spending too much time outdoors. He had a terrible quarrel with his father, who cut off his allowance and he returned to Paris where he shared a studio with Bazille. Monet finally sold two of his Normandy landscapes after they had been accepted in the 1865 Salon, the official exhibition held every year in Paris. His works were praised by critics for capturing the freshness of the moment. That summer he stayed in Chailly-en-Bière, where he worked on *Luncheon on the Grass,* a large scene inspired by a work of the same name by Edouard Manet. Bazille and a nineteen-year-old woman named Camille Léonie Doncieux, the daughter of a local businessman, posed for the picture. The figures on the canvas are painted with broad, flat brush strokes, while the background is painted in dots and patches of color.

In the fall Monet went to Trouville on the English Channel near Le Havre, where he met James McNeill Whistler, an American artist who was living in England and France.

In Paris that winter Monet painted *Woman in the Green Dress,* using Camille as his model, and exhibited it in the Salon of 1866. Critics praised the painting as a symbol of modern life. Camille and Monet were living together at the time, but their families did not approve of their relationship and refused to give them support. The couple moved to Sèvres, a Paris suburb, where Monet worked on *Women in the Garden.* Camille posed as all four of the fashionable women in the scene.

Monet did not have enough money to pay his rent and he was evicted by his landlords. He was forced to leave Sèvres because of his debts. In summer he left Camille in Paris and went to Honfleur where he found Boudin and Courbet. When he returned to Paris Bazille came to his rescue by inviting him to stay in his studio in Paris and by buying *Women in the Garden,* to be paid for in monthly installments. Renoir, who was also staying in Bazille's studio, went about Paris with Monet, painting views of the city with him.

In August 1867 a son was born to Camille in Paris and was named Jean. Monet was spending most of his time with his aunt Sophie in Sainte-Adresse. His family refused to meet Camille, but his aunt gave him money to return to Paris, and the following spring he won a silver medal at an exhibition in Le Havre. Unfortunately he was penniless, and his paintings were seized by his creditors because he did not pay his bills. The same wealthy Le Havre shipowner who had bought his still life in Rouen bought the works from the creditors and commissioned the artist to paint his wife's portrait. Monet took Camille and Jean to Étretat, near Le Havre, where he rented a cottage.

Back in Paris he submitted two paintings to the Salon of 1869, but they were rejected. That winter Edouard Manet invited him to join his friends, including the writer Émile Zola, when they gathered at the Café Guerbois. In the summer he settled at Bougival, not far from Paris, and painted with Renoir, but he was so poor he could not afford paints. Renoir was staying with his parents who lived nearby, and he brought his friend bread from his mother's table so he would not starve. The two of them painted at La Grenouillère, a popular spot for boating on the Seine River on the outskirts of Paris. Working side by side they painted in a fresh manner, with rapid brushwork, building up the picture surface with small strokes of paint. They used spots and dots to capture atmosphere, and the figures were formed without definite lines.

A self-portrait of Claude Monet at the age of forty-six. *Art Resource/The Rijksmuseum, Amsterdam.*

The following spring, in 1870, Monet's works were again refused at the Salon. In June he finally married Camille, and she received a dowry from her parents. Aunt Sophie died two weeks later. On July 19 France declared war on Germany, setting off the Franco-Prussian War. Bazille joined the army, and was killed in action. Monet fled to London to avoid being called into the army, and continued painting, choosing boats on the Thames River as his favorite subject. Camille soon followed with Jean. Several friends of the artist were in London at this time, including Pissarro. Paul Durand-Ruel, a French art dealer, opened a gallery in London and bought several of Monet's pictures. He then arranged an exhibition, but was unable to sell the pictures.

The artist's father died in January 1871, the same month that the French surrendered to the Prussians. In late spring Monet took his family to Zaandam in Holland, where he painted views of the canals. Camille managed to earn a little money by giving French lessons.

The artist became interested in brightly colored Japanese woodblock prints after a store clerk wrapped his groceries in one of them. He returned to the store and bought all they had and continued to collect the Japanese prints with great enthusiasm. The bold colors and unexpected arrangements of figures in space influenced his own work.

When Monet returned to Paris in the autumn of 1871, he found the city in ruins as a result of the war. In December he went to Argenteuil, a charming suburb on the Seine River north of Paris, where he could be closer to nature. Argenteuil had been occupied by the Prussians and its bridges were destroyed, but it was being rebuilt. Monet was perfecting his style, painting with thick, brilliant colors and short brush strokes. He used color to capture the forms of objects and record the effects of changing atmosphere.

In Argenteuil he lived in one rented house, then another. He sometimes painted the activities of the town, but he did not make friends with the people who lived there. Durand-Ruel was back in France and paid him well for his pictures.

The artist lived well, enjoying a good life-style in Argenteuil, and had his own garden, where he raised roses and dahlias. Yet he was always late with his rent and was still borrowing money. Even when his pictures were selling well he spent everything he earned and kept writing his friends, pleading for money, telling them he was going to be thrown in jail by his creditors. No matter how much money he had he wanted more.

In 1873 Monet bought a barge and built a cabin on top to use as a floating studio, so he could paint right on the water, studying the play of light and the reflection of the clouds on the liquid surface. He would work from dawn until evening, even in the hot sun or freezing cold. Sometimes, Renoir and Manet came to Argenteuil to paint with him.

That year, he and his friends, who liked to paint subjects from modern life in a fresh, new style, decided to put on their own exhibition in which works would not be chosen by a jury, as they were at the Salon. The group called themselves the Société Anonyme, later changing their name to A Group of Independents. The next year thirty artists, including Renoir, Pissarro, and Alfred Sisley, exhibited their paintings in a photographer's studio. Few people came to the exhibition, and those who did laughed. One critic said, "Monet declared war on beauty." Another referred to the group as "These impressionists," taking that word from Monet's painting *Impression: Sunrise*, a view of Le Havre with two small boats in the harbor. Even though people made fun of his work Monet was persistent, and he continued to believe in his own art. He was very independent, never caring much about what other people thought.

In 1876 Camille fell ill and Monet was not selling his paintings. He could not even afford paints and brushes, and the second Impressionist exhibition was no more popular than the first. Ernest Hoschedé, the owner of a Paris department store, who collected Impressionist painting, came to Monet's rescue by inviting him to paint four large panels to decorate the dining room in his country estate at Montgeron. As a guest of the Hoschedé family, the artist enjoyed a luxurious life while working on the project.

Afterward, he set out for Paris, where the wealthy painter Gustave Caillebotte, whom he had met a few years earlier, rented a small studio for him near the Saint-Lazare, a huge glass and iron railroad station. Monet's main interest was in nature and the sea, but he was also fascinated by trains, a modern symbol of achievement in the growing industrial development of the time. He painted crowds of travelers in a hazy atmosphere of clouds of steam rising from the locomotives. He usually worked directly from the subject, seldom making drawings before painting on the canvas. Painting at his easel in the crowded train station, however, was so difficult that he had to finish much of the work in his studio. Seven of his Saint-Lazare paintings, along with more than twenty of his other works, were shown in the third Impressionist exhibition of 1877. The public still did not like his pictures, with their dots and splashes of color painted in rough brushwork. Sales were poor, and he was penniless again. In January 1878 Manet and Caillebotte lent Monet money so he could move from Argenteuil.

Camille had a second son, Michel, in March of 1878, and the family moved to Vétheuil on the Seine. Ernest Hoschedé, the Parisian department store owner, and art collector, had gone bankrupt and his family, which included his wife, Alice, and six children, moved in with Monet. The artist continued to paint landscapes, and sold a few but did not have enough money to heat the house during the winter. And there were eight children to feed! To make matters worse, Camille was suffering from cancer. Alice Hoschedé took care of her in her illness, and Caillebotte, once again, lent them money to live on. In the spring of 1879, when the Impressionists exhibited for the fourth time, the American artist Mary Cassatt, who had joined the group, advised a friend of hers to buy one of Monet's paintings.

When Camille died in September, her husband painted her portrait, to record the effects of the light as it fell on her face. Afterward he was shocked by his own lack of emotion and wrote in a letter, "Finding myself at the deathbed of a woman who had been and still was very dear to me, I caught myself with my eyes focused on her tragic temples in the act of automatically searching for the succession, the arrangement of color gradations that death was imposing on her motionless features." Another freezing winter followed, and all eight children were ill. Caillebotte again lent Monet money, and the artist's brother Léon helped as well.

When the fifth Impressionist exhibition was held in 1880 Monet, Renoir, and Sisley refused to participate, having quarreled with Degas. Monet announced his independence from the group and submitted two of his works to the Salon. One was accepted and one rejected. That year he had a one-man show sponsored by *La Vie Moderne,* a weekly publication. By now the critics seemed more understanding of his work, although the general public still found it shocking.

Having moved from one house to another, the artist decided late in 1881 to settle in Poissy, near Paris, where he could put his sons in a good school. Alice Hoschedé and her children joined him in spite of her husband's objections. The artist showed thirty-five works in the seventh Impressionist exhibition the next year. By then he was making a good living, and he moved to the quiet rural village of Giverny in the Seine River valley, where he would live for the rest of his life. Durand-Ruel, who was selling Monet's work in his London gallery, had a one-man exhibition of his paintings that year. The dealer advanced him money to rent a house in Giverny, which he moved into with his two sons and Alice Hoschedé and her six children. One of Alice's daughters, Blanche, wanted to be an artist and often went into the fields with Monet and painted by his side.

The villagers liked to watch him when he went out in his wooden shoes, with a beret on his head. He was a stocky man, bold and energetic, with bright eyes and a dark, heavy beard. His mood often changed quickly when he was dissatisfied with himself, and he would sometimes get depressed. He had a terrible temper and would have fits of anger if the weather changed while he was in the middle of a painting. He burned pictures he did not like and once threw his brushes into the river.

Forty-nine of Monet's works were included in the first American exhibition of Impressionist art in 1886, and the following year, thanks to his friendship with Whistler, two of his paintings were shown in London by the Royal Society of British Artists. In 1887 Théo van Gogh, an art dealer whose brother Vincent was a struggling painter, directed a one-man exhibition of Monet's work in Paris. He was applying his paint more heavily, using broader brush strokes, and capturing the effect of light as it changed. His work was being accepted, and by the late 1880s he had a very good income, getting high prices for his work. Yet he continued to beg for money from his friends.

In 1890 he bought a farmhouse with enough land to plant flower beds and vegetables. He hired a gardener, built a greenhouse, and turned a barn at the end of the house into a studio. He bought additional land with water and created a pond. He had become such a celebrity that a group of American artists settled in Giverny so they could work near him. But Monet stayed within his garden walls and paid no attention to the Americans. The only visitors he would see were important French artists, such as Paul Cézanne, who admired Monet; prominent statesmen, including Georges Clemenceau; and eminent authors. Among these were Stéphane Mallarmé; Gustave Geffroy, a critic who wrote Monet's biography; Octave Mirbeau; and Émile Zola, who wrote a novel about an artist. When Zola took a courageous stand against anti-Semitism during the Alfred Dreyfus affair, the famous French court case of a Jewish army officer tried for treason, Monet supported him.

Monet was a hardy person and en-

Monet in his studio at Giverny with the duke of Trévise. © *Roger-Viollet*.

joyed taking trips. In winter he liked to go to Étretat, where the rock formations on the seacoast are spectacular. He dressed in fisherman's clothes and weighted his easel so it would not blow away in a strong wind. He had an accident and nearly drowned in 1885. He had set up his easel beneath a cliff and a huge wave came along and threw him against the cliff. The wave washed him into the sea and dragged him down. Luckily he managed to clamber out of the water and onto the shore, but

his easel and painting were destroyed.

Monet also traveled south to the Riviera, and went to London, where he loved seeing the city's buildings through the winter fog.

Ernest Hoschedé died in 1891, and the next year Monet and Alice were married. By now Monet had begun developing his works in series, painting the same stacks of grain that stood in the fields near his home, in different seasons, at different times of day, showing the changing effects of light and color. He would paint several pictures at the same time, working on each one for only a few minutes, then moving on to the next when the light changed. The following day he would return to each picture at the same time as the day before. Sometimes he worked from his floating studio on the river, painting fields of flowers or rows of poplar trees on the shore. He got so involved in his series paintings that he bought a row of poplar trees that were for sale so that he could finish painting them before they were sold to someone else and chopped down.

In 1892 and 1893 he spent several months in Rouen, where his brother Léon lived, studying its famous cathedral from a shop on the second floor of a building overlooking the church. The sunlight passing across the facade of the church, and the changing atmosphere became the subject of these pictures, with only a blurred outline of the Cathedral appearing as if in a mist. His series pictures were exhibited and sold in other countries as well as in France.

In Giverny Monet loved to work with the flowers in his garden. In 1893 he bought more land in order to create a water garden with lily pads floating on the surface and he planted new species of water lilies. At one end of the pond he built a curving wooden footbridge, like those he had seen in Japanese prints, where he could stand and watch the lily blossoms open and close. He began painting the water lilies in 1902, and the blossoms became his favorite subject. Now his work was so successful that he was able to buy even more land to increase the size of his water garden.

People were beginning to buy their own motor cars, and Monet bought an automobile that he drove to Madrid, Spain, in 1904 to see the paintings in the Prado Museum. Alice had never liked it when he went off by himself and this time he took her along. Four years later they went to Venice, Italy, together. By then Monet's eyesight was failing and he was in ill health. In 1909, forty-eight of his paintings of water lilies were exhibited in Durand-Ruel's London gallery and they were well received. Later, the Museum of Fine Arts in Boston gave him a one-man show of forty-five paintings.

In the spring of 1910 Alice became ill and died a year later. The artist was grief-stricken and fell into a deep depression, rarely leaving his house and garden. Moreover, he was developing cataracts and had to wear thick glasses. Early in 1914 his son Jean, who had married Blanche Hoschedé, died after a long illness. Blanche came to live with Monet and looked after him.

The artist kept working, continuing with the water lily theme and using large brushes to paint broad strokes. Some of these works were on such large panels that, in order to work on them, he had to build another studio, with an immense skylight.

He had always painted directly from nature, but now he painted in his studio from drawings that he had sketched outdoors. When he was not satisfied with the results he would burn them.

After World War I broke out, in July of 1914, Monet watched his son Michel leave for active duty, and he constantly worried about his safety. He continued working quietly in Giverny during the war, taking only one trip to Normandy to visit the favorite seaside places of his youth. After the war ended, in November 1918, Premier Georges Clemenceau, a longtime friend of Monet, persuaded him to give twelve big water lily panels to the French government, to be hung in a special building. The panels would eventually be installed in large oval rooms in the Orangerie, near the Louvre Museum, after the artist's death.

Although Monet's eyesight was growing continually worse, he continued to work, painting his Japanese footbridge in series. He had cataract surgery in 1923, then developed lung cancer and failed rapidly. Clemenceau, no longer premier, lunched with him in November of 1926 and was at his bedside when he died on December 5. Monet was eighty-six. As he had requested, he was buried quietly, with no religious service, in the churchyard at Giverny.

Claude Monet had worked all of his long life painting light as it appeared in nature, moment by moment and transferring its fleeting effects into lasting works of art. His paintings are so highly admired that the main street in Giverny is now called the rue Claude Monet.

The French government has made his home into a national landmark, and visitors from all over the world can stroll through his gardens, walk over his Japanese footbridge, and gaze down into his pond at the water lilies that gave him so much pleasure and brought him fame.

Georgia O'Keeffe

1887–1986   American painter with an orginal style known for her
New Mexican landscapes and enlarged flowers

Georgia O'Keeffe was a legend in her own time. She had an independent personality, as reflected in her life, and her own special way of seeing, as reflected in her art. She was born on November 15, 1887, in Sun Prairie, Wisconsin, the daughter of Francis and Ida Totto O'Keeffe, and grew up on a large wheat farm. She had a brother two years older, a younger brother, and four younger sisters. Her grandparents lived on farms nearby. There was not much display of emotions among the O'Keeffes and the family was never close. O'Keeffe and her mother rarely agreed on anything, and she felt her parents did not approve of her. She did get along reasonably well with her sisters. She did not like to talk about her family history, saying,

"Where I was born and where and how I lived is unimportant."

The children went to school in a one-room schoolhouse. When O'Keeffe was a little girl she spent long hours playing with a homemade dollhouse. She was very independent at an early age and said, "I was satisfied to be all by myself." She sewed clothes for her dolls and for herself, even after she grew up. She loved to be outdoors and was curious about things she saw in nature. Even as a tiny child she was aware of light and of colors; in time, strong colors would become important in her painting.

When O'Keeffe was eleven she and two of her sisters took drawing lessons at home. She continued to draw at Sa-

129

cred Heart Academy, a Catholic boarding school near Madison, Wisconsin, where her parents sent her when she was twelve. She told another child, "I'm going to be an artist." She later said, "I found things I could say with color and shapes that I couldn't say in any other way . . . things I had no words for." After a year at Sacred Heart she went to Madison, Wisconsin, to live with an aunt. She attended a local school, where the art teacher taught her to look closely at flowers.

Her family sold the Wisconsin farm in 1903, and moved south to Williamsburg, Virginia, for a warmer climate. They sent O'Keeffe to Chatham Episcopal Institute, a boarding school for girls in the foothills of the Blue Ridge Mountains. She became art editor of the school yearbook and played on the basketball and tennis teams. She also liked to play poker and taught her friends the game.

O'Keeffe was different from the other girls and they thought her strange. She was plain and not interested in boys and clothes like the other girls. She dressed simply and wore her hair pulled back and braided. She was poor in spelling, but good in drawing. Her art teacher encouraged her to enroll in the school of the Art Institute of Chicago after she graduated in 1905.

In Chicago O'Keeffe stayed with an aunt and uncle. When she went home to Williamsburg for summer vacation she fell ill from typhoid fever and remained in Virginia the next year. Then in 1907 she moved to New York, where she studied with the American artist William Merritt Chase at the Art Students League. Chase taught traditional European methods of drawing and painting, yet encouraged his students to experiment in their own individual way.

The work of modern European artists was being introduced to the American public by the famous photographer Alfred Stieglitz who had a gallery at 291 Fifth Avenue. O'Keeffe went with her classmates to 291, as it was called, when drawings by the French sculptor Auguste Rodin were being shown and went back again to see the works of Henri Matisse.

In 1908 O'Keeffe's father was having business problems and could not afford to support her in New York. She returned to Chicago in November 1908 to work as a commercial artist in the advertising business. Two years later, she contracted measles, which temporarily affected her eyes, and again returned to Virginia. Her parents had separated, but that was a subject she never discussed.

During the next school year O'Keeffe taught art briefly at her old school in Chatham and during the summer attended art school at the University of Virginia in Charlottesville, where her mother now lived. Her instructor, Alon Bement, introduced her to the ideas of his own teacher Arthur Wesley Dow, a famous professor at Columbia University's Teachers College in New York City. O'Keeffe was inspired by Dow's methods, which encouraged students to learn about design instead of trying to copy things as they looked, and to express their feelings by inventing their own abstract patterns. Dow had studied in France with Paul Gauguin and had also studied Japanese art, with its flat composition and simplified forms.

In the fall of 1912 O'Keeffe took a job in Texas as the head of art education for the elementary schools in Amarillo. She loved "the openness, the dry landscape, the beauty of that wild world." She enjoyed being in the "wild west," the setting of stories that her mother had read aloud to the children when they were little. And she was amused by the cowboys when they came to town. She did not agree with the teaching methods of the Amarillo school system, however. She kept to herself, spending her free time taking long walks over the plains. Alon Bement invited her to be his summer school assistant at the University of Virginia and she taught with him for three years.

In 1914, after her second year in

Georgia O'Keeffe as a girl. *Catherine Krueger.*

Amarillo, she went to New York to study with Professor Dow at Teachers College. There she made friends with Anita Pollitzer, a classmate, and together they visited Stieglitz's "291" to see exhibitions of American modern art and of the painters Georges Braque and Pablo Picasso.

In the autumn of 1915 O'Keeffe went to Columbia, South Carolina, to teach at a junior college. Meanwhile she worked on her own drawings and paintings, trying to represent the basic form of an object rather than its exact appearance. She had decided to paint to please herself and not be influenced by other artists. She liked to create abstract forms out of her imagination, always experimenting with her own original style. Often her subject was flowers. She said, "A flower touches everyone's heart."

O'Keeffe had begun writing letters to Anita Pollitzer, a correspondence that would last more than half a century. She sent Pollitzer some of her charcoal drawings, telling her not to let anyone else see them. Nevertheless, Pollitzer showed them to Stieglitz, who was impressed with their fresh beauty, and he and O'Keeffe began writing to each other.

In May 1916 O'Keeffe quit her teaching job and went back to New York, to Teachers College. The next month, without O'Keeffe's knowledge, Stieglitz exhibited her work in a group show at 291. O'Keeffe was angry because she felt her drawings were too private for everyone to see. She went to Stieglitz and demanded that he take them down. However, he talked her into leaving them up and into having lunch with him.

That fall O'Keeffe was teaching again, this time at a teachers college in Canyon, Texas, where she refused to teach according to the school's standard method. She was different from everyone else and the people in Canyon did not like her. In her simple black dress with a white collar and her hair pulled back in a bun, she looked old-fashioned. She kept to herself, and when everyone else was in church, she took long walks, admiring the vast, flat prairie and the clear, blue sky, with little white clouds. She even liked the dust storms and the violent thunderstorms.

The following spring, on April 3, 1917, three days before the United States declared war on Germany and entered World War I, Stieglitz gave her a one-woman show at 291. At the end of the school term she was back in New York, a city filled with nervous excitement over the war. During her visit, Stieglitz took his first pictures of her, photographing her face and her hands, which were beautiful, with strong, slender fingers. She never wore makeup to soften her features, and her strong will showed in her face. Her nose was prominent, her mouth and chin firm, and her thick eyebrows arched over large brown eyes.

After a brief stay in New York O'Keeffe returned to Texas. Her youngest sister was living with her at that time because their mother had died. In late summer the two young women took a trip to Colorado. On the way, O'Keeffe got her first glimpse of the bare hills and green piñon trees of New Mexico. On the way back to Texas they stopped in Sante Fe, New Mexico, and she fell in love with the clear mountain air and the brilliant light of the desert.

That fall O'Keeffe's relationship with the people in Canyon was even more strained because they felt patriotic and she was against the war. In February 1918 she fell ill and left Canyon to live with a friend on a farm in Waring, Texas. Stieglitz was worried about her and sent his assistant, the young photographer Paul Strand, to Texas to bring her back to New York. In early June she and Strand were on a train heading east.

In New York Stieglitz arranged for O'Keeffe to live in his niece's studio and encouraged her in her art. The friendship between them grew close, leading to Stieglitz's separation, and later divorce, from his wife. He continued to photograph the artist in every pose. She said, "He photographed me until I was crazy!"

Stieglitz exhibited his photographs of O'Keeffe beginning in 1921 and continued to exhibit her drawings and paintings, asking high prices for them. As her style developed she simplified forms and enlarged them, working mostly in watercolor, charcoal, and pastel on pa-per. And she began to work with oil paints on canvas. In 1923 Stieglitz arranged to have one hundred of her works exhibited in a one-woman show at the Anderson Galleries; he had closed 291. People thought her work was clear and direct, but out of the ordinary. Critics called it feminine, which O'Keeffe did not like. She was proud to be the only woman accepted in Stieglitz's group, which included Arthur Dove and John Marin, friends of hers whose work she admired. Yet she strongly objected to being called a "woman artist." She insisted, too, that her work was not related to any art trend or style and she did not want people to read meaning into her works.

In the summertime Stieglitz's family and a steady stream of guests gathered together in the Adirondack Mountains, at Lake George, New York. The family house was in a lovely spot overlooking a clear lake in a setting of dense green woods and rolling hills. O'Keeffe liked to garden. She painted in an old shack called the Shanty, which was off in a field. Her first close-ups of a single flower magnified to enormous proportions were painted at Lake George in 1924. She felt that if she enlarged a flower people would take time to look at it. She would use the same subject over and over, reworking it and calling the results a series. (See reproduction in the color section of this book.)

Stieglitz loved to have people around. He was a friend of the poet William Carlos Williams, the writer Gertrude Stein, and the many American modernist artists whose work he encouraged. O'Keeffe needed privacy and would sometimes go off to Maine without him. There she would collect seashells on the beach and use them as subjects for paintings. Sometimes she would magnify a single clam shell as she would a flower.

On December 11, 1924, O'Keeffe and Stieglitz were married. Although she was now his wife she did not like being called Mrs. Stieglitz, and if someone called her that she would say, "I am Georgia O'Keeffe!" Her work continued to be the center of her life, as it had always been and always would be. In 1925 both O'Keeffe and Stieglitz were included in an exhibition at the Anderson Galleries along with the four painters: Arthur Dove, Marsden Hartley, John Marin, and Charles Demuth, and the photographer Paul Strand.

O'Keeffe and Stieglitz lived in rooms thirty floors above the street, in the Shelton Hotel in New York City. They were surrounded by skyscrapers and could see the East River. The views inspired O'Keeffe to paint a series of cityscapes, including *Shelton Hotel No.*

1 and *Radiator Building—Night, New York.* Some of her best works were painted in the late 1920s and included the series *Black Iris.* Her paintings were shown at the Brooklyn Museum in 1927, and the following year five of them were included in an exhibition at the new Museum of Modern Art in New York.

Besides painting, the artist worked in Stieglitz's galleries framing pictures, putting them in storage, and hanging all of the works for the shows. She supervised the installation of the pictures when he opened the Intimate Gallery in 1925.

However, relations with Stieglitz were growing strained. Both were self-centered and had strong personalities, and O'Keeffe was jealous of Stieglitz's friendship with a woman named Dorothy Norman.

In 1928 while they were at Lake George, Stieglitz had a heart attack. The next summer she went to Taos, an artists' colony in New Mexico, with Paul Strand's wife, Rebecca, even though Stieglitz objected. They were guests of Mabel Dodge Luhan, a wealthy easterner who was married to a Navajo Indian, and who liked to paint and to surround herself with artists and writers. O'Keeffe rode Luhan's white horse over the desert and went on pack trips with other guests. She loved the dry

Radiator Building—Night, New York. Fisk University Museum of Art. Carl Van Vechten Gallery,
Alfred Stieglitz Collection.

Georgia O'Keeffe and Alfred Stieglitz. *The Bettman Archive.*

mountain air, the vast open spaces, the bold desert colors, and the strong sunlight of New Mexico. The desert hills and flowers, and the adobe church in Ranchos de Taos, became the subjects of her New Mexican paintings.

In 1929 the stock market crashed, and the Great Depression followed. At this time many people felt that art should have serious subject matter and carry a social message, so O'Keeffe's paintings were not always well received.

The following summer she was back in Taos. As she took long walks, she col-

lected animal skulls and bones that were bleached from the sun and worn smooth by wind and sand. She said, "To me they are as beautiful as anything I know." She shipped a barrel of bones back to the East as symbols of the desert. Later she would arrange and paint them in her studio. The best known of these works is *Cow's Skull: Red, White, and Blue.* In the summer of 1932 O'Keeffe traveled to the Gaspé Peninsula in eastern Canada. Her paintings of white barns were inspired by this trip.

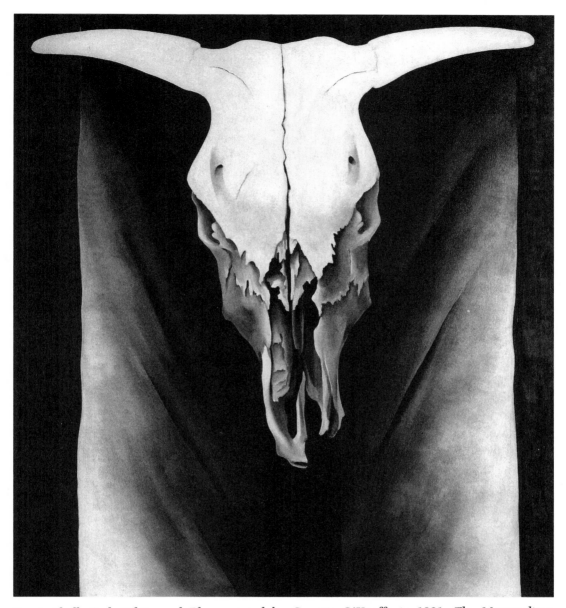

Cow's Skull: Red, White and Blue, painted by Georgia O'Keeffe in 1931. *The Metropolitan Museum of Art. The Alfred Stieglitz Collection, 1949.* (52.203)

When Radio City Music Hall was being built in New York City's Rockefeller Center, a competition was held to choose an artist to paint a mural in the powder room. Against Stieglitz's objections, O'Keeffe entered, and her design *Manhattan* won. However, when she began to paint the mural she saw that the canvas lining the powder room wall had not been properly attached and she walked off the job. Feeling she was a public failure and suffering stress from her troubled marriage, she had a nervous breakdown. She did not begin to recover until the end of 1933, following a stay in the hospital and a trip to Bermuda.

New Mexico seemed to O'Keeffe to be just the right place for her, and the next year, 1934, she went back there, staying at Ghost Ranch, a summer resort seventy miles from Taos. She now owned a Model A Ford and would drive it across the desert until she reached a spot where she wanted to stop and paint. Whether she painted a landscape, a bone, or a flower, she concentrated on the object, removing it from reality, simplifying its forms and giving it a new meaning. She said of the flowers, seashells, rocks, pieces of wood, and "beautiful white bones on the desert . . . I have used these things to say what is to me the wideness and wonder of the world as I live in it." In the evening she liked climbing to the roof to watch the sunset.

In 1938 O'Keeffe traveled to Arizona and Colorado, taking a pack trip on horseback to Yosemite with the photographer Ansel Adams. Adams took the photographs of Yosemite, for which he became famous, and O'Keeffe sketched. The artist's reputation was growing, and articles were written about her. That year the College of William and Mary gave her an honorary degree, and in time there would be others, including one from Harvard University.

In 1939 when Eleanor Roosevelt and Helen Keller were chosen two of twelve outstanding women of the previous fifty years, O'Keeffe was also chosen. The artist's painting *Sunset—Long Island* was included in an exhibit at the 1939 New York World's Fair. That year, the Dole Pineapple Company sent her to Hawaii to produce paintings that would advertise their product. Back in New York Stieglitz was ill and O'Keeffe was nervous, so she went to the Bahama Islands in the Caribbean Sea, to recover.

She continued to return to Ghost Ranch and in 1940 bought her own house with eight acres of land where she had no telephone. She had horses to ride and Siamese kittens as pets. She set up a studio to work in which she always kept in perfect order. No one was allowed in the room while she was painting.

When the United States entered World War II O'Keeffe felt safe in that isolated spot in New Mexico. Butter and meat were rationed during this time and ranch hands were being drafted into the army, but she felt far from the war, unaware that the atom bomb was secretly being developed not far from her, in Los Alamos. While the war was still on, in 1943, the Art Institute of Chicago held a one-woman exhibition of her work.

Two years later O'Keeffe bought an old, abandoned adobe building on three acres of land in the tiny village of Abiquiu. This home, which she called The Faraway, was about sixteen miles from Ghost Ranch and was completely hidden from the road. Although Spanish was the only language spoken in that remote area, O'Keeffe never learned to speak it. She did not make friends with the local people, nor was she interested in observing the Indians whom many other artists came to New Mexico to paint. In fact she never painted people at all, nor did she make self-portraits. She preferred to paint bones, using the blue sky as background.

The Museum of Modern Art had a one-woman show of her work in 1946. After the opening, she returned to New Mexico, traveling by air for the first time. In July she received word that Stieglitz was seriously ill. She immediately flew back to New York and was with him when he died. He left her his large art collection and his photographs, which she distributed to museums and helped to organize exhibitions to show them. Finally, in 1949, she returned to New Mexico to live, installing an irrigation system in Abiquiu, planting a garden, and creating a studio in which to work and a vault in which to store her paintings.

Once she was settled, O'Keeffe began to travel, first to Mexico in 1951 where she met the painter Diego Rivera and then to France and Spain. Unlike other American artists who went to Europe to study art when they were young, O'Keeffe crossed the Atlantic for the first time when she was sixty-five. Then she took a trip to Peru in 1956 and in 1959 she went around the world, visiting the Orient, Southeast Asia, and islands in the South Pacific. Views from the airplane inspired her to paint clouds. At age seventy-five, she took her first rafting trip down the Colorado River, with the photographer Eliot Porter, sleeping under the open skies. She continued rafting until she was in her mid-eighties.

The Worcester Art Museum in Massachusetts gave the artist a one-woman show in 1960. In 1962 she was elected to the American Academy of Arts and Letters. Four years later the American Academy of Arts and Sciences elected her as a member. The Amon Carter Museum in Fort Worth, Texas, had an exhibition of her works that later traveled to Houston and Albuquerque. When an exhibition was held at the Whitney Museum in New York City in 1970, she insisted it be held in the largest space available and that she supervise the printing of the catalog. That same year the National Institute of Arts and Letters awarded her a gold medal. Later she would receive the Medal of Freedom from President Gerald Ford in 1977, and the National Medal of Arts from President Ronald Reagan in 1985.

In New Mexico the artist had a comfortable life, spending winters in Abiquiu and summers at Ghost Ranch, with a housekeeper, gardener, and secretary to help her. She rose at dawn to exercise and ate organic food grown in her garden. When visitors tried to see her she could be terribly rude. As she grew older the wrinkles and lines in her face grew deeper and her hair turned white, yet she stayed slender and erect. She continued to look the same in her plain black or white dress and flat-heeled shoes. In 1971 she had serious problems with her eyesight and stopped painting.

In 1972 O'Keeffe met a tall, handsome young man named Juan Hamilton and hired him to do odd jobs. Then he became her assistant and business manager. There were rumors they would marry. Hamilton, who had studied pottery and sculpture, taught O'Keeffe to make pottery and encouraged her to paint again. She first began with watercolors and then turned to oils, but her paintings were highly simplified, and she had assistants in her studio to help work on them. Hamilton also encouraged her to cooperate in making a 1975 film for television about her life and work. In addition, they produced a book together that was published in 1976 which included her own brief, poetic text. On her ninetieth birthday in 1977, she was honored with a celebration at the National Gallery of Art in Washington, D.C.

Because of her close relationship with Hamilton, O'Keeffe broke off with most of her old friends. Her former agent, whom she dismissed after thirty years, sued her, and this received nationwide publicity. In 1984 O'Keeffe had a heart attack. Hamilton moved her to Santa Fe in order to be near the hospital. She died on March 6, 1986. The bell in the adobe church rang loudly to announce her passing. At her request there was no funeral or memorial service: her ashes were scattered over the ground near her house at Ghost Ranch.

The one hundredth anniversary of O'Keeffe's birth was celebrated by an exhibition at the National Gallery of Art. In years to come perhaps her personality will be forgotten, but Georgia O'Keeffe will always be remembered for her powerful and original art.

Pablo Picasso

1881–1973   Spanish painter whose name became a symbol of revolution in art

During his own lifetime Pablo Picasso was one of the most famous men in the world. Some people love his work and some make fun of it, but everyone finds it interesting because it is so original. Picasso discovered new means of expression that changed the way we look at things. He had a powerful personality and a private life so closely related to his art that each change in his life led to a major change in his style of painting.

Pablo Ruiz y Picasso was born October 25, 1881, in Málaga, Spain, on the brilliant, sunlit coast of the Mediterranean Sea. His father was José Ruiz Blasco and his mother María Picasso López. According to Spanish custom when naming a child, the father's family name is followed by the mother's. Picasso used Ruiz, his father's name, to

sign his pictures until he was twenty. After that he signed only Picasso, his mother's family name. Pablo had a younger sister Conchita, who died very young, a loss that affected him deeply.

José Ruiz was an art teacher and curator of the city museum. He painted still lifes and made cutouts of paper and cardboard. It is said that Pablo could draw before he could talk, but he was not a good student and he would often pretend to be ill so he would not have to go to school. When José Ruiz dropped him off in the morning the boy was always afraid that his father would forget to come back for him. On Sunday afternoons Ruiz often took his son to the bullfights, a popular amusement in Spain. A bullfight is the subject of Picasso's earliest-known work, a painting he did when he was eight or nine years old.

In 1891, when Pablo was ten, the family moved to La Coruña in northwestern Spain, on the windy, rainy Atlantic coast, where José Ruiz taught art in a high school. He instructed his son in drawing and painting, and sometimes the boy finished details in his father's pictures. At this time portraits of his family and their friends were the subject of Picasso's paintings. He continued to do portraits of people who were close to him for the rest of his life.

After four years in La Coruña the family moved east, across the country to Barcelona in the province of Catalonia on the Mediterranean coast, near the French border, where José Ruiz had taken a position as professor at the School of Fine Arts. Pablo took an examination for the advanced class in the school, called La Lonja, even though he was only fourteen. At this time one of his paintings was accepted for an exhibition in Barcelona.

After studying at La Lonja for a year he got bored and felt he had nothing more to learn from his teacher. So he and a friend from La Lonja, Manuel Pallarés, rented their own studio. Picasso's early paintings were in the traditional style acceptable to the public. One of his works, *Science and Charity,* in which his father posed as the model

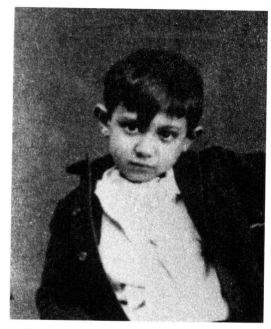

Pablo Picasso at the age of seven. *Musée Picasso, Paris.*

for a doctor sitting at the bedside of a woman who is dying, earned an award in Madrid and a gold medal in Málaga. Later in his life the artist said that he did not like the pictures he had done at that time.

In Barcelona he spent his free time in the café Els Quatre Gats (The Four Cats), where avant-garde, or forward-looking, artists and writers with advanced ideas gathered. One of them, the poet Jamie Sabartés, became his lifelong friend. His companions were bohemians, rebelling against traditional social behavior and proclaiming concern for all humanity. They were willing to live poorly and suffer hardships for the sake of their art.

In the fall of 1897 Picasso went to Madrid, the capital of Spain, where he was quickly accepted at the Royal Academy of San Fernando. He studied the works in the Prado Museum, especially those of Diego de Velázquez, Francisco Goya, El Greco, and Titian, all of whom he admired. He was sixteen years old and had a tiny allowance from an uncle, but he did not have enough money to live on. In Madrid he enjoyed the cafés and the life around him, often forgetting to go to the Academy.

In the spring he came down with scarlet fever and had to return home to Barcelona to recover his health. He spent that summer with Manuel Pallarés and his family at their home in the mountain village of Horta de Ebro, now called Horta de San Juan. Picasso enjoyed the natural beauty of the area. He admired the simple peasants who worked in the fields and made sketches of them. He and Pallarés rode about on mules, and for a time camped out in the hills to be close to the earth while Picasso made landscape studies.

Back in Barcelona he continued to see his friends at Els Quatre Gats. He went about town in a shabby black suit and a hat, filling his sketchbook with drawings of people he saw on the street. A feeling of loneliness shows in the faces of those he sketched. Local artists could hang their works on the walls at Els Quatre Gats. In 1900 Picasso exhibited one hundred and fifty drawings at the café, mostly portraits of his friends. Reviews of his work were published in two periodicals.

Picasso had an independent spirit that was leading him away from the traditional method of painting that he had learned from his father. He and his friends were interested in modern styles, especially the exciting trends that were developing in Paris. One of his works was selected for the Spanish section of the world's fair of 1900 in Paris.

In early autumn the artist, still in his teens, took a train to France with a friend, the poet-painter Carles Casagemas. They stayed in Montmartre, a section of Paris that attracted both French and foreign artists. Picasso went about town painting city life, especially people in the streets. One day he met fellow countryman Pedro Mañach, an industrialist from Catalonia. Mañach took an interest in Picasso's work and offered to pay him an allowance in return for his paintings. At this time the artist sold three bullfight pictures to an art dealer, Berthe Weill.

Unfortunately Casagemas became deeply depressed, and by the end of the year the young men were back in Spain. That winter Casagemas committed suicide. The tragedy threw Picasso into deep depression. He painted *The Dead Casagemas* in memory of his friend.

In the spring the artist started an art publication in Madrid, with a friend, Francisco de Asís Soler. However, it failed after two issues. Soon Picasso was in Paris again, where Mañach organized an exhibition of sixty-four of his works. A critic praised him in a journal. At this time he met Max Jacob, a Jewish poet and art critic who went about wearing a top hat and a monocle, an eyeglass that covers one eye.

A self-portrait of Picasso in 1901 shows he had grown a beard, which was dark and shiny like his hair. He was five-feet-three-inches tall, powerfully built and strong muscled, with a head that seemed large in relation to his body. His deep-set eyes were round, black, and penetrating. He could be charming when he was in a good mood, and was said to be courteous, but he could easily get angry or bored. And sometimes he was gloomy for long periods of time.

Picasso showed an interest in performers of all kinds, especially Harlequins. His pictures at this time, now called his blue period, were painted almost entirely in shades of blue, and the mood is always melancholy. Works from his blue period have a haunting power. People suffering from loneliness and hardships, such as beggars, street musicians, and blind men, were his major subjects. The figures are large, painted in an empty setting.

Life in Paris was difficult. He lived for a time in a one-room apartment with Max Jacob, sharing one bed between them because they were so poor. Jacob had a job, so he slept at night; Picasso stayed up all night and slept during the day. Conditions were so bad that he broke his contract with Mañach and returned to Spain. Back in Barcelona he continued to create icy blue paintings, revealing sadness and suffering in his characters, as in *The Old Guitarist*.

Picasso had been moving back and forth between France and Spain, and then in 1904 he settled permanently in Paris. Although he lived in France for the rest of his life, he always remained a Spaniard. In Paris he visited art galleries and museums, especially the Louvre, where he absorbed art from all ages. Although his work shows the influence of different styles and periods, Picasso always kept his own individuality.

The artist lived in a run-down tenement, a former piano factory that had been converted into studios, which his friends called the *Bateau Lavoir* (Laundry Boat). The building had no gas or electricity, and only one toilet and water tap for all thirty studios. Picasso could not afford to buy enough coal for the stove that heated the room; it would get so cold that tea left in a cup overnight would freeze. His 1904 painting *The Frugal Meal,* showing a thin, pathetic-looking couple with only a crust of bread to eat, may well be based on his own experience.

Nevertheless, he entertained a steady stream of poets and artists who had great fun together and wanted to find new ways of expressing themselves. He was the leader of a close group of friends, known as *la bande à Picasso* (the Picasso gang). They had poetry readings in a café where Picasso paid the owner in paintings instead of money when he ran up a bill. One of the group, the poet Guillaume Apollinaire, wrote an article about Picasso in 1905 that helped make the artist known.

Picasso had great creative energy, painting with speed and producing an enormous amount of work. He painted late at night, then slept through the morning. He had a magnetism that attracted people, and a good sense of humor. His wit often comes through in his work. When friends visited, he might put on a false mustache or a funny hat from a large collection that he kept in his studio, or show them the white mouse that made its home in a drawer.

The artist and his friends loved going to the circus to watch the jugglers, acrobats, and clowns. He created portraits of these characters whose performances were magical, even though they lived in poverty. Sometimes his own image can be seen in the paintings.

Shortly after moving into the *Bateau Lavoir,* Picasso met a beautiful young woman, Fernande Olivier, who became his constant companion. He turned to subjects filled with beauty and calm, using warm shades of pink in his paintings. This stage in his work became known as his rose period. He modeled his figures with firm outlines and no unnecessary details, painting only what was needed for his message. His 1905 *Family of Saltimbanques* shows the artist's feelings of tenderness toward circus performers, who had to be constantly on the move with their families. (See reproduction in the color section of this book.) That same year, Leo Stein, a well-to-do American who was living in Paris, visited Picasso's studio with his sister Gertrude, a writer, and they began collecting his work.

Soon afterward Picasso began painting Gertrude Stein's portrait. It took him months to complete; she posed for him more than eighty times. He had trouble painting her face. In the end he treated it like a mask, modeling it after an ancient sculpture that had recently

Picasso in his studio in 1929. © *Harlingue-Viollet.*

been excavated in Iberia, the Spanish peninsula, and exhibited at the Louvre.

The Steins were at the center of the art and literary world in Paris. They invited the artist to their home where they had weekly dinner parties for writers and artists, including one of the foremost painters of the time, Henri Matisse, who considered Picasso a rival. These evenings were difficult for the Spaniard, who spoke no English and very little French, but he made important contacts. The figures in Picasso's pictures were becoming more rounded,

with firmer lines, looking almost like classical sculpture. In *Boy Leading a Horse,* painted in 1906, the full-length figure of the nude youth reflects the artist's interest in Greek statues.

Picasso continually invented new ways of expressing his art. In 1907 he created an experimental work called *Les Demoiselles d'Avignon* (The Young Ladies of Avignon), which was composed of five female figures. Instead of showing the human forms in a conventional way, the figures are angular, drawn with simplified lines, and the foreground and background merge. Some of the figures are seen from different angles at the same time and some of the faces look like African masks. Picasso admired African tribal art, which he would have seen on visits to the Trocadéro Museum of Ethnology in Paris. He found it interesting that these works were created for a magic purpose. He was impressed with the simplified structure and distorted proportions of the forms and with the way that African sculpture expresses the idea of a figure instead of its actual appearance.

When his friends saw *Les Desmoiselles d'Avignon,* they were shocked and disturbed by it. They could not understand it, and they thought the artist was mad. Matisse accused Picasso of making fun of modern art, and Leo Stein laughed at him. Picasso rolled up the painting and stored it in his studio, where it remained for many years before it was shown publicly.

In the autumn of 1907 Picasso met Daniel-Henry Kahnweiler, a German art dealer who owned a gallery, and Kahnweiler began selling his paintings. Some months later he met a wealthy Russian art collector from Moscow named Serge Shchukin who began buying his works, acquiring more than fifty of them during the next few years.

In the summer of 1908 Picasso went to a quiet spot in the country and painted landscapes. The French painter Georges Braque spent that same summer in the south of France. When Picasso returned to Paris in the autumn he saw that he and Braque had been painting landscapes in a similar style. They were representing nature with geometric forms, breaking them up and reassembling them in the manner of Paul Cézanne, whose work had been shown at an exhibition in Paris. Cézanne is known to have said, "You must see in nature the cylinder, the sphere and the cone."

Braque's paintings were rejected by the official Salon that autumn, 1908, but they were shown at Kahnweiler's gallery. Picasso and Braque worked closely together, even though they were different in many ways. Almost every evening they would visit one another's studios to see what each had been doing that day. Sometimes they dressed alike in mechanics' overalls. They thought of themselves as inventors, identifying with the brothers Wilbur and Orville Wright, who invented the airplane. In works of this period by Picasso and Braque natural objects are broken apart into flat, angular shapes, and rearranged, superimposed, and compressed into a shallow space. Few traces of the original objects can be recognized. The main interest was in the forms that make up the objects, not in the objects themselves. The style was so very revolutionary it was given the name Cubism, even though there are no cubes to be seen in the pictures.

By then Picasso's talent had been recognized internationally and his paintings were selling well. He enjoyed going to Spain in the summer, but sometimes he liked to go to the south of France, where he could be near Braque. In autumn 1909 he moved into a large, comfortable apartment in Paris with an adjoining studio, where he and Fernande Olivier had a maid to wait on them. The space was filled with paintings by Picasso's friends and with objects he liked to collect, such as African masks and musical instruments. Because he was an avid collector and never allowed anything to be thrown away, Picasso's home and studio were always cluttered.

The artist was constantly falling in love. He was domineering with women and would often treat them rudely. After awhile he would get restless, would try to free himself, and would soon become interested in someone new. In 1911 he fell in love with a pretty young woman named Eva Gouel, whom he met at Leo and Gertrude Stein's home. His pet name for her was *Ma Jolie* (my pretty one), taken from a popular song. Picasso and Braque had begun putting letters and numbers on their works to stand for ideas. Now Picasso wrote the letters that spell out *Ma Jolie* on one of his paintings.

In the winter of 1912 Picasso's work was included in an exhibition in Moscow and then in various shows in Germany. That spring he pasted a piece of oilcloth, printed to imitate caning on the seat of a chair, onto an oval painting and framed it with heavy rope. *Still Life with Chair Caning*, which brings everyday objects into a painting, was his first collage. Picasso and Braque experimented with the new art form, sticking cutout shapes and scraps of cloth, cardboard, newspaper clippings, and other objects onto a flat background, often drawing or painting over them. In 1913 eight of Picasso's works were included in an exhibition at the Armory Show in New York City.

When World War I broke out in 1914 Braque was drafted into the army and Guillaume Apollinaire enlisted. Both fought in the trenches and were seriously wounded in action. The art dealer Kahnweiler, as a German, was an enemy alien and had to leave France. He fled to Italy, and the works in his gallery were confiscated. Gertrude Stein went to England. Picasso remained in Paris and continued his life much as he had before. He was a citizen of Spain, a neutral country, and he would have nothing to do with the war. Very few of his friends were left in Paris. Eva was ill with tuberculosis, and he took her to Avignon in the south, where the climate was mild. She died in a nursing home in December 1915, leaving the artist sad and depressed.

About a year later his spirits rose when the poet Jean Cocteau invited him to design the scenery and costumes for his new ballet *Parade,* to be performed by Sergei Diaghilev's Russian Ballet dance troupe. In February 1917 Cocteau and Picasso left for Rome, where Diaghilev was making his headquarters during the war. Costumes that Picasso designed for *Parade,* which was inspired by the circus, were cardboard cubist constructions. The production opened in Paris, and when the curtain went up, the audience booed! They were not prepared to see such a modern ballet.

Nevertheless, Picasso enjoyed being in the theater world, associating with this new group of interesting, creative people. When the company performed in Barcelona he went along. Then Diaghilev took the ballet company to South America, but Picasso did not go. One of the dancers, Olga Koklova, stayed behind with him. She and Picasso had fallen in love. A year later, in 1918, they were married in Paris and went to Biarritz, an exclusive seaside resort, for their honeymoon. Picasso had drifted away from his bohemian friends and was spending time with more fashionable people. The couple moved to a large, two-story apartment with servants to look after them, where Olga enjoyed entertaining. His work reflected a sense of calm and peace.

World War I ended in 1918. Braque, who had suffered head wounds during the war, returned to Paris. He and Picasso had grown apart; their friendship would never be the same. Now Matisse and Picasso had a joint exhibition in a gallery. In 1919 the artist went to London to design the costumes and scenery for another ballet, *The Three-Cornered Hat,* for which he painted a bullfight arena as the scene for the backdrop curtain. The production was a great success. Through the years he continued to work on ballets, including *Pulcinella* in 1920, with music by Igor Stravinsky and choreography by Léonide Massine.

In February 1921 Olga gave birth to a son, Paulo. The artist would paint lovely portraits of him as he grew up. One shows him in the costume of a Harlequin, another holding a lamb, and Paulo is mounted on his donkey in a portrait that is especially charming.

Picasso's imagination had broad range. His visit to Italy inspired an interest in ancient Greek and Roman stat-

Picasso's 1924 portrait of his son Paulo. *Giraudon/Art Resource/Musée Picasso, Paris.*

ues. He was also influenced by the Neo-Classical style of the nineteenth-century French master J. A. Dominique Ingres. These years are known as his Neo-Classical period. He created huge nude female figures, using firm outlines, with few details, in simple settings. At the same time he continued working in the Cubist style, with figures becoming larger and flatter. And he experimented with paintings that showed multiple views of a single person, so the front and back would be visible at the same time. The *Three Musicians* of 1921 is one of his masterpieces from this period.

Picasso loved to be at the seaside. In summer he went with his family to fashionable resorts on the French Riviera where he enjoyed the beach. In Paris he always associated with the avant-garde, the most up-to-date, forward-looking group of advanced thinkers. Artists were becoming interested in the ideas of Sigmund Freud, the psychoanalyst in Vienna who expressed theories about imagination and the subconscious mind. Freud was interested in the way one thought flows into another, and how people's dreams reveal their suppressed thoughts. Picasso and his friends wanted to understand how dreams and repressed feelings affected the creative process. They tried to record their subconscious fantasies, cre-

ating Surrealist works, which were startling and mysterious. Familiar objects were broken up and reassembled and combined in surprising combinations. In 1924 André Breton wrote the *Surrealist Manifesto*, expressing the ideas of the group, and the following year Picasso participated in their first exhibition of surrealist painting, held in Paris. His work was getting harsher. His female figures are violent and distorted, having been taken apart and reconstructed, as in *The Three Dancers* of 1925.

By now the artist was nearly fifty. He was discontented with his personal life and with his traditional, middle-class family, and he yearned to be free of it. He said of himself, "I am not a gentleman." In 1930 he bought a two-hundred-year-old castle in the Normandy countryside, the Château Boisgeloup, and turned the stables and coach houses into painting and sculpture studios. He had grown interested in a beautiful young woman named Marie-Thérèse Walter, and her likeness began appearing in his paintings and sculpture.

Picasso had always liked to work in three dimensions, to create works of sculpture; he was now welding metals, using the same Cubist forms as in his paintings. He produced huge heads with distorted features out of plaster and did engravings to illustrate books. His first retrospective exhibition, covering two hundred thirty-six works from all of the periods in his career, was held in an art gallery in Paris in 1932. He was so famous by then that an art magazine published a special edition about him.

Even though Picasso lived in France he never gave up his Spanish citizenship. In 1933 and 1934 he took trips to Spain. He continued to enjoy the bullfights and use the bull as a subject in his works, sometimes turning it into a Minotaur, half-man, half-bull. The Minotaur, a mythological figure part human, part beast, part divine, was an important symbol to Picasso. A huge exhibition of the artist's works was shown in 1935 in Paris, London, and New York. That year, Marie-Thérèse gave birth to a baby girl who was named Maya.

The difficulties in Picasso's personal life at this time made it impossible for him to concentrate on his painting. He told a friend, "It's the worst period of my life." For several months, beginning in May 1935, he did not paint at all. However, he did express his feelings by writing Surrealist poetry. He wrote in both French and Spanish. Paul Éluard, a poet, who had become his friend, encouraged Picasso in his poetry, and, in the winter of 1936, Éluard introduced him to an attractive photographer named Dora Maar.

That summer the Spanish General Francisco Franco led the Nationalist military forces that supported Fascism in an uprising against the liberal Republican government, leading to the outbreak of the Spanish Civil War. Picasso was firmly opposed to the Nationalists, who had the support of the Nazi German leader Adolf Hitler. Fearing that bombing raids might soon begin, the Spanish government sent the paintings in the Prado Museum in Madrid to a secret hiding place, and Picasso was appointed absentee director of the museum. The artist was deeply troubled by the Spanish Civil War. *The Dream and Lie of Franco,* a series of etchings accompanied by a poem, published soon after the war broke out, expresses his rage.

The following year, on April 26, 1937, Hitler sent German fighter planes to bomb Guernica, a village in a beautiful valley in the north of Spain. The event took place in the middle of the afternoon while people gathered in the marketplace. After bombing the center of town the Nazi planes swooped down to machine-gun the citizens who had taken refuge in the fields. The world was shocked that civilians far from the battlefield were deliberately and ruthlessly killed.

Guernica. Giraudon/Art Resource/Prado, Madrid.

When Picasso received the news that Guernica had been wiped out and innocent civilians had been killed, he was enraged at the cruel and needless destruction. He had been invited by the Spanish Republican government to create a mural for the Spanish Pavilion at the 1937 Paris International Exhibition. Now he knew he had the perfect subject. He began working on a huge painting which would express his anger. To compose the work, which was twenty-six feet wide and eleven feet high, he made at least fifty sketches for the various figures. Dora Maar photographed each step as he progressed, taking pictures of him as he mixed his paints and climbed up a stepladder with a long brush to work on the painting, which he called *Guernica*.

The painting shows the victims of the tragedy in various poses, revealing their fear and agony. A building burns. Women's faces are knotted in pain, as if screaming in terror. A mother holds a dead baby in her arms. Figures are distorted to emphasize the artist's message. *Guernica* was an outcry against all war and human suffering. After it was exhibited at the world's fair in Paris it traveled to Chicago, Los Angeles, and San Francisco. In 1939 it was shown at the Museum of Modern Art in New York City, along with three hundred of his other works, in "Picasso: Forty Years of His Art." In keeping with the artist's wishes, *Guernica* remained on loan to the museum until Spain was free of Fascism and a new democratic government was formed. It was sent to Spain in 1981, six years after General Franco's death, and is now exhibited in Madrid.

When World War II broke out on September 3, 1939, Picasso stayed in France. People urged him to go to the United States or Mexico, where he would be safe, but he refused. Hitler's troops marched into Paris, and the Germans occupied France the following summer, but he still insisted on staying in Paris. Sometimes he would go with Dora Maar, his old friend Jamie Sabartés, who had become his secretary, and his Afghan hound Kasbec to the seaside resort of Royan. Some of his friends had to hide from the Germans, and many left the country. The Surrealist writer André Breton went to the United States. The Jewish poet Max Jacob stayed in a monastery in France and the Nazis forced him to wear a yellow star because he was Jewish. Then he was arrested and sent to a concentration camp where he later died.

Life was difficult under wartime conditions. Picasso could not get enough food or art materials, and the Nazis would not let him exhibit his work, which they considered degenerate. A great sculptor as well as a painter, he collected objects that people discarded as junk to use for sculpture. He transformed a leather bicycle seat and iron handlebars into the head of a bull. During the war he wrote a Surrealist play,

Desire Caught by the Tail, which was performed for a small audience in someone's home.

Paris was liberated from the Germans in 1944, and Picasso's friends began returning. Soon afterward the artist joined the Communist party and became an active member, attending international conferences through the years. His drawing of a dove, standing for peace, was used by the Communists for a poster and became a universal symbol.

Now for the first time the artist showed his work at the official autumn Salon exhibition and was given a large gallery all to himself for seventy-four of his paintings and five of his sculptures. Even though he was a foreign artist he was the guest of honor. Outside the building there were anti-Communist demonstrations against him.

Themes from classical mythology that reflect his joyful mood are revealed in some of Picasso's works from the period following the war. Françoise Gilot, a young art student whom he had met in 1943, became his model and constant companion, and in the spring of 1947, a son Claude was born to the couple. Two years later, a daughter Paloma was born.

Picasso loved the clear, dry air of the Mediterranean and enjoyed taking daily swims in the sea. When he was in Antibes, on the French Riviera, in 1946 the curator of the Antibes Museum, located in the Grimaldi Palace, invited him to use some of the rooms for a studio. Paintings that he created there, including the mythological composition *La Joie de Vivre,* remained in the palace to form what would become the Picasso Museum.

Antibes is not far from Vallauris, a quiet village in the hills above the Riviera that is noted for its ceramics factory. Picasso saw an exhibition of Madoura pottery in 1946 and was invited to visit the workshop. The next summer he became very active working with the local potters creating vessels out of clay. He modeled highly original sculptural forms and made designs on the surface with a brush. He involved himself in every stage of production and continued this activity for the rest of his life. Soon he bought a yellow, two-story villa, La Galloise, high in the hills of Vallauris, where he could be near the pottery works. He produced such vast quantities of pottery that he had to rent an abandoned factory to hold it. The factory served as his studio for sculpture as well as for painting. It was large but always cluttered.

Picasso continued to be interested in sculpture, using everyday materials that he found: one of the most famous is *Baboon and Young.* Two toy cars were used for the head of the mother ape,

the handle of an old pitcher forms her ears and shoulders, and a strip of metal becomes her tail.

Françoise Gilot left Picasso late in 1953, taking Claude and Paloma with her to Paris. He was depressed because he missed the children. There were important exhibitions of his work in Rome and Brazil that year and a celebration by the Communists in his honor the year following, then shows in Paris and Germany the year after that. In the spring of 1955 he moved to La Villa Californie, a large, sunlit house surrounded by gardens with palm and eucalyptus trees, in the hills above Cannes in the south of France. Goats grazed in the gardens, and the artist installed his bronze animals all about. His Afghan hound Kabul was always at his side. He kept a dovecote on a balcony and would feed the birds grain when they wandered into his studio.

In 1957 Picasso's seventy-fifth birthday was celebrated by a huge exhibition of his work at the Museum of Modern Art in New York City. The exhibition later traveled to Chicago and Philadelphia. It attracted record-breaking crowds. Picasso was recognized internationally as the greatest artist of the century. He did not have to depend on patrons to commission works, so he could be independent and express his own ideas. His paintings were selling for record prices, which he kept raising.

He was a rich man and owned valuable property, yet he did not change his basic life-style, his careless manner of dressing, and simple tastes and habits.

In 1958 Picasso bought a fourteenth-century château in Vauvenargues, fifty miles from the sea, near Aix-en-Provence, in a valley surrounded by forests. It was an ideal place to retreat to when he needed privacy. The chateau is located amid scenery that is the subject of Paul Cézanne's landscapes, paintings that Picasso admired. The area reminded Picasso of his beloved Spain. That year a huge mural that the artist painted for the United Nations Building in Paris was installed.

Over a period of time the artist experimented with paintings that were based on the works of great artists of the past. He produced variations of *The Women of Algiers* by Eugène Delacroix, *Las Meninas* (Maids of Honor) by Diego de Velázquez, and *Déjeuner sur l'herbe* (Luncheon on the Grass) by Edouard Manet. He painted portraits of himself and of Jacqueline Roque, his new companion. He also painted circus themes and bullfight subjects that recall his Spanish heritage.

The artist continued to be restless even in old age. He grew uncomfortable at La Villa Californie when high-rise apartments went up around him and neighbors could look into his garden. In 1961 he bought *Mas Notre-Dame-de-Vie,* a villa on a hilltop at Mougins near Cannes with a view of the Mediterranean Sea. That March, shortly before he turned eighty, he married Jacqueline Roque. She was constantly at his side, sheltering him from the outside world and preventing tourists and unwanted visitors from entering their home. It was sometimes difficult even for his own children and his old friends to see him.

As Picasso grew older and his friends died he retreated even more. He continued working although his work was not well received. He was rarely seen without a paintbrush in his hand. He used loose brush strokes, yet his paintings reflected strength. The Spanish government opened the Picasso Museum in a fifteenth-century palace in Barcelona in 1963. Works owned by his family and friends and by the artist himself were donated to the museum. The artist was now world renowned. His works were exhibited in Japan and Israel as well as in America and Europe.

To celebrate Picasso's eighty-fifth birthday in 1966 the French government organized a large exhibition of his paintings, sculpture, drawings, and prints at the Grand and Petit Palais in Paris. The next year a gigantic sculpture sixty feet high, designed by Picasso, was installed in front of the Civic Center in Chicago. He turned down payment of one hundred thousand dollars because

Picasso making his last piece of ceramic in his studio, August 1966. © 1981 Roberto Otero/Black Star.

he wanted it to be his gift to the people of Chicago.

On Picasso's ninetieth birthday the president of France honored him at the Musée du Louvre in Paris, and he was named an honorary citizen of the city. Even now he continued to be productive, but he rarely went out.

On Sunday April 8, 1973, Picasso died at the age of ninety-three in his studio at Mas Notre-Dame-de-Vie. He was buried in the garden of the Chateau de Vauvenargues, in a quiet ceremony, in the presence of Jacqueline and his son Paulo. His bronze statue

Woman with a Vase was placed on his grave.

So ended the long, productive life of Pablo Picasso. Three years after his death the French government and Paris City Council announced plans to start a Picasso Museum in Paris with his personal collection. In addition, his works are displayed in the museums at Antibes and Barcelona. No other artist in history has ever had so many museums devoted to his work, and no other has made such a great change in the art of his own time. The name *Picasso* will always be a symbol of revolution in art.

Rembrandt van Rijn

1606–1669   The greatest genius of Dutch painting

Rembrandt Harmensz. van Rijn, the greatest of all Dutch painters, enjoyed much success during his lifetime and he became so famous that he is known to the world by his first name. However, his periods of happiness were brief, while his sorrows were deep and long lasting. Perhaps his personal tragedy helped him develop a deep understanding of people. He was able to express the emotions of his subjects by focusing on their inner lives rather than on the outside world. The greatness of his work lies in his humanity.

Leiden, Holland, where Rembrandt was born on July 15, 1606, is an important center of learning; the first Protestant University in the Netherlands was founded there. At this time Holland was nearing the end of a successful struggle for independence from Catholic Spain and was on its way to becoming a world power. The boy was the eighth child in his family, but only four had survived; a ninth was to follow. Rembrandt's father, Haarmen Gerritsz. van Rijn, was the fifth generation in his family to be a miller. Their family name van Rijn came from the name of the mill (Rijnmill) near their home.

The van Rijns were simple people, moderately well-to-do. Rembrandt's mother, Neeltgen Willemsdr van Zuytbrouck, was a religious woman, the daughter of a baker. The boy's parents wanted to prepare their son for a profession, so they entered him in the Latin School in Leiden when he was seven. In addition to Latin, he learned religion, history, and classical literature.

When he was fourteen, he enrolled in the University at Leiden. However, it soon became clear that he was determined to paint, so he began a three-year apprenticeship in the workshop of Jacob van Swanenburgh, where he was trained in the basic technique of painting. Showing great promise he went to Amsterdam for further training in the studio of Pieter Lastman, who specialized in historical scenes in the Italian manner. The young student was quick to understand his subjects and he soon became a master of portraying facial expressions. After six months he returned to Leiden to work on his own.

While most young painters wanted to travel to Italy to study, Rembrandt chose to remain in Holland, finding subjects in his surroundings and using members of his family as studies. When someone asked him why he did not go to Italy, he replied that he could see enough Italian pictures at home.

In Leiden Rembrandt became a teacher himself and continued to be an important teacher throughout his lifetime. As was common practice he brought his own pupils and assistants into his studio to work with him on his paintings. In addition to portraits he chose subjects from history, mythology, and the Bible, especially the Old Testament. Rembrandt sketched constantly, and his genius shows through in his drawings and etchings as well as in his paintings. Most of his drawings were kept in albums for his private use. He produced nearly seven hundred drawings and three hundred masterful etchings in his lifetime.

By the time he was in his early twenties Rembrandt was firmly established as an artist. Holland had become a rich, seafaring nation in the seventeenth century, with colonies in Asia and America, and Amsterdam was now an important center for commerce and banking. Merchants who had grown wealthy wanted to live like the nobility. They needed paintings to hang in their homes and encouraged Dutch artists to produce them. Rembrandt painted pictures for local citizens and for Frederick Henry, prince of Orange, the most important person in the country, who hung them in his art gallery in The Hague.

In 1631 Rembrandt left Leiden to settle permanently in Amsterdam. There he stayed in the home of Hendrick van Uylenburgh, a wealthy art dealer, artist, and publisher and supervised his studio. He did well with portrait commissions. In 1632 he was asked by the Surgeons' Guild to paint a group portrait of a prominent physician, Dr. Nicolas Tulp, and his students. Most group portraits have no movement, but this one portrays action. Rembrandt

Self-portrait of Rembrandt. *Alinari/Art Resource/National Gallery, London.*

showed Dr. Tulp giving his students a lesson in anatomy. The picture helped establish Rembrandt's reputation as Holland's leading portrait painter.

In 1634 Rembrandt married Hendrick van Uylenburgh's cousin Saskia, and five years later bought a large, expensive house in the Jewish section of Amsterdam, on a street where other artists lived. Rembrandt had a special admiration for the Jewish people and their Old Testament, and he often used them as his models; his painting *The Jewish Bride* is among his best known. At the time, he painted quiet scenes and dramatic landscapes with changing skies.

The artist had many friends—well-educated scholars, preachers, writers—with whom he enjoyed conversations. He also enjoyed collecting paintings and engravings by other artists, art books, natural specimens such as shells and coral, antique statues, and even weapons. He kept armor and foreign costumes of fancy materials and fur in his studio for his sitters to wear when they posed for portraits.

He was happy with Saskia, who bore him four children but only one survived, a son Titus. Saskia died in 1642 when Titus was only a year old. All of the deaths in his family made the artist very sad.

In 1642 Rembrandt finished his best-known and largest painting, commonly called *The Nightwatch*. Its real name is *The Company of Captain Frans Banning Cocq and Lieutenant William van Ruytenkured.* (See reproduction in the color section of this book.) Instead of arranging the figures in stationary poses for an ordinary group portrait Rembrandt gives the men movement by representing them vibrating with life as they start to march. His startling approach lends dramatic meaning to the picture. *The Nightwatch* expressed Rembrandt's originality and independence, although it was not well received at the time it was painted.

For the next few years he led a very quiet, private life. As a widower he needed someone to look after Titus, so a woman named Hendrickje Stoffels came to live with them in the big house when the child was about eight years old. In time she became the artist's common-law wife and she bore him a daughter named Cornelia in 1654. Unfortunately, Rembrandt's expensive house with its lavish furnishings was more than he could afford and he was running into debt. He was a poor manager of money, and he was not selling many paintings, so he was unable to pay his bills. The city of Amsterdam took over Rembrandt's grand house and its furnishings to pay his creditors. He had to move into a smaller home and his

Flemish Nobles Visiting Rembrandt's Studio, a painting by Adolphe-Alexandre Lesrel. *From* Great Men and Famous Women, *Vol. VIII, ed. Charles Horne (New York: Selmar Hess, 1894).*

valuable possessions were auctioned off. Titus and Hendrickje Stoffels tried to help him pay his debts by setting up an art business in their own name in order to avoid his creditors.

In spite of his financial difficulties, the artist continued to work productively, as he did throughout his lifetime. He used his family as models and painted self-portraits, as he always had. Rembrandt's extraordinary self-portraits, painted from youth through old age, offer a penetrating record of his character and his changing appearance. His work grew calmer as he grew sadder. During this period of difficulty he received an important commission from an Italian nobleman who collected works by the finest European artists of the day. The Italian wanted a portrait of a philosopher, and Rembrandt created the masterpiece *Aristotle Contemplating a Bust of Homer.*

In time, the painter's income increased, but tragedy struck once more in 1663 when Hendrickje Stoffels died, and yet again in 1668 when Titus died, just a few months after his marriage. Cornelia, still living with her father, was the only child to survive. Even his daughter-in-law, Titus's widow, died before he did. Rembrandt's life came to an end in 1669, when he was sixty-three, and he was buried in Westerkerk, a church in Amsterdam. The grand house that he loved but lost is now a public museum, and thousands of tourists flood into the Rijksmuseum in Amsterdam every day year-round to admire *The Nightwatch*.

Diego Rivera

1886–1957   Mexican artist who painted murals to express his political ideas

Diego María Rivera and his twin brother, José Carlos María, were born on December 13, 1886, in Guanajuato, Mexico, where their father Diego Rivera and mother María del Pilar de Barrientos were schoolteachers. Both of their grandfathers were involved in silver mining. The Rivera family lived in a three-story house on a narrow cobblestone street. José Carlos died when he was only a year-and-a-half old, and then a sister María was born when Diego was five. Diego began drawing as soon as his little fingers could hold a pencil. He liked to draw pictures of locomotives and trains, and thus was nicknamed "the engineer."

His father, who had liberal political ideas, left Guanajuato in 1892 and took the family to Mexico City to live. Rivera was homesick and he fell ill, but his great-aunt Totata took loving care of him. He was devoted to her and always remembered how she let him play with some of her favorite things that she kept in an old trunk. When he was eight years old he enrolled in a Catholic school, and at the age of ten he started an evening art course at the Academy of San Carlos, the official art school of Mexico. He liked to play soldier and was interested in military history, so when he was twelve his father enrolled him in a military school. He lasted only two weeks because he hated the discipline and drill. Next he enrolled as a full-time student in the Academy of San Carlos on a scholarship. There he learned the fundamentals of drawing and painting from Santiago Rebull, the landscape painter José María Velasco, and Gerardo Murillo, known as Dr. Atl, who had studied in Europe. At the Academy Rivera developed an appreciation of the Mexican landscape and of pre-Columbian art. After six years he won a medal in a painting class, and his work was included in the annual exhibition.

The governor of the state of Vera Cruz, who met Rivera's father after he had become an inspector for the Department of Public Health, was impressed with Diego's talent and granted him a small scholarship to study in Europe. The young artist made enough money for his passage by selling some of his works. He sailed for Madrid, Spain, in 1907. There he studied with the Realist painter Eduardo Chicharro y Agüera and copied paintings in the Prado Museum by Flemish and Spanish masters, especially Francisco Goya and El Greco. Chicharro recognized his student's talent and included his pictures in group exhibitions in Madrid and Paris.

Rivera was an intelligent, energetic, and good-natured young man with large, bulging eyes and a dark, curly beard. He was well over six feet tall and had always been fat. As the years went by he became huge, weighing as much as three hundred pounds, although his hands were small and dainty. The bulky young Mexican could be seen around Madrid in a broad-brimmed hat wearing wrinkled clothes that did not fit. He soon made friends with a group of avant-garde writers and painters, people with advanced ideas, who met in cafés. Rivera enjoyed telling tall tales about himself to amuse the group. It is hard to know what the true facts are about his life because he made up so many stories. In Spain he was sympathetic to workers who were striking for better wages and working conditions, just as workers in Mexico were doing.

In 1909 the young artist moved to Paris where he studied paintings in the museums and sketched outdoors along the Seine River. That summer he traveled to Bruges, Belgium, where a Spanish friend María introduced him to Angeline Beloff, a slender, blue-eyed, blond Russian artist who illustrated children's books. From Belgium the three of them went to London to visit museums and sketch outdoors in poor industrial areas. By the end of the year Rivera was back in Paris. The following year his works were accepted for exhibition with the Society of Independent Artists.

In June 1910 he returned to Madrid and by October was back in Mexico. Shortly after his arrival Rivera's paintings were exhibited at the Academy of San Carlos to celebrate Mexico's one hundred years of independence from Spain. His work was highly praised and it sold well. Several of his paintings were bought by the wife of President Díaz; the government bought many of the others.

The week that the exhibition opened a band of peasants rose up against the dictatorship of President Porfirio Díaz, and a long, bloody conflict, a revolution that would last a decade, began. In later years Rivera claimed that he was a "revolutionary with the peasant army of the leader Emiliano Zapata for six months." The truth is that he returned to France in June 1911 and did not go back to Mexico until the Revolution was over.

Paris was the city he loved and where he wanted to make his home. He and Angeline Beloff set up housekeeping in Montparnasse, the bohemian section of the city, where artists and other people not concerned with social convention liked to live. Angeline became his common-law wife.

In Paris Rivera's long list of friends included artists, poets, and political revolutionaries, not only from Mexico but from all over the world. One of his companions was the Italian painter Amedeo Modigliani. The two young artists went about town playing pranks, sometimes behaving outrageously.

Diego and Angeline traveled to Toledo, Spain, in spring 1912, where the artist was so influenced by the works of El Greco that he worked for a time in El Greco's style, with elongated, angular forms. When he returned to Paris Rivera showed his work in the Autumn Salon exhibition. Works of other artists made a big impression on him, especially those by Paul Cézanne. He was also inspired by Georges Braque and Pablo Picasso, who were experimenting with Cubism. These artists turned away from traditional styles and were reducing forms to geometric shapes, breaking them up and reconstructing them. Rivera was painting in the Cubist style by 1913, but his works were more colorful than those of other Cubist painters and he included Mexican motifs. In 1914 a young Chilean artist introduced him to Picasso, who praised Rivera's paintings.

Because of the Mexican Revolution the artist's scholarship was cut off and he had to support himself and Angeline through the sale of his works. In spring 1914 he had a one-man show in Paris at an art gallery, and his paintings sold well. He also exhibited in group shows that were held in Czechoslovakia, Holland, and Belgium. That summer he went on a walking and sketching tour in Spain with Angeline and a group of friends. He was painting landscapes on the island of Majorca when World War I broke out. In the winter the group moved on to Madrid, where his work was included in an exhibition of Cubist works. From there he and Angeline went on to Barcelona and in the spring they returned to Paris.

A son was born to Angeline in 1916. They named him Diego but called him Diegito, "little Diego." The boy died of influenza when he was two years old.

In March 1917 at a dinner party in Paris, Rivera got into a fight with a writer who had criticized one of his paintings. Their hostess's china was broken and there was even talk of a duel. As a result of the incident other artists were angry with Rivera and they avoided him. All the while he was searching for his own personal style in his art. He gave up Cubism and turned to a more realistic style of drawing and painting.

Like his father, Rivera had liberal political ideas, and changes taking place in Russia were of interest to him. After Czar Nicholas II was overthrown in the October Revolution of 1917, leading to the establishment of the Soviet Union and the beginning of the Communist regime, Rivera applied for a visa to go to Russia, but it was denied. In February 1920 he left for Italy. He traveled about for a year and a half, studying Italian art, especially Renaissance frescoes, murals, which are painted on walls

while the plaster is still wet so that the colors will sink in. He also made sketches to use as models for paintings on canvas. In June 1921 he left Angeline behind in Paris and departed for Mexico. The Revolution was over, and now he began to focus on his native land, expressing a truly Mexican art based on the beauty of the people, their tropical surroundings, their festivities, and their daily lives. In November 1921 the government sent him with a group of artists and writers to the state of Yucatán to visit ruins of the ancient Maya and learn about Mexico's past.

In 1922 Rivera married Guadalupe Marín. Two years later a daughter was born, whom they named Guadalupe, nicknamed Lupita. Another daughter followed, named Ruth, nicknamed Chapa.

Rivera joined the Communist party in 1922 and became very active politically. He felt that the Communists would make the world a better place for Mexican peasants and other workers. When he began painting large murals for the walls of the new cultural institutions of the government he worked for the same low wages that an ordinary workman would earn, which amounted to about two dollars a day.

Rivera was the leading artist of *Los Tres Grandes,* the three great painters of the Mexican mural movement. The other two were José Clemente Orozco and David Alfaro Siqueiros. These artists were determined to create a national "art for the people" that would express the realities of Mexican society. They used mural painting to express their ideals of social revolution and the struggle for Mexican cultural identity. The murals, painted in the fresco technique, were created in public places and are monumental in size, as they are meant to be seen by everyone. Rivera was skillful at organizing the large spaces to create complex compositions that carry a message. He simplified the forms of the figures and painted broad areas of bright colors with strong outlines.

The first mural that Rivera worked on was begun in 1922 in the auditorium of the National Preparatory School in Mexico City. The subject is the creation of the world. The next, on the theme of everyday life of the Mexican people, was on the walls of the Ministry of Education's extensive new headquarters in Mexico City. This project, which was enormous, took more than four years. The murals carry a strong political message on the need for social change to bring about an ideal society with a better life for ordinary workers. Newspaper articles attacked these murals and students with conservative political ideas rioted in protest against them.

In 1926 Rivera started on a project in Chapango, at the National School of Agriculture, on the subject of revolutionary social change and good government. Scenes relating to the revolution reflect his admiration for Emiliano Zapata, who led the peasants in the movement to recover the land that had been taken away by the dictatorship government. Zapata was a colorful leader and he became a national hero and favorite subject for Mexican painters.

To paint a mural Rivera had to climb up on a wooden scaffold, sometimes putting in more than twelve hours a day. While working in the chapel in Chapingo in 1927 he fell off the scaffold and was knocked unconscious. It took three months for him to recover from his injuries.

After completing the mural project in Chipango in August he departed for the Soviet Union with an official delegation. A Union leader had arranged the visit to celebrate the tenth anniversary of the October Revolution. When Joseph Stalin, the Soviet dictator, made a speech to the Mexican visitors Rivera sketched his portrait. The artist was honored by the School of Fine Arts in Moscow and invited to paint murals for the Red Army Club. He made a few sketches, but the project was never completed.

After nine months in Russia Rivera returned home. In murals that he painted after his return he included the Russian revolutionary symbols of a red star and hammer and sickle, as Communist propaganda to carry the message of unity to all workers.

Meanwhile he continued to produce drawings and paintings, many of them for patrons in the United States. His works were admired for their purely Mexican subject matter and for the simplified forms of the figures in a balanced composition. Colorful scenes at the flower market with the peasants who sell the flowers was a popular theme. He also painted portraits, successfully capturing the character of the person. One of his favorite subjects was himself, sometimes painted with humor.

Among Rivera's most important murals are those in the National Palace where the president had his office, in the main square of Mexico City. He began them in the summer of 1929 and worked on them on and off for decades. The subject is the history of Mexico, beginning with the pre-Columbian people. His representation of the Spanish conquest of 1521, led by Hernán Cortes, shows the Aztecs as noble Indians who were enslaved by greedy, cruel Europeans.

Earlier in 1929 he had been appointed director of the Academy of San Carlos. He planned to make drastic changes but was forced to resign the following year. In the meantime he had broken up with Guadalupe and at forty-four he married nineteen-year-old Frida Kahlo. Frida was the daughter of a German Jewish photographer and a Mexican woman of Spanish and Indian descent. As a child she had been stricken by polio and wore a brace on one leg. While in high school she was in a streetcar accident on her way home from school. Her internal injuries left her unable to have children.

Frida Kahlo was also a painter. Her work is highly autobiographical. The subject of her paintings reflect her lifelong suffering resulting from her many illnesses and from the cruel way in which Rivera sometimes treated her. After having a miscarriage she used the experience as a subject for her art.

In December 1929, at the invitation of Dwight Morrow, United States ambassador to Mexico, Rivera began work on frescoes in the Cortes Palace in Cuernavaca to be a gift to the people of that city. A year later he and Frida went to San Francisco, California, for the opening of a large exhibition of his work. Rivera painted a mural in the Pacific Stock Exchange, praising the richness of the earth in California and the progress of its people. His next mural

A la Señora Elizabet D.V. Morrow
Homenaje de respeto y afecto.
Diego Rivera. 1932

Diego Rivera in front of an unfinished mural at Cuernavaca, Mexico, in 1932. *Smith College. Sophia Smith Collection.*

Diego Rivera and Frida Kahlo in New York in 1932. *The Beinecke Rare Book and Manuscript Library, Yale University. Photograph by Carl Van Vechten.*

was in the California School of Fine Arts, on the making of a fresco. Frida made a hit in California in her long Mexican dresses and silver jewelry, and the couple were a big social success.

While at work in San Francisco the artist was called back to Mexico City by the government to finish his project in the National Palace. He returned to Mexico City in June 1931. While there he began building two adjoining houses

in the suburb of San Angel where he and Frida could live and work.

The Museum of Modern Art in New York City was opening an important exhibition of Rivera's work late that year, so he and Frida sailed to New York on an ocean liner. The show was very well received and set new records for attendance. The next year the ballet *Horse Power* by the Mexican composer Carlos Chávez opened in Philadelphia with scenery and costumes designed by Rivera. The orchestra was conducted by Leopold Stokowski.

One of the most important murals in Rivera's career was painted in Michigan in 1932 in the courtyard of the Detroit Institute of Art, on the subject of the automobile industry, celebrating the new Ford V-8 model. To understand the technology the artist spent months studying the machinery at the Ford Motor Company plant.

His next mural created a scandal that has not been forgotten. In 1933 he was invited by the Rockefeller family to decorate a wall in the RCA Building in Rockefeller Center. Sketches for the work, *Man at the Crossroads*, had been approved, but Rivera defiantly changed the design by including a portrait of Vladimir Ilyich Lenin, who founded the Soviet Union and ruled as dictator. Rivera's purpose was to praise Communism and show Capitalism as an evil sys-

Hugh Curry, Jr., a watchman in the RCA Building, poses for the central figure in Diego Rivera's mural in 1933. *UPI/Bettmann.*

tem. The Rockefellers were angry and asked Rivera to remove the portrait of Lenin from the composition, but the artist refused, so the unfinished mural was covered over with canvas and later destroyed. "The Battle of Rockefeller Center" received attention in newspapers all over the world. As a result of the incident General Motors canceled its plan for a Rivera mural in its building at the 1933 Chicago World's Fair.

The artist and Frida sailed for Mexico City in December 1933. For some months Rivera was ill and too depressed to work, but when he started painting again he re-created the Rockefeller Center mural in the Palace of Fine Arts. His next mural in Mexico City was for the owners of the Hotel Reforma on the theme of Mexican festivals. Another unpleasant incident occurred because he included unflattering portraits of some well-known people. The owners painted out some of the figures without Rivera's consent and the artist sued them. He won the case, but the murals were removed from the walls.

Rivera and Frida were now living in San Angel in their villa surrounded by a wall of tall cacti, in two houses, one pink, one blue, that were simply furnished. Rivera was one of the first people to appreciate pre-Columbian art. They had a large collection of these artifacts by the ancient Indians of Mexico. They also collected Mexican folk art that they bought in the marketplace. The artist's interest in these objects can be seen in his beautiful paintings, which reflect their native surroundings. The couple had two daschunds for pets. They also had monkeys, parrots, a little deer, and cats. Many of these animals are included in Frida's paintings.

Rivera continued to be politically active. When the Communists expelled the revolutionary leader Leon Trotsky from the Soviet Union in 1936 the artist urged the Mexican president to grant him refuge. Rivera invited Trotsky and his wife to stay in Frida's family home in Coyoacán, and it was put under heavy guard. The Riveras and Trotskys saw one another often until the two men had a political argument and the Mexican put his Russian guests out of the house.

The French writer André Breton also came to Mexico to visit. He was impressed with Frida's paintings and helped to have them exhibited. In November 1938 twenty-five of them were shown at a gallery in New York where Georgia O'Keeffe came to see them. Then they were exhibited in Paris, with Frida present. Pablo Picasso and other leading artists in France came to see her work. After Frida returned to Mexico she and Rivera separated and divorced, although they continued to see each other.

In 1940 Rivera was invited to paint a mural celebrating the Golden Gate International Exposition, the San Francisco World's Fair. He went to California in June and began work on a large fresco on the subject of friendship between the United States and Mexico; events in the history of each country were included. Thousands of people came to watch him on the scaffold. In the meantime Trotsky had been assassinated in Mexico. Rivera, fearing for his own life, hired an armed guard to be stationed on his scaffold to protect him as he painted. Frida joined him in San Francisco and they remarried in December, the same month that an exhibition of his works was held in the San Francisco Museum of Art. They returned to Mexico two months later. In May 1942, after a German submarine sank two Mexican tankers, Mexico declared war on Germany. During World War II Rivera continued working on various projects.

The artist enjoyed publicity and in 1947 he began a mural in the Hotel del Prado that he knew would cause another scandal. The subject was the simple theme of his childhood memories of Sunday visits to Alameda Park, but he included the slogan "God does not exist." A mob of protestors, most of them Catholic students, damaged the fresco and threw stones at Rivera's house. The mural was withdrawn from view for a time and not shown to the public again until nine years later, after the artist had removed the unpopular slogan.

In 1949 more than a thousand of his works, created over a fifty-year period, were exhibited at the Palace of Fine Arts in Mexico City. The President of Mexico made a speech calling the artist a "national treasure."

Frida went into the hospital the following year for operations on her spine and remained there for nearly a year. During this long, painful period Rivera faithfully stayed in a room next to hers to be near her. At this time his paintings were exhibited in Venice, Italy, and he was honored by the Mexican government with the National Art Prize.

In 1952, during the Korean War, Rivera was commissioned by the National Institute of Fine Arts to produce a large painting to be sent on a tour through Europe. In this work, *The Nightmare of War and the Dream of Peace,* he included a portrait of Joseph Stalin, the dictator of the Soviet Union, and showed South Korean soldiers hanging and shooting North Koreans,

the Communist invaders of South Korea. The director of the Institute refused to exhibit the painting, returning it to the artist. Later, with the help of the Communist Party, Rivera managed to exhibit it to the public in Paris and in the People's Republic of China.

Frida's right leg had to be amputated in August 1953 and she died the following July. The house in Coyoacán in which she had grown up was given to the Mexican people for a museum. In July 1955, a month after the doctors told him that he had cancer, Rivera married his art dealer Emma Hurtado. The couple went to Russia at the invitation of the Moscow Fine Arts Academy and while there Rivera had an operation. In March they went to Czechoslovakia, Poland, and East Germany, all countries under Communist rule. They were back in Mexico in April.

That December Rivera's seventieth birthday was celebrated by the nation. On November 24, 1957, he died of heart failure in his San Angel studio. Funeral services were held at the Palace of Fine Arts, with official honors, and he was buried in the Pantheon de Dolores in Mexico City. Rivera's murals can still be seen by the public on the walls in many cities in Mexico and the United States. And today Frida Kahlo is recognized as an outstanding artist, perhaps even equal to her husband.

Peter Paul Rubens

1577–1640   Flemish painter, diplomat, and scholar

Peter Paul Rubens was a bright star. A brilliant painter with extraordinary creative power, he was also a renowned diplomat of boundless energy and a cultivated scholar who led a princely life. He was born in Siegen, Westphalia (in what is now Germany), on June 28, 1577, the son of Jan Rubens, a lawyer, and Maria Pypelincx, whose father was a dealer in tapestries. Nine years earlier Jan Rubens had fled Antwerp, Flanders (now Belgium), with his wife and their four children, to avoid religious persecution. He had become a Protestant while Flanders was under the rule of Catholic Spain. Peter Paul and an older brother, Philip, also born in Westphalia, were tutored by their father. Jan Rubens died when Peter Paul was only ten years old. His mother, who was a

Catholic, took her children back home to Antwerp. This Flemish city was a busy commercial, cultural, and artistic center, in spite of a prolonged war with the Protestant Dutch to the north. Peter Paul and Philip attended a Latin school, where they were instructed in Latin and Greek. Both boys developed a lifelong interest in ancient art and classical culture. Philip would become a classical scholar, and Peter Paul would use his skills in reading Latin and his knowledge of mythology and ancient literature when illustrating classical subjects in his paintings. Because of financial difficulties Maria Rubens took her sons out of school when Peter Paul was thirteen and placed him in the household of a countess. There he served as a page, perfecting his manners and learning a courtly way of acting.

The boy really wanted to be an artist. In 1591, at fourteen, he became an apprentice to a landscape painter for a brief period and then went into the studio of the portrait painter Adam van Noort. An apprentice's duties included grinding and mixing colors for the master painter, preparing his canvases, and cleaning his brushes and palette. After about four years Rubens was apprenticed to Antwerp's leading master, Otto van Veen, also called Vaenius, whose guidance was especially helpful. Then in 1598 he was accepted into the Guild of Saint Luke as a master and was able to take on a pupil of his own.

Two years later, in May, when he was not quite twenty-three, Rubens set out for Italy. He went first to Venice, where he saw the works of the great Venetian painters, especially Titian, who would come to be his favorite. Later, when he grew wealthy, he collected nine or ten Titians of his own. While in Venice Rubens met Vincenzo I Gonzaga, duke of Mantua, who invited him into his service. The duke, an enthusiastic patron of the arts, wanted Rubens to copy masterpieces of Renaissance paintings, including works by Michelangelo and Leonardo da Vinci, to add to his personal art collection. This gave the young man an opportunity to view the art treasures in the ducal palace and the wonderful art collection of the duke's princely relatives in Florence, the powerful Medici family. When Vincenzo's sister-in-law Maria de' Medici married King Henry IV of France in the cathedral of Florence in October 1600, the artist attended the ceremony. But the king himself was too busy with his affairs in France to travel to Florence for his own wedding to the bride he had not yet met. The marriage took place by proxy, with the grand duke of Tuscany standing in for the king.

Through his service to the duke, the young Rubens had a chance to travel around Italy to study the works of artists he admired—including Raphael, Titian, Leonardo de Vinci, Michelangelo, and Caravaggio. Before long the duke sent Rubens to Rome, which was the artistic capital of the world, to copy Renaissance paintings, and there he was able to pursue his study of ancient art as well. When making drawings of ancient sculpture he filled them with life, and when copying a picture he always made slight changes, adding movement and energy. A new dynamic Baroque style with a strong emotional quality was developing in Italy. Rubens quickly absorbed it into his own fast, fluent method of painting. Baroque works, with their dramatic effects of light and dark, give an illusion of reality and a feeling of endless space.

While in Rome Rubens received his first important church commission: to paint three altarpieces for a chapel. This enabled him to stay in Rome for more than a year and to be with his brother Philip, who was getting an advanced degree at the university. The young painter was an attractive, courteous man; well read and fluent in several languages. Moreover, he was dignified, self-confident, and thoroughly reliable. Through his service to the duke he was developing his etiquette of court life.

In 1603 Vincenzo decided to send Rubens on a diplomatic mission to Spain to deliver precious gifts to the court of King Philip III. These included a beautiful carriage with six fine horses, exquisite perfume, and sixteen paintings. It was a difficult journey over land and sea in rainy, windy weather, and the paintings were badly damaged by water. Rubens was responsible for restoring them. For one of them he substituted a work of his own to present to the king's powerful minister, the duke of Lerma. It won him high praise and a commission to paint an equestrian portrait of the duke astride a spirited white horse.

While in Madrid the young Flemish artist saw works by Titian and another great Renaissance artist, Raphael. The experience helped him develop his judgment in art as well as his own skill in painting. When he returned to Italy, Vincenzo appointed him curator of his art collection and an advisor to him on purchases.

After two more years in Mantua, Rubens persuaded the duke to allow him to return to Rome. There he lived with his brother Philip, who was working as a librarian to an important cardinal. Together the brothers produced a book on ancient Roman art and language, which Philip wrote and Rubens illustrated. At the same time the painter began building up a collection of ancient Roman coins and sculpture. Rubens achieved great success in Rome, even though there was no shortage of fine Italian artists. He was asked to paint the high altarpiece in the new church of Santa Maria in Valicella. In the midst of the work Vincenzo called him to Mantua, for a time, to paint a series of portraits.

In the meantime Philip returned to Antwerp where their mother was ill, and in the autumn of 1608 he sent a message to his younger brother to come quickly. Unfortunately their mother died before Rubens could reach her bedside. To honor her memory the young artist placed over her tomb the magnificent first version of his painting for the high altar in Rome.

With eight years of experience in

Rubens with his wife Isabella Brant in 1609. *Alte Pinakothek, Munich.*

Italy, that formed the basis of his style, he now settled down in Antwerp. In 1609 he married Isabella Brant, whose father was a lawyer and whose aunt had recently married Rubens's brother, Philip. Isabella gave birth to a daughter, Clara Serena, who would live only twelve short years; fortunately two sons born later, Albert and Nicolaas, survived. Rubens and Isabella also brought up Philip's son after Philip's death.

The artist built a house for his family that was in the Italian style with a large courtyard, a formal garden, and a spacious studio for his workshop. A gallery was later added to exhibit his collection of ancient statues, gems, and coins. He also collected paintings and drawings by outstanding European artists. He attended Mass every morning and for recreation he rode horseback and read books on a wide range of subjects that included zoology and botany.

Rubens, who was the leading artist in the Spanish Netherlands, served as court painter to the royal rulers who governed the land, the archduke Albert and the archduchess Isabella, who was known as the Infanta, or Spanish princess. He also did work for private patrons and for the Church. At that time a Twelve Years' truce was being negotiated between Spain and the United Provinces of the Netherlands to the north (the Dutch Republic), whose leaders wanted to form a separate Protestant state. The city of Antwerp commissioned Rubens to paint a picture to decorate the room in the town hall where the papers would be signed.

In addition to portraits and biblical scenes the subjects of the artist's paintings included mythological, historical, hunting and battle scenes, and landscapes. His works are filled with muscular figures in swirling movement in large scale, dramatic compositions. Among his important commissions is a series of cartoons, or preparatory sketches, illustrating the story of the Roman general Decius Mus, who is said to have sacrificed his life so his army could be victorious. The scenes were used as designs that were woven into large tapestries.

With so much work to do Rubens needed a large number of young assistants in his studio to help on the paintings. The master would create a sketch for his pupils to use as a guide for a large painting, or he would make a drawing in chalk which the young painters would fill in. Afterward, he would finish the picture himself. The most talented of his pupils was Anthony Van Dyck, who became a great master in his own right. Sometimes Rubens's friend Jan Brueghel or another established artist would collaborate with him on a large work. The other painter

Decius Mus Addressing the Legions, painted by Rubens probably in 1617. *National Gallery of Art, Washington, D.C. Samuel H. Kress Collection.*

might fill in still life details or land-scapes, while Rubens would paint the figures. Engravings were made of many of his pictures and these were widely circulated as his fame spread all over Europe.

In 1622 Maria de' Medici, whose son had become King Louis XIII of France, invited the Flemish painter to portray twenty-one events in her life to deco-rate the new Luxembourg Palace, her residence in Paris, for a fee of twenty thousand crowns. Rubens, who spoke fluent French, proceeded to Paris where he was received by the royal family. He presented the Queen Mother Maria de' Medici with a small dog and also a jeweled collar, gifts from her friend the Infanta Isabella.

The Queen Mother had led an event-ful life. Shortly after her wedding to Henry IV, the king had been assassinated and she served as regent for their son. But in time she was exiled from the court because of her power struggles with the young king's ministers, and it was years before King Louis allowed his mother to return to Paris. When Rubens painted the episodes in her life he showed her surrounded by ancient Greek and Roman gods to give the impression that her reign had been divinely inspired.

Between the years 1622 and 1625 the artist made three trips to Paris to work on the palace decorations. Life was not easy in the French court, but he was admired for his honesty and fairness and he made some good friends. Among them was the scholar Nicolas-Claude Fabri de Peiresc, with whom he corresponded for the rest of his life. Another was the English nobleman George Villiers, duke of Buckingham, who came to Paris for the wedding of King Louis's sister Henrietta Maria to Charles I of England. The duke persuaded Rubens to paint his portrait on horseback and eventually to sell him his collection of ancient marble statues and jewels.

In 1621 both Philip III of Spain and Archduke Alber died, and King Philip IV ascended the throne. The Infanta Isabella now ruled the Spanish Netherlands as governor on behalf of her nephew King Philip. The Twelve Years' Truce between the United Provinces and the Spanish Netherlands had expired, and Isabella was eager for permanent peace. The Infanta was impressed with Ruben's character and she drew him into her service, bestowing on him the title of Gentleman of the Household to her Majesty's Serene Highness. He became her secret advisor. As a court painter he could easily move about from one country to the next for his diplomatic missions without arousing suspicion.

In 1626 Isabella Brant, the artist's beloved wife, died, probably from the plague that had stricken so many in Antwerp. After her death Rubens's diplomatic activity increased, and he traveled about negotiating an end to the fighting between Spain and England. In 1628 he was summoned to Madrid. There he lived in the royal palace, painted portraits of the king and his family, and made copies of paintings by Titian that were in the royal collection. Diego de Velázquez, the young Spanish court painter to Philip IV, also had rooms in the palace and the two became friends.

While Rubens was in Madrid news came that England might be willing to make peace with Spain. He was given the title Secretary of the King's Privy Council of the Netherlands and he departed for London in 1629 to try to negotiate a settlement. As always he combined painting and politics. He created historical paintings to present as gifts to King Charles I, who was keenly interested in art, and the king asked him to decorate the ceiling of his new banqueting house in Whitehall with scenes of nine events in the glorious reign of Charles's father, King James I. The project would prove a great success, although the king was slow in paying the fee of three thousand pounds. In appreciation of his talents the king dubbed Rubens a Knight of the Golden Spur and presented him with a jeweled sword, a diamond ornament, and a ring from his own finger. While the artist was in England, Cambridge University gave him an honorary Master of Arts degree. Most important of all, the diplomatic mission was to prove a success; King Charles agreed to make peace with Spain.

Rubens had grown tired of the business of international diplomacy with its petty jealousies and intrigues, and he was worried about his children back in Antwerp under the guardianship of relatives. Also he was eager to settle down at home so he could work in his own studio. In March 1630 he returned to Antwerp, and by the end of that year he took as a bride Hélène Fourment, the beautiful daughter of an old friend who was a local silk and tapestry merchant. The groom was fifty-three by then and the bride only sixteen, the same age as Rubens's son Albert. The artist gave his bride wonderful wedding presents of gold and diamond jewelery. She served as an inspiration and a model for his paintings for the rest of his life. Four children were born during their years together, two sons and two daughters. A fifth child, another daughter, was born eight months after the artist's death.

His marriage did not keep him from diplomatic obligations. In 1631 Maria de' Medici arrived in Flanders, having been exiled from France by her son King Louis. An admirer of the Queen Mother, Rubens came to her aid and was pressed into her personal service. Also, there was much more to be done in the quest for lasting peace in the Netherlands. The Infanta Isabella, still trying to reunite a divided Netherlands, sent Rubens on a secret diplomatic mission to the Dutch capital, The Hague. In 1631 King Philip knighted Rubens, conferring on him the title of nobility and granting him a coat of arms.

When the Infanta died in 1633 she was succeeded as governor by her nephew the Cardinal-Infante Ferdinand, brother of King Philip IV. A triumphal procession was planned to celebrate his official entry into Antwerp in 1635. Rubens was responsible for the decorations for this festive occasion. He set to work designing nine temporary

A self-portrait of Rubens. *Art Resource/Kunsthistorisches Museum, Vienna.*

Daniel in the Lions' Den, painted by Rubens around 1615. *National Gallery of Art, Washington, D.C. Ailsa Mellon Bruce Fund.*

timber structures. These included several triumphal arches for Ferdinand to pass under along the processional route through the streets of Antwerp, and a series of stages for official ceremonies along the way. He also designed paintings, as well as floats for the procession and fireworks to add to the festivity. To carry out this enormous undertaking he had to organize a team of artists and craftsmen.

The new ruler arrived in Antwerp by boat and took two hours to wind through the city on horseback. Included in his schedule was a visit the next day to the home of the artist, who lay in bed exhausted and ill. Ferdinand thanked him for the impressive decorations and eagerly accepted as a gift some of Rubens's pictures that he had painted for the occasion. The following year the Cardinal-Infante named Rubens his court painter.

King Philip was also an enthusiastic patron of the artist. In 1636 he commissioned a huge series of paintings of mythological subjects to decorate his summer palace and hunting lodge outside of Madrid. The artist bravely proceeded with his work in spite of his crippling arthritis and frequent attacks of the gout. He was spending more and more time in his country house, the Château de Steen, eighteen miles south of Antwerp, which he had purchased in 1635. There, as lord of the castle, he led a quiet life with his family and was inspired to paint wonderful landscapes for his own pleasure.

When Rubens died on May 30, 1640, following a severe attack of the gout, he was buried in the parish church of Saint James in Antwerp. The artist, often called "the Prince of Painters," was considered the most illustrious citizen of Antwerp. More than five hundred masses were sung for him in churches and convents. Later a memorial chapel was built in the parish church of Saint James, with one of his paintings over the altar. His own paintings fetched high prices, as did his collection of antiquities and paintings by other artists. In his will he generously left bequests not only to his family but to all kinds of people he knew. His will stipulated that the collection of his own drawings was to be inherited by any of his children who became a painter or married one. Failing this, the drawings were to be sold after the youngest child turned eighteen. When it was clear there were to be no more artists in the family, Rubens's drawings, together with his paintings, were sold at auction in 1657 and were widely dispersed. His works continue to enrich the world of art and to inspire artists to this day.

Titian (Tiziano Vecellio)

?–1576 Leading Venetian artist of the Italian Renaissance and favorite painter of princes and kings

The artist known as Titian, who was really named Tiziano Vecellio, was born sometime between 1488 and 1490 in Pieve di Cadore, a village high in the Italian Alps north of Venice. The exact date and even the year of his birth are unknown. His father, Gregorio Vecellio, served as an official in the local government and his grandfather, Count Vecellio, fought in the Venetian army. All we know about his mother is her name, Lucia. Tiziano was one of five children: we know the names of two sisters—Orsa and Catterina—and an older brother—Francesco. His background was fairly modest, yet Titian became a well-to-do nobleman and one of the greatest artists who ever lived.

When he was around nine years old, his family sent him to Venice, a beautiful city on the coast of the Adriatic Sea that is built on dozens of small islands with canals running between them. At that time Italy was made up of small states and independent cities; Venice was a separate republic with a culture of its own. It was an important center of maritime trade between East and West and a strong political and commercial power. In Venice Titian lived with an uncle and went into the mosaic workshop of Sebastiano Zuccato, who recognized the boy's talent. He then became an apprentice to Gentile Bellini, who taught him the basics of painting. Gentile's methods seemed old-fashioned to the boy, who drew with speed and boldness, so Titian also studied with Gentile's brother Giovanni, the greatest artist in Venice.

Finally he chose the brilliant artist Giorgione to be his teacher. In 1508 Giorgione asked Titian to work with him on the frescoes, or wall paintings on wet plaster, on the outside walls of the Fondaco dei Tedeschi, the warehouse of the German merchants in Venice that was the commercial center for trade with the north. Giorgione was jealous when Titian was praised, but he appreciated the young man's talent and once said of him, "He was a painter even in his mother's womb." The styles of Titian and Giorgione are so similar that it is sometimes impossible to tell their paintings apart. After Giorgione died from the plague two years later, Titian finished some of the works his master had started.

In the late autumn of 1510 Titian was invited to paint three large murals in nearby Padua on the subject of the miracles of Saint Anthony. He stayed in Padua until the winter of the following year. When he was invited to Rome to the court of Pope Leo X in 1513 he turned down the offer preferring to stay in Venice. In the spring he applied for the privilege of painting a battle scene in the Great Council Hall of the ducal palace to replace an old one that was falling into ruins. He asked for only enough money to pay for his paints, the salaries of two helpers, and for an official position, when it would become available, that would pay him a salary. He was given the position of painter to the Venetian Republic after Giovanni Bellini's death, and started receiving the income in 1517, but it took him more than twenty years to complete the mural. He kept putting it off until officials forced him to do the painting.

Titian opened his own workshop in 1513. His work, which was exciting and original, was in demand. The figures that he painted were solid, and the scenes, filled with dramatic action, seemed to glow. He used colors skillfully and was able to make his figures come to life against landscape backgrounds that add reality to the picture. In 1516 he was asked to create a painting for the high altar of the Church of the Frari in Venice on the popular Catholic subject of the Assumption of the Virgin. The work, finished in 1518, was powerful and exciting, one of the finest paintings of the Italian Renaissance. The Renaissance was a period beginning in the fifteenth century when there was a rebirth of learning. An interest in the culture of ancient Greece and Rome was revived, and there was a new appreciation of mankind and of nature. While Titian was working in Venice, Michelangelo and Raphael were working in Rome and Florence, the other great centers of Italian Renaissance culture. Titian probably knew of Michelangelo's works from drawings that were brought back to Venice by travelers.

Some of the princely families who ruled over the small states and independent cities of Italy recognized Titian's talent. He had been invited to Ferrara in 1516 to create paintings on the subject of ancient Greek mythology for the ruler Alfonso d'Este, duke of Ferrara, to hang in his castle, and the duke summoned him back to Ferrara in 1519. While there Titian must have seen a painting by Raphael that Alfonso owned. In Ferrara he painted a portrait of the duke that was admired by Charles II of Spain who later became the Holy Roman emperor Charles V. The picture ended up as a gift to the king.

On another visit to Ferrara in 1523 Titian met Federigo Gonzaga, marquis of Mantua. He would become Duke of Mantua and an important patron to Titian. In later years he would ask Titian to design silver for the court of Mantua and to paint a portrait of the first gazelle to be seen in Italy. It had been brought from Egypt to Venice.

Back in Venice Titian created other works, including religious pictures and a battle scene for the aristocrat Jacopo Pesaro, who was an archbishop and former naval commander. He also painted an altarpiece for the family chapel, which incorporated members of the Pesaro family in a religious scene.

In November 1525 the artist married a young woman named Cecilia, who had been living with him and was the mother of their two sons, Pomponio and Orazio. (Orazio grew up to become a painter, working with his father, while Pomponio followed a career in the church although he was not well suited to the life. He turned out to be a disappointment to his father.) Their mother was ill when the boys were small and died in August 1530 after giving birth to a daughter Lavinia. When she grew up Lavinia married Cornelio Sarcinnelli of Serravalle and had six children. The artist was so grief-stricken by Cecilia's death that he could not finish a portrait of her that he was painting. He sent for his sister Orsa to take charge of his household and look after his children. She dutifully served her brother and his family for the rest of her life.

By 1531 Titian was socially prominent and wealthy enough to rent spacious quarters in a luxurious palace in an area known as the Biri Grande, on the outskirts of Venice. It had a wonderful view of distant mountains, and lovely gardens that extended to the edge of the sea. Five years later he rented the entire house. He was courteous and hospitable and gave lavish dinner parties, inviting other artists,

An engraving entitled *A Celebration at the House of Titian. The New York Public Library Picture Collection.*

authors, and historians. His guests were entertained by musicians as they dined on fine food and good wines. Titian loved music and owned several musical instruments.

The artist became a good friend of the architect-sculptor Jacopo Sansovino from Florence and of the writer Pietro Aretino, who came to Venice from Rome in 1527. Aretino took charge of Titian's relations with patrons and wrote letters for him. He helped make Titian's name known and boosted his reputation

as a portrait painter. The artist had many wealthy patrons.

In 1530 Titian went to Bologna for the coronation of Charles V, when he was crowned Holy Roman emperor by Pope Clement VII. When the emperor returned to Bologna in 1533, the artist went there again and painted his portrait with a big dog. It is said that the emperor was so impressed with the work that he refused ever to be painted by anyone else.

A story is told that Charles V had

Titian's portrait of Emperor Charles V astride his horse. *Art Resource/Prado, Madrid.*

such admiration for Titian that when the artist dropped his paintbrush on the floor the emperor picked it up.

Back in Spain, the emperor issued a royal decree conferring on Titian the rank of nobleman, giving him the title of count of the Palatine. He made the artist a Knight of the Golden Spur and presented him with a golden chain of honor, the highest honor an artist could receive.

Titian was a confident, courteous gentleman, admired as a painter of genius by all the princes of Europe. He was highly successful in portraying the identity and true character of his sitters so that the viewer feels drawn into their thoughts. He also revealed their social status and political standing while placing his subjects in their historical setting. The coloring he used makes the figures so natural they seem to come alive. People said they looked like real people "lacking only the breath of life."

In 1536 Federigo Gonzaga asked Titian to paint a series of twelve Roman emperors for a room in his ducal castle in Mantua. The artist studied ancient Roman marble statues and gems and coins with emperors' portraits to use as models. He painted the rulers dressed in Renaissance armor, each in a slightly different pose. It was said that the images are so lifelike that everyone who looked at them thought they were real

men, and people traveled to Mantua just to see them. To paint a portrait of King Francis I of France, whom he never met, Titian used as a model a medal that was designed by Benvenuto Cellini.

In 1541 Titian went to Milan to see Charles V. The emperor granted the artist an annual pension for life, but there was never enough money in the royal treasury to pay it, so it was years before Titian began to collect his allowance.

The artist Giorgio Vasari came to Venice that year. He visited Titian in his studio and admired his coloring and lively style of painting. When Vasari wrote a book on the lives of the important Renaissance artists, he included Titian.

After Vasari left Venice Titian was asked to complete ceiling paintings on subjects from the Old Testament in the church of Santo Spirito in Isola that had been started by Vasari. Titian was at the height of his fame and was considered the most important painter of his time.

In 1543 he was in Busseto at the invitation of Pope Paul III, who was meeting with Charles V. The emperor commissioned Titian to paint a portrait of his wife Isabella who had died four years earlier. Then he went to Ferrara with the pope and his court and painted the pope's portrait. Paul III was related to Cardinal Alessandro Farnese of Ferrara, who also commissioned works from the artist but failed to pay for his pictures. In 1545 Titian went to Rome with his son Orazio, where he was welcomed with ceremony by the papal court. He painted a group portrait of Pope Paul with his nephews. Titian's group portraits are remarkable for the way in which the subjects interact with one another.

In Rome the artist was invited to stay in the Vatican in Belvedere Palace and given a studio. The pope gave him the opportunity to study ancient and Renaissance art in his collection. Vasari, who guided Titian around Rome, showed him temples and statues from ancient times that were being found buried underground. Titian saw Michelangelo's paintings in the Sistine Chapel of Saint Peter's Church, and Vasari took him to Michelangelo's studio. Titian admired the work of Michelangelo whose solid muscular figures influenced his own style. In June of the following year Titian was made an honorary citizen of Rome and left for Venice, making a stop in Florence for his first visit to that city.

In early January 1548 the artist set off for the imperial court in Augsburg at Charles V's command to attend the ceremonial opening of an important political meeting, the Diet of Augsburg. He

An engraving from Titian's self-portrait. *The New York Public Library Picture Collection.*

was accompanied by Orazio and a nephew. To get there they had to travel through deep snow across the Alps in bitterly cold weather. During the next nine months he painted Charles V on horseback and made portraits of the emperor's family and other people in his court. Charles V's sister Mary of Hungary asked Titian to paint scenes from Greek mythology to decorate the great hall in her new palace near Brussels in the Spanish Netherlands. On his return to Venice he stayed at Innsbruck where he began portraits of King Ferdinand, brother of Charles V.

He was home only a few weeks when the emperor asked him to come to Milan to do portraits of his son Prince Philip, who would inherit the throne. Titian painted the prince in full armor, creating a great masterpiece. In the autumn of 1550 Philip called him to Augsburg again for the announcement of Charles V's retirement from public life. After Titian returned to Venice and settled down again, the prince continued to write him asking for new paintings, including works to decorate his apartments at the Escorial, his palace near Madrid. Prince Philip and Titian began a correspondence that continued for the rest of the artist's life. Philip kept asking for more and more new paintings and Titian would keep asking to be paid.

In 1556 Charles V abdicated, passing the crown of the Holy Roman emperor to his brother, Ferdinand I. The prince became King Philip II, ruler of Spain, the Spanish possessions in America, and the Italian dominions. Titian was offered payment in full of the pension that the emperor had awarded him years before. Orazio went to Milan and collected the money but unfortunately was severly wounded when Leone Leone, engraver of the Imperial Mint, attempted to rob him. Some years later, when Titian was a very old man, he arranged to have the pension transferred to Orazio.

Titian's pictures were very much in demand and he had a large workshop at his house in the Biri Grande, with assistants and apprentices to help him produce them. Orazio was his chief assistant, and Doménikos Theotokópoulos, a Greek artist who became known as El Greco, assisted in the studio for a time before going on to Spain. The aging master remained strong, alert, and productive, developing new ideas in composition and design. He worked and reworked his paintings, trying to make them perfect. As he grew older he applied his paints boldly in patches of color, using loose brush strokes. Sometimes he rubbed paint onto the canvas with his fingers.

The artist was so admired by royalty that when Henry III stopped in Venice in 1574 on the way to his coronation as king of France, he visited Titian's studio. The artist was working on a large religious painting, *The Pietà*, which he wanted to have placed in the Chapel of the Crucifix in the Church of the Frari. He was still writing letters to Philip II asking to be paid for his work.

Titian died in his home on August 27, 1576, a victim of the plague. His remains were carried in solemn procession from his house to the Frari, where he was buried beneath the crucifix.

The severe epidemic of the plague raging in Venice took Orazio's life two months later. The house, full of paintings and precious objects, was looted, and the Titian workshop was dissolved. The artist's house was sold by Pomponio five years later. The magnificent works Titian had created during his lifetime set the course of European paintings for centuries to come. His influence on artists who followed him enriches our cultural heritage.

Vincent van Gogh

1853–1890   Dutch Post-Impressionist painter who worked in a highly original style

Few artists are as famous as Vincent van Gogh, whose paintings are so original that anyone might recognize them at a glance. Yet all of his works, more than two thousand drawings and paintings, were produced within the short span of only ten years. And even though his brightly colored pictures bring instant pleasure to those who see them, his short life was one of exhausting struggle, poverty, and suffering.

Vincent Willem van Gogh, named after his two grandfathers, was born March 30, 1853, in the Netherlands, in the small village of Zundert in the quiet province of Brabant. He was the son of Anna Cornelia Carbentus and the Reverend Théodorus van Gogh, a strict Protestant clergyman whom Vincent deeply admired. When Vincent Willem was born, he was given the same name as his brother who had been born dead exactly one year earlier. The future artist thought of himself as the second Vincent. A brother, Théodorus, came along in 1857 and was Vincent's best friend throughout their lives. There were also three sisters, Anna, Elizabeth, and Wilhelmina, and another brother, Cornelius. A constant stream of letters that Vincent wrote to his family, mostly to his brother Théo, reveals the artist's thoughts and feelings and the intense difficulties caused by his inner turmoil.

Van Gogh attended a village school, and in 1864, when he was eleven years old, he went to boarding school for two years in the village of Zevenbergen. Then he went to secondary school at Tilburg, where he did well in foreign languages. He could speak Dutch, German, French, and English.

An uncle was a partner in Goupil and Company, international art dealers based in Paris and the company had a branch in The Hague. Van Gogh went there to work as a junior clerk in the summer of 1869. It was a happy period for him. He did well in the business, got to know some artists, and learned how to handle works of art. He read all of the art journals and built up a collection of prints, which he would use in the future to help him in his own work. His brother Théo later joined the firm, working in the branch in Brussels, Belgium.

After five years Vincent was transferred by the company to London, where he lived in a boardinghouse. He fell in love with his landlady's daughter, Eugénie, and asked her to marry him, but she turned him down. He was so upset and got so depressed that the company sent him to Paris, hoping the change would help him, but he returned to London the following spring, in 1875. The company insisted he go back to Paris, but the change did not help. He showed no interest in his work and spent all of his time reading the Bible. In 1876 van Gogh was dismissed from Goupil.

He decided to teach at a boarding school in England, where he also helped out as a preacher. He was happy doing this, but his employer could not afford to pay him. After he had spent Christmas with his family, who were living in Etten, an uncle got him a job at a bookstore in Dordrecht. Van Gogh did not take an interest in his work. He spent his time taking long walks in the countryside and looking at nature with the eye of a painter. Soon he started drawing.

Next he decided to study theology and become a preacher like his father. He had a deep feeling for social justice and sympathy for the poor. In May 1877 he moved to Amsterdam where he lived with one uncle while another arranged for studies that would prepare him for entrance examinations for theological school. However, after fifteen months of study he failed the exams and was turned down by the University. Then he enrolled in a school to take a course for missionaries, but he failed there too.

In December 1878 van Gogh went to work as a mission preacher to the coal miners of the Borinage region in Belgium. In an effort to improve working conditions for the miners he tried to be like them: he rubbed coal dust on his face and hands and even went down into the dangerous mine shafts. He shared the little bit of money he had with the workers, gave away his bed, and slept on the floor. When he had arrived in Belgium he was wearing a nice suit, but soon he started going about the village in an old soldier's tunic and a shabby cap. Then he gave away his tunic and made shirts out of sacks, and he went about without socks. His behavior was so strange that he was sent away.

Unwilling to give up his missionary work, van Gogh continued in another community, but this did not last either. By the end of summer 1880 he realized that he should become an artist. He made simple sketches of miners and peasants and broad landscapes, which were awkward and stiff, yet forceful. He felt a deep sympathy for simple peasants and admired the work of the French artist Jean-François Millet, whose paintings showed poor farm people hard at work in the fields.

In October 1880 van Gogh went to Brussels to study art. Until then he had used printed pictures as models, but in Brussels he had live models to pose for him. Théo sent him money to live on and would continue to support him for the rest of his life.

In April 1881 van Gogh went back to Holland to live with his parents at Etten. When a young, widowed cousin, Kee Stricker Vos, came to visit he fell in love with her, but she did not return his love. Unable to accept her rejection he followed her home to Amsterdam, but Kee's parents refused to let him see her.

He pleaded with them, thrusting his hand into the flame of a lamp and saying, "Let me see her for as long as I can keep my hand in the flame." Shocked, they blew out the lamp and sent him away.

At the end of 1881 van Gogh went to The Hague, where he stayed for more than two years. Anton Mauve, a painter of peasant life who was married to van Gogh's cousin, gave him painting lessons, and he studied the works of the Dutch masters Rembrandt van Rijn and Frans Hals. He began doing street scenes and landscapes as well. An uncle who was an art dealer commissioned him to draw twelve city views of The Hague.

The artist was so deperately poor and lonely that he took in from the street a pregnant woman called Sien and her five-year-old daughter. His friends and relatives did not approve of Sien and stopped seeing van Gogh. He broke off with her in September 1883 and went to Drenthe on the North Sea to paint its natural beauty, but when winter came, he was lonely and cold. In December, in spite of disagreements he had been having with his father, he returned to his parents, who were living in Nuenen, at this time, but his odd behavior often embarrassed them.

While living in Nuenen he met a young woman who was a next-door neighbor. She wanted to marry him, but her parents objected. She was so upset she attempted suicide. The incident caused a scandal, and van Gogh had to leave his parents' home to live in a rented studio nearby. That fall, 1884, he gave a few art lessons, and a goldsmith commissioned him to decorate the walls of his dining room.

Some of the artist's most original paintings from this period had as their subject the poor peasants around him who lived off the potatoes that they raised. He felt this subject "should make people think of a way of life entirely different from that of our refined society." For his paintings van Gogh used earth colors, with dark shades of green and gray. The most important of these works is *The Potato Eaters,* a close-up of angular, earthy figures in their humble cottage. The painting is considered to be his first masterpiece.

Van Gogh painted his first self-portrait during this period, showing himself as an artist at work in front of his easel, wearing a blue peasant's smock and holding a palette and brush. He had reddish hair, cut short so it stood on end, and a stubbly beard. He was of medium height, broad shouldered, and strong. His blue eyes were deep set and narrow. Someone who knew him said, "His face was homely and covered with freckles, but changed and brightened wonderfully when warmed with enthusiasm." Although he was only thirty-two he had lines in his face and wrinkles in his forehead.

In March 1885 van Gogh's father died unexpectedly, and the artist was deeply affected.

That November he departed for Antwerp, Belgium, where Peter Paul Rubens, whose work he admired, had lived. After studying Rubens's works he began to lighten the colors in his own paintings. He found Japanese prints in secondhand book shops and was impressed with their bright colors, flat forms, and the action of the figures. He bought them and hung them on the walls of his room.

To improve his skill, van Gogh enrolled at the Academy of Fine Arts, but even there he upset the director with his odd behavior. The young artist often had to go hungry in order to buy art supplies. He was ill, too, and longing to be with family, so in early March of 1886 he went to Paris where Théo was an art dealer. The brothers lived together in a comfortable apartment, which was cluttered with works of art. Van Gogh went to art school, where he drew from live models and plaster casts of ancient masterpieces of sculpture. He usually dressed in an ordinary way, but in the studio where he painted he wore a blue workman's shirt splashed with dots of color on the sleeves. Among the artists he met were Emile Bernard and Henri Toulouse-Lautrec. Bernard would invite van Gogh to his parents' home in the country until he had a fight with them and stormed off. Bernard loved van Gogh for his good heart, however, and corresponded with him for the rest of his life. "He was the most noble man one could think of," he said of van Gogh, "free and open, extremely lively . . . an excellent friend . . . completely free from egoism and ambition."

Van Gogh also met Théo's artist friends Claude Monet, Edgar Degas, and Paul Gauguin. He found it stimulating to get together in cafés with these men and discuss their work. He liked to drink absinthe, a liquor that can cause bizarre behavior.

The last Impressionist exhibition was held while van Gogh was in Paris. He was able to study the shimmering color and vibrant brush strokes of Impressionist works and to experiment by painting in that style. By now the Neo-Impressionists Georges Seurat and Paul Signac were painting in the Pointillist style, a method of using tiny dots of color to construct forms. While developing his own style, van Gogh also absorbed new ideas from them. He experimented with bright colors, piling them on with long, firm, rhythmic brush strokes. He painted quickly, with a fierce restlessness, capturing a feeling of life. He copied Japanese prints and even included them in some of the portraits he painted.

In the spring of 1887 the artist organized a group exhibition in a café and at that time he began signing his pictures Vincent, supposedly because van Gogh was too difficult to pronounce for anyone who was not Dutch. He painted still lifes with flowers, which were gay and colorful, yet flat. He also produced a great many self-portraits.

The artist was highly nervous and did not know how to behave as others did. Théo found him hard to get along with, and his friends stopped coming to see him because Vincent would quarrel with them and get into wild arguments. In Théo's words, "It seems as if he were two persons: one marvelously gifted, gentle and refined, the other egotistic and hard-hearted. . . . It is a pity that he is his own enemy, for he makes life hard not only for others but also for himself." Nevertheless, Théo remained devoted to his brother all of his life.

Van Gogh's health was suffering from his stressful life in Paris, and he needed a warmer, quieter place to live and work. He decided to go to the south of France, where he felt he could live close to nature and express himself artistically. He had the notion that the

Van Gogh's self-portrait at his easel. *Van Gogh Museum, Amsterdam.*

south of France would be like Japan and he could develop a Japanese way of seeing nature.

In February 1888 he settled in Arles in Provençe, on the Rhone river, about thirty miles from the Mediterranean Sea. It was cold when he arrived but when spring came he enjoyed working in bright sunlight in his beautiful new surroundings, drawing with a pen cut from a reed, creating a simple, broad, flat pattern with a few rhythmic strokes. He went to the orchards to paint fruit trees in blossom, using swirly lines and intense colors. He worked with mad concentration, as if in a frenzy to create, and had to keep asking Théo for paints and canvas to produce more pictures. The artist made a series of still lifes of a sunflower, close-up, saying, "Yellow is the symbol of love and kindness, the color of the all-warming sun." His intense energy was reflected in his work, and he developed a distinctive style of his own. He wrote, "I work without noticing that I am working. Sometimes the brushstrokes seem to come by themselves, one following the other, connected like words. . . . I lose all consciousness of myself and painting comes as if in a dream."

That spring van Gogh exhibited three of his paintings at the Salon des Indépendants. And he continued to send Théo paintings in the hope they would sell. In the middle of June he took a trip to Saintes-Maries-de-la-Mer, a medieval town on the seacoast. There he painted slender fishermen's boats that reminded him of those in Japanese prints.

The artist made a few friends in Arles. Among them was the postman Joseph Roulin, who was interesting to talk to. Another was Paul-Eugène Milliet whom he taught to draw. Milliet was a second lieutenant in the Zouaves, a company of Algerians serving in the French army. Milliet described van Gogh as "a pleasant chap when he was in a good mood, which was not always the case. . . . This youth with a taste and talent for drawing became a fanatic as soon as he touched a paint brush. . . . When he started painting I either left right away or refused to express my opinion; otherwise we quarreled." The portraits van Gogh painted of Milliet and of Roulin and his wife and children all have a living quality.

In September he created one of his famous night works, *Starry Night*, painted outdoors by the light of a street lamp. The dazzling stars and swirling nebula create an explosive effect.

All along van Gogh had been dreaming of an ideal community of artists who would work together and relieve his constant loneliness and feeling of emptiness. He was intent on starting an

L'Arlesienne, a portrait of Mme. Joseph-Michel Ginoux painted by van Gogh while he lived in Arles. *The Metropolitan Museum of Art. Bequest of Sam A. Lewisohn, 1951. (51.112.3)*

artists' colony in Arles, convinced that "painters of the future will come to work in the south," and he was hopeful that Paul Gauguin, who was down on his luck in Paris, would be the first to join him.

Théo sent his brother money to prepare his yellow house for a guest. It was a clean, simple home with red tile floors and sturdy furniture. Van Gogh described it in a letter to his sister Wilhelmina, "My house is painted the yellow color of fresh butter on the outside with glaringly green shutters: it stands in the full sunlight in a square which has a green garden with plane trees, oleanders and acacias." Van Gogh's own bedroom, which can be seen in one of his most famous paintings, had light blue walls and a solid yellow bed. He painted sunflowers to decorate the room that he used as a studio.

Gauguin kept postponing his visit, but after a great deal of urging from Théo, who gave him some money, he finally went to Arles on October 20, 1888. In Arles, the two artists worked together, with Gauguin acting as "studio head," and at night they drank together at a café, which is shown in Van Gogh's well-known painting *The Night Café*. Neither of the men, however, was easy to get along with, and tensions developed. One night, van Gogh threw a glass filled with absinthe at Gauguin. Then, two nights before Christmas, after a quarrel, Gauguin threatened to leave Arles. Van Gogh, in a fit of mental unbalance, threatened Gauguin with an open razor, and then went home and cut off a piece of his own ear. Gauguin, who spent the night in a hotel, was questioned by the police and left for Paris.

Van Gogh was taken to the hospital in Arles, and Théo came to his bedside but stayed only briefly before returning to Paris. After a short period of recovery the artist returned home to continue working. A well-known self-portrait of van Gogh shows him with a bandaged ear.

Life became more and more difficult for van Gogh. People in the community claimed he was violent and had him taken back to the hospital by force. The exact nature of his illness is not known, but when he was stricken by seizures he had hallucinations and would hear strange voices. He also suffered from depression. Mental illness seems to have run in the family, for Théo himself was suffering from nervous attacks. Nevertheless, Théo married Johanna Bonger in Amsterdam on April 17, 1889.

Van Gogh was now too frightened to live alone and had himself admitted to the asylum of Saint Paul-de-Mausole on

May 8, 1889, in the hope of gaining mental stability. The asylum was in a twelfth-century monastery in Saint-Rémy, about twelve miles from Arles. A room was provided as a studio, and he was able to go outdoors to paint the wheat fields and olive orchards surrounding the asylum. Through iron bars, he painted the view from the window of his studio.

In Saint-Rémy van Gogh found beauty in the trees—the olives, the pines, and the cypresses with their flamelike rhythms surging upward. He also painted still lifes of flowers and plants that filled the whole canvas. He wrote to Théo, "I am working like mad and feel a blind rage to work more than ever. And I believe that this will contribute to my recovery."

By then his work was beginning to attract attention. Ten of his paintings were shown at the Society of Independent Artists exhibition and an article praising him was published in a French paper. In addition five paintings were shown in an important exhibition in Brussels, where one of them, *The Red Vineyard*, sold for four hundred francs.

Van Gogh was pleased when Théo's wife had a son on January 31, 1890, and named the baby after him. For his nephew's bedroom, he painted a lovely picture of branches covered with white almond blossoms against a white sky.

That spring he suffered a serious attack of depression that lasted all season. He had been thinking of leaving Saint-Rémy and finding new surroundings. He wanted to place himself under the care of Dr. Paul-Ferdinand Gachet, a physician and amateur artist, in Auvers-sur-Oise, a country village about twenty miles from Paris. In May he was released from the asylum and went to Paris to visit Théo and his family. He stayed only three days before going on to Auvers, but now he was close enough to Paris to return for visits and for his brother and family to visit him.

In Auvers he rented an attic room from the Ravaux family, who operated a café. He enjoyed painting the small houses with thatched roofs in the town and the endless wheat fields. He worked with great intensity, sometimes with such incredible speed that he produced a painting every day. At times he applied paint directly onto the canvas from the tube.

The artist became a friend of Dr. Gachet, who encouraged him in his work. Van Gogh painted the doctor's portrait. Their relationship became strained, however. Van Gogh felt discouraged, fearing another attack and having no hope of recovery.

One day he managed to discover where his landlord hid his revolver, and he took it with him when he went out-

Van Gogh's painting *The Church at Auvers. Giraudon/Art Resource/Musée d'Orsay, Paris.*

doors to paint. On July 27, while in the fields painting haystacks van Gogh shot himself in the chest. He was severely wounded, yet managed to crawl back to the house where he was staying. Mr. Ravaux called the doctor and Théo rushed to his brother's bedside. Van Gogh died two days later, on July 29, 1890. Théo was so affected by the death of his beloved brother that he went mad three months later, and his wife took him back to Holland where he died three months after that.

The three memorial exhibitions that were held in van Gogh's honor would have pleased Théo, who had worked so hard to have his brother's work known to the public. One hundred years later van Gogh's paintings would bring the highest prices in history.

Van Gogh once wrote, "I have walked this earth for thirty years and out of gratitude I want to leave a token of remembrance in the form of drawings or paintings—not made to please a certain taste in art, but to express a genuine human emotion." If that was his wish, then it did come true.

Diego de Velázquez

1599–1660   Painter and courtier to King Philip IV of Spain

Diego Rodríguez de Silva Velázquez was born in 1599 in Seville, Spain, in the region of Andalusia. His father, Juan Rodríguez de Silva, whose parents came from Portugal, was said to be descended from minor nobility. His mother, Jerónima Velázquez, whose family were natives of Seville, gave birth to seven children. Diego, who was the eldest, adopted his mother's name, as was the custom in Andalusia.

Seville, on the Guadalquivir River, was an important port of entry to the Atlantic Ocean and the wealthiest city in Spain. Gold brought from the extensive Spanish possessions in America and textiles from the Orient made the city an important center of trade. Seville attracted artists and learned people who added to the liveliness of the city. They would gather around the marketplace and the cathedral, an important center for the Catholic religion.

Little is known about Velázquez's family life. As a young child he had a good education. And he was gifted in art. In 1610, when he was eleven years old, he was apprenticed to Francisco Pacheco, who painted religious pictures for the Catholic church, and went to live in the master's home. Pacheco, who was only a mediocre artist, is better known for writing about art and for his poetry than he is for his painting. He was a friend of other artists, poets, and scholars, who would often meet in his home. The young apprentice had the opportunity to listen to the conversations of these learned men. As Pacheco's apprentice Velázquez learned the techniques of painting, making drawings from nature, and he drew portraits, using local models.

After serving his six years as an apprentice Velázquez passed the examination to become a member of the Painter's Guild in Seville. In 1617 he was granted a license to practice the art of painting and he opened his own studio. In April of the following year he married Pacheco's daughter, Juana de Miranda. A baby girl, Francisca, was born to them in 1619 and another, Ignacia, two years later.

The young Velázquez showed remarkable talent in his study of character and also in his ability to capture a single moment in time. Most of his works were of ordinary people in their daily lives. He would go out on the street to find interesting subjects and would represent simple people with understanding and sympathy. Still-life studies of everyday objects within the paintings were included with great care. He had an extraordinary ability to reproduce the textures of different surfaces with accuracy. Ordinary objects in his paintings are as realistic as the solid figures of people. *Old Woman Cooking* and *The Waterseller of Seville,* two masterpieces from this period, seem timeless. He also painted portraits and some religious subjects.

The king of Spain, Philip IV, who had ascended the throne the year before at age sixteen, loved painting and had inherited a fine art collection, which he was constantly enlarging. In 1622 Velázquez went to Madrid at the encouragement of Pacheco, in the hope of painting King Philip and Queen Isabella. He was unsuccessful, but managed to see the royal art collection and meet some important people.

The following year the prime minister, Don Gaspar de Guzmán, the count of Olivares, who was from Seville, summoned Velázquez back to Madrid to paint a portrait of the king. The monarch was so pleased with the brilliant results that he appointed the artist painter to the king in October 1623. Velázquez was given a studio in the palace and was paid a monthly allowance, with additional payment for each painting that he produced. He would be the king's painter and would have Philip's respect and friendship for the rest of his life. Yet he did not feel accepted in society, since craftsmen, who worked with their hands, could not be considered aristocrats. The painter had a burning desire to improve his social status and did everything possible to establish painting as a noble profession.

In the palace in Madrid Velázquez studied the great masterpieces of art that the royal family had collected.

Works by Venetian painters, especially Titian, influenced his style and he began using flowing brush strokes and clearer, brighter colors. At the same time, he was improving his extraordinary ability to capture the individuality of his subjects and record them at a fixed moment.

In 1627 Philip IV honored Velázquez with state duties, appointing him as gentleman usher at court. The artist fit in perfectly as a courtier in the service of the royal family, disciplining himself to follow the strict routine. He observed the people around him who were trying to win favor with the royal family. He was clever at playing court politics and protecting his own position. Those who were less successful in gaining royal favor were jealous, especially because the king enjoyed spending time with him. Philip would come to the studio to watch him work and loved to have long conversations with him.

Velázquez was a cultured man, calm and restrained, with no conflict in his life. But he was a quiet, secretive person. So little is known of his private life that he is sometimes considered to be mysterious. Always foremost in his mind was his ambition to have his noble heritage acknowledged and to establish a high social position for his family.

In 1628 the Flemish painter Peter Paul Rubens arrived at the Spanish court in Madrid as a special diplomat for the Infanta Isabella, King Philip IV's aunt. Isabella governed Flanders, which was under Spanish rule. Velázquez admired Rubens's work and was impressed with him because he was considered a painter-gentleman: Rubens had gained high status in society, even though artists were usually thought of as socially inferior by people of the aristocratic class. Velázquez accompanied the visitor to El Escorial, the royal palace and monastery north of Madrid, to see the art collection. Rubens was especially enthusiastic about the splendid paintings of mythological subjects by Titian and encouraged the young Spaniard to study the Italian masters.

The following year Velázquez asked King Philip to allow him to travel to Italy to perfect his art. The king gave him permission along with expense money and letters to Italian princes introducing him as court painter. The artist sailed from Barcelona on August 10, 1629, in the company of a prominent Spanish general. Two weeks later he arrived in Genoa, where he stayed with the Spanish ambassador, and then traveled to Milan on his way to Venice. At times he was suspected of being a spy, and an escort would be supplied for his protection when he went sightseeing to look at works of art. He made sketches of masterpieces that impressed him and painted copies of some of the pictures.

From Venice Velázquez went to Rome, the great art center, where he was invited to stay in rooms in the pope's Vatican Palace. There he could copy works by Raphael and Michelangelo, but his rooms in the Vatican were isolated and he was lonely, so he got permission to spend the summer in the villa of the Medici family. There he studied and sketched the important Medici collection of ancient marble statues. From Rome he went to Naples, which was under Spanish rule, where he painted a portrait of Philip IV's sister Doña María, who was passing through Italy following her wedding to the king of Hungary. After his visit to Italy, the artist's brushwork was lighter and freer, and he had perfected his technique.

He was back in Madrid early in 1631. While he had been away Queen Isabella gave birth to a son who was named Baltasar Carlos. The king was pleased to have an heir to the throne and had been waiting for Velázquez to return, as he would let no other artist paint a portrait of the prince. Nor would he allow anyone else to paint his own portrait.

Velázquez did portraits of Philip IV, the king's parents, his queen, and the young prince Baltasar Carlos on his favorite pony. The portraits were painted with simplicity, even when the subject was the king, who had more power than any other monarch in the world, with territories stretching from the Mediterranean to the Philippines. Velázquez also created battle scenes illustrating Spain's victories in the Thirty Years War. In *The Surrender of Breda,* one of his most famous works, the victorious Spanish general and the defeated commander meet with dignity on an equal plane, as the Dutch leader surrenders by handing over the keys to his fortress.

King Philip also put Velázquez to work decorating the Buen Retiro, a magnificent pleasure palace that he was constructing on the outskirts of Madrid, where lavish court festivals would be held. Some of the paintings to decorate the walls were bought in Italy and Flanders, while others were created in Spain. Velázquez also worked on pictures to decorate the Torre de la Parada, the royal country lodge outside Madrid, which was being redesigned. The king stayed in the lodge when he went hunting, his favorite amusement. Velázquez painted portraits of members of the royal family in outdoor settings, dressed for the hunt with their favorite hunting hounds by their sides. He also painted portraits of the count of Olivares, scenes from mythology, and a series of portraits of the dwarfs and jesters in the court, whose function was

Velázquez's portrait of the duke of Olivares. *Alinari/Art Resource/Prado, Madrid.*

to entertain the king. The artist treated these pathetic subjects with sympathy and understanding, revealing their character and showing them with a sense of dignity.

In 1633 the artist's daughter Francisca married Juan Bautista Martinez del Mazo, a painter who had become her father's closest assistant. When Velázquez was promoted to Gentleman of the Wardrobe in 1636 he transferred the title of Gentleman Usher to his son-in-law. He was advanced to Gentleman of the Bed Chamber in 1643 and given a key as an additional honor. Appointments to other offices were to follow. The artist became progressively more important in court life as his relationship to the king grew stronger.

Spain was at war with France at the time and the king went to Aragon, a region in the north of Spain, to lead his troops against the French. Velázquez accompanied the monarch on his military campaigns in 1644 and painted the leader dressed for battle. The artist worked under difficult conditions. An easel had to be made by a carpenter, and a window, to provide light, had to be cut into the royal lodgings while the king posed for his portrait. Then, windows were cut into a wall in the artist's lodgings so he would have enough light to finish the portrait.

While the king was on the battlefield, Queen Isabella died in Madrid. Philip's grief was overwhelming. Two years later tragedy hit again when Prince Baltasar Carlos died a week before his seventeenth birthday. The king suffered deeply from losing his wife and his only son, the heir to the throne. In spite of his personal grief, and a shortage of money in the treasury, Philip continued to make the royal residence larger and more splendid. He bestowed on Velázquez the power of supervisor and administrator of the project.

The artist was producing fewer paintings as his additional court responsibilities took him away from his art. He was sometimes considered lazy because he worked so slowly. One reason he took so long is that he painted directly on canvas rather than doing preparatory drawings as studies and therefore he often had to do a good deal of reworking.

In 1648 Velázquez received a royal order to take another trip to Italy, to buy paintings and ancient statues for the king's art collection. He was granted a fine carriage to ride in and an extra mule to carry pictures. His travel companions were the official group going to Italy to bring King Philip's niece Mariana of Austria back to Spain. It had been arranged for Baltasar Carlos to marry his cousin Princess Mariana, but after the prince's death, Philip decided to marry her himself to ensure political stability.

The group left Madrid in November

1648, traveled south to Málaga, and sailed from there to Genoa, Italy. Velázquez then headed for Venice, where he bought some important paintings by Titian, Paolo Veronese, and Tintoretto. In Bologna, his next stop, he met with two artists who specialized in wall paintings and arranged for them to come to Madrid to participate in the decoration of the palace. He stopped in Florence and then Rome, where he ordered casts to be made of the finest ancient statues and molds to send to Madrid for casting other statues.

Pope Innocent X commissioned Velázquez to paint his portrait. A story is told that the artist had not picked up a brush since he had left Spain and felt he needed practice before undertaking the Pope's portrait. He had his slave-assistant, Juan de Pareja, who was a painter from Seville, of Moorish ancestry, pose for him. When the portrait was exhibited it caused a sensation. The subject looked so real that people did not know whether to talk to the picture or the man. In November 1850 Velázquez signed papers granting Juan de Pareja his freedom so that he could work as an independent painter after he returned to Spain.

Velázquez was welcomed by all of Rome and was commissioned to paint portraits of several members of the papal court. His portrait of the pope was a great success. He chose not to flatter his subject but to reveal his cruel nature. When the pope first saw the results he said, "All too true." The portrait brought the artist great respect. He was honored by membership in the Academy of Saint Luke in Rome and given a gold papal medal on a chain. He took advantage of his popularity to further improve his social status so that he would be recognized as a noble. He had a burning ambition to become a knight in a Spanish military order, an honor reserved for noblemen.

Velázquez was happy in the beautiful city of Rome, where he enjoyed a leisurely life free of court duties. He was involved with a new friend and did not want to return to Madrid, even though the king was impatient and wrote him several letters urging him to hurry home. The artist remained in Rome for a year before returning to Spain.

Finally he reached Madrid in June 1651 with the works of art he had purchased for Philip IV. The following year the king named him Palace Chamberlain. His duties included all of the operations within the royal residence. He was responsible for the activities and clothing of the king and the court and the ceremonies and decorations in which Philip was involved outside of the palace. This included looking after important foreign visitors.

The artist was given a four-story

apartment in the Casa del Tesoro, which was connected to the palace. He lived comfortably. Among his possessions were a good number of books on architecture, science, philosophy, history, and poetry. He was earning a lot of money, but could not collect it. Payments were often held up due to lack of funds in the royal treasury.

The burden of Velázquez's duties gave him little time for his art, yet he managed to create some of his greatest masterpieces. He painted four scenes from mythology to hang in one of the halls he was decorating in the royal palace. Paintings that had been brought back from Italy were installed in El Escorial, and there were others acquired from the superb art collection of the English king Charles I after he was beheaded.

In 1656 Velázquez created his last great work and his most famous painting, an enormous portrait of the royal family, *Las Meninas.* (See reproduction in the color section of this book.) The *meninas* are the young noblewomen who are the attendants of the Infanta Margarita, heir to the throne and daughter of King Philip IV and his second wife, Mariana of Austria. The noblewomen surround the young princess in a salon of the palace. Servants, dwarfs, jesters, and a large dog are also in attendance. The king and queen are shown in the background, as if reflected

Demingo's portrait of Velázquez in his studio. *The Bettmann Archive.*

in a mirror, and Velázquez included himself, paintbrush in hand, looking out from the picture. This is his only known self-portrait. The king hung *Las Meninas* in his private chamber.

Another painting of 1656 represents the myth of Arachne, a mortal who claimed she could weave like a god. She challenged the goddess Minerva to a weaving contest. Their tapestries were judged equal, but Arachne had insulted Minerva, so the goddess changed her into a spider.

Velázquez also painted portraits of Queen Mariana, and the royal children. These subjects, dressed in bright colors, look like dolls in fancy clothes with chalk-white makeup, rouged cheeks, huge wigs, and elaborate jewels.

The artist was highly successful in his career, yet he would not be satisfied until he attained a worthy position of nobility that would descend in his family. This was especially difficult because, as a painter, he worked with his hands like a craftsman and sold his works like a tradesman. Philip IV was eager to elevate Velázquez to knighthood but could not confer this honor unless the purity of his bloodline could be firmly established. Witnesses were called in and questioned, one hundred forty-eight altogether. Doubts still remained about the nobility of one of Velázquez's grandparents, but in the end the king managed to get a special order from the pope, and in November 1659 the king named Velázquez a knight of the Order of Santiago, the most important order of chivalry in Spain. The knighthood confirmed his noble birth, and his title could be passed on to his descendents.

In 1660 King Philip's daughter Infanta María Teresa married King Louis XIV of France in an elaborate ceremony on the Isle of Pheasants in the middle of the Bidosa River, which divides the Spanish and French frontiers.

The wedding was important politically: France and Spain signed a treaty ending their long war. As chamberlain, Velázquez organized and directed the elaborate marriage ceremony and all of the festivities, including a bullfight to entertain the royal couple.

The trip was tiring for the artist. A month after his return he fell ill from a fever. The king sent his court physicians to look after him and went to his bedside to see him. A few days later Velázquez died. According to the king's wishes a funeral was held that was appropriate for a noble courtier. Velázquez, dressed in the robes of the Order of Santiago that he had waited so long for, was buried in the Church of San Juan Bautista in Madrid, in the presence of the King. A week after his death, Juana Pachecho, who had been his quiet, dutiful wife for more than forty years, died of the same fever. The artist's son-in-law and assistant Juan Bautista Martinez del Mazo became painter to the king.

After Velázquez's death little attention was paid to his work for a century and a half. In the early nineteenth century his paintings were admired and copied, but he was out of fashion. Then, later in the century, the French artist Edouard Manet visited Madrid on a trip to Spain and was struck by the pictures he saw. He wrote to a friend in

France saying, "Velázquez alone is worth the journey. . . . He is the painter of painters. . . . He has captivated me." Manet brought Velázquez back into the public eye. Today his work seems as fresh as it did in his own time, and he is considered one of the great masters of European painting.

Johannes Vermeer

1632–1675   Dutch painter of quiet interior scenes

The life of Johannes, or Jan, Vermeer, one of the great seventeenth-century masters, is something of a mystery. Few of his works survive—only thirty-four paintings—and he left no drawings or prints. Vermeer was neither well known nor appreciated outside of his own town. There is little information that tells about his professional activities, and he made no self-portraits, so we do not even know what he looked like.

Johannes Reyniersz Vermeer was born in Delft in the Netherlands in October 1632 and lived there all of his life. He had a sister Gertruy who was twelve years older than he. Delft was a quiet, prosperous city with rows of neat houses built along crisscrossing canals. The family lived in one of Delft's small canal houses. Vermeer's mother, Digna Baltens, came from Antwerp in Flanders (now Belgium). His father Reynier Jansz, who adopted the name Vermeer, was a silk weaver. The year before his son was born, Reynier Jansz joined the Guild of Saint Luke, an association of artists, so that he could register as an art dealer. Ten years later he bought the Mechelen, a large building on Delft's Great Market Square in the center of town, which the family lived in and ran as an inn. Young Vermeer would have been able to look at paintings his father bought and sold and to meet artists. His father was deeply in debt when he died in 1652. His mother inherited the Mechelen.

Little is known about the boy's childhood. It is not known where he learned the techniques of his craft. It has been suggested that he was a pupil of the well-known painter Carel Fabritius, who had been a pupil of Rembrandt's. He must have served as an apprentice to a master artist since in 1653 he was admitted to the Guild of Saint Luke as a master painter. This permitted him to sell pictures by other artists as well as his own work. He seems to have been highly respected and recognized as an important artist in Delft, for he was twice elected as an officer of the Guild of Saint Luke and he supervised new decorations in the guild hall. When an art dealer was selling paintings that he attributed to famous artists, and there was a question about whether the pictures were authentic, Vermeer would be called to The Hague, the Dutch capital, to give a final opinion.

Shortly before he was admitted to the guild Vermeer married Catharina Bolnes, the daughter of a wealthy woman named Maria Thins. Vermeer's family was Protestant, the official religion recognized by the Dutch state. Maria Thins, who was Catholic, did not approve of her daughter's marriage to the young artist. He probably converted to Catholicism around this time. Fifteen children were born to the couple, but only eleven survived infancy. The names of just nine of these are known.

Vermeer and his family may have lived for a time in the Mechelen. He had a hard time supporting so many children. It is not known if he tried to sell the pictures that he painted; he may have painted mostly for his own pleasure and for a small circle of friends. And little is known about his relations with other artists. While other Dutch artists went to Italy to study and to paint the landscape, Vermeer stayed at home. Although he did not travel to learn from great masterworks of art, the paintings he and his father handled as art dealers surely influenced his own technique. Some of these pictures appear in backgrounds of his interior scenes.

Early in his career Vermeer painted biblical and mythological scenes, but most of his works are Dutch interiors with one or two people in them. Members of his family posed for him. The paintings represent quiet, thoughtful views of his own private world. An everyday activity is suspended in a moment in time: People are playing musical instruments, reading, or writing letters. The forms are firmly silhouetted and each object is precisely recorded, in an atmosphere of clear light and harmonious color. Vermeer's success in capturing light falling on a surface has never been equaled.

The artist was fascinated by optics, the effect of light on the way we see things. This interest in optics is not sur-

Vermeer at work in his studio. *Culver Pictures, Inc.*

prising. Christiaan Huygens, the scientist who improved the telescope and made important astronomical discoveries, and Anthony van Leeuwenhoek, the naturalist who perfected the microscope and studied the minute structure of matter, were both born in Holland around the same time as Vermeer. Geography must have been of interest to Vermeer as well, because he showed maps in accurate detail on the walls of the rooms in his paintings.

The artist always had money troubles, and his financial situation grew even worse when an economic depression hit the country as the result of war between Holland and France. His mother-in-law came to the rescue. By

Vermeer's *Girl Reading a Letter,* painted in 1657. *Art Resource/Gemaeldegalerie, Dresden.*

1660 Vermeer was living with his wife and children in Maria Thins's house. A room in the front of the house served as his studio. His mother-in-law helped support the family, and apparently the artist helped her run the household.

Vermeer died in 1675 at the age of forty-three and was buried in The Old Church in Delft. He left his widow deeply in debt, with eight of their children still minors. Most of his pictures went to his creditors for unpaid bills; the baker took two of them to satisfy a debt for bread. Twenty-six paintings were turned over to an art dealer in Amsterdam. Anthony van Leeuwenhoek was appointed trustee to administer Vermeer's estate. Catharina Vermeer was forced to declare herself bankrupt.

Vermeer's work went more or less unnoticed after his death. In 1804 an art gallery in The Hague purchased *View of Delft*, but the artist was nearly forgotten for almost two hundred years. (See reproduction in the color section of this book.) Pictures painted by Vermeer were even said to be by better-known artists so they would be considered more valuable. Then in the mid-nineteenth century, a French journalist visiting Holland saw *View of Delft* in The Hague and was so impressed with it that he searched for all of Vermeer's other works. He wrote about the painter, praising his art, and people began to take notice.

In fact Vermeer's reputation soared and he became so popular that artists began imitating his work and signing his name to their own paintings. The most famous forger was Hans van Meegeren, whose court trial in 1945 caused a sensation. Van Meegeren had sold a so-called Vermeer to the prominent Nazi Hermann Göring, Adolf Hitler's field marshal. The Dutch people objected to the sale because the Germans had been at war with Holland. By then Vermeer's works had become so highly esteemed by the Dutch that Van Meegeren was accused of being disloyal by selling a national treasure. To prove that he had not betrayed his country, he had to admit that he had forged the painting. Today, the few authentic Vermeers that exist are considered the finest Dutch paintings of their kind.

James McNeill Whistler

1834–1903   American artist who lived in London and painted the famous portrait known as "Whistler's Mother"

James McNeill Whistler was a talented artist and colorful character, so eccentric and witty that his personality is as well known as his art. An American, he was born James Abbott Whistler in Lowell, Massachusetts, on July 11, 1834, but spent most of his life in Europe. His father, Major George Washington Whistler, a graduate of West Point, was a civil engineer who specialized in building railroads. His mother, Anna Matilda McNeill, whose simplicity and quiet dignity are revealed in the portrait known the world over as "Whistler's Mother," was a strict, religious woman from a Scottish family that had settled in North Carolina. His paternal grandfather had come to America with the British army during the Revolutionary War. When the war was over he married in England and sailed back to America to settle in Maryland and become a major in the United States Army.

Jimmy, as Whistler was called, had two younger brothers, William and Charles, and a half brother and sister, George and Deborah, from their father's first marriage. Major Whistler's work took him around New England, so the family moved about. Then in 1842 Czar Nicholas I invited him to supervise the building of a railroad that would run from Saint Petersburg to Moscow, so he set off for Russia. The family followed, but it was a long, hard journey and, sadly, Charles died en route.

The beautiful czarist capital of Saint Petersburg was an interesting place to

James McNeill Whistler and his youngest brother, Willie (*seated*), painted in Europe in the mid-1840s. *The Library of Congress, Washington, D.C. Pennell Collection.*

live, and the experience had a lifelong influence on Jimmy, who was nine years old. Although most of the family's friends were other Americans working with the railroad, the boy had a chance to be around Russian nobles in the czar's court. He observed their actions and absorbed some of their sophisticated culture. He learned to speak fluent French, attended dancing school, and enjoyed ice-skating on the river.

The family had several servants, including an Irish maid who had come with them, a governess for the boys, and a Swedish tutor. When Jimmy was ten his parents enrolled him in a drawing course at the Imperial Academy in Saint Petersburg because he had shown an intense interest in drawing from the time he was four.

In the summer of 1847 Mrs. Whistler took the children to England to visit cousins. There Deborah met Francis Seymour Haden, a young physician, and they were married in October. After the wedding the family returned to Saint Petersburg, and the following summer they went to England again. Jimmy, whose health was fragile, suffered in severely cold weather, and a cholera epidemic was raging in Saint Petersburg; so in the fall when the mother went back to Russia she left him with Deborah and her husband. Dr. Haden encouraged his young brother-in-law in his art, even though his parents never wanted him to become an artist. Haden was intensely interested in collecting and producing etchings, prints created by scratching a picture on a copper plate. He got the boy interested in etchings, too, and together they pored over prints by Rembrandt.

That winter Major Whistler fell ill from cholera and died in the spring of

1849. His wife returned to America by way of London and settled with her sons on a farm in Pomfret, Connecticut, where the boys attended a school headed by an Episcopal clergyman, who was a West Point graduate. During the two years Whistler was a student at the school, he did little that was noteworthy except to draw, producing portraits of his friends and scenes of local events.

In 1851 he managed to get into West Point, then under the command of Colonel Robert E. Lee, who went on to become leader of the Confederate army during the Civil War. While there he changed his middle name from Abbott to McNeill, his mother's maiden name. At West Point he was at the top of his drawing class, which was taught by the distinguished teacher Robert W. Weir; however, he was at the bottom of his chemistry and philosophy classes. Furthermore he could not learn to ride a horse, an important requirement for the military, and he got into fights and disobeyed rules. In June 1854 he was dismissed with over two hundred demerits against him, and his military career came to an end.

In November he went to work for the United States Coast and Geodetic Survey in Washington, D.C., making official government maps. The work was highly technical, and to relieve his boredom Whistler would make little sketches on the official maps. He was always late for work or he would not show up at all. He lasted only a few months on the job until February 1855. However, he received excellent training in etching and the experience helped him to become a brilliant master in this craft, which he would practice with great success for the rest of his life.

While living in Washington Whistler enjoyed a busy social life. He rented a studio where he painted a few portraits, but he longed to study in Paris, the art center of the world. He was able to convince his mother to let him go and to provide him with a small allowance, and that summer he set off for Europe. He never again returned to the United States, although he always considered himself an American.

On his way to France he stopped in London to visit Deborah and her husband. In Paris, he immediately began living the free and easygoing life of a bohemian, making no attempt to conform to the usual restrictions of society. He was slender, short, and had a full head of dark curly hair and a mustache. He liked to attract attention and wore a white suit and a broad-brimmed straw hat with dangling ribbons. In later years he would stroll about in a frock coat and top hat, sporting a monocle on one eye, and swinging a tall cane. The artist

Edgar Degas, who was conservative in dress, once told Whistler that he looked ridiculous.

The young American spent two years apprenticing in the studio of the painter Charles Gabriel Gleyre, but again he was absent much of the time. During his student days he stayed out late every night. He was always reckless with money so he was constantly broke.

In 1857 he went to Manchester, England, to see an exhibition of the Old Master paintings. Among them were Dutch paintings and etchings and fourteen works by the Spanish artist Diego de Velázquez, whom Whistler deeply admired. The following year he traveled around France and the Rhineland and produced his first set of twelve etchings from nature, called the *French Set*. Soon he got his own press and learned to print etchings himself.

In Paris Whistler's friends were avant-garde artists and writers, talented young men with advanced ideas who experimented in new ways of expressing themselves. Among them were the French poet Charles-Pierre Baudelaire and the painters Alphonse Legros and Henri Fantin-Latour. The three artists—Whistler, Fantin, and Legros—who called themselves the Société des Trois, enjoyed one another's company, sitting in a café and talking late into the evening. Fantin introduced his American friend to the artist Gustave Courbet, whose realist style Whistler deeply admired. He also met Edouard Manet, with whom he would later spend a good deal of time.

Courbet encouraged the young men to paint subjects from modern life, not history. All the while, Whistler was developing an original style of his own that would have an effect on the new direction in art that would take place in the late nineteenth century and lead to twentieth-century Modernism.

One of his best works from this period, called *At the Piano*, is a painting done in 1858, a portrait of his half sister Lady Seymour (Deborah Haden) and her daughter Annie. It is a lovely picture, reflecting a quiet mood and showing the realist influence of Courbet. Although it was admired by other artists the jury of the official Salon in Paris turned it down for exhibition. Fantin, whose own paintings were also rejected by the Salon, arranged to have the painting exhibited in a studio along with other pictures that had been rejected. There it met with success.

In 1859 Whistler moved to London, but he would return to Paris to visit, and he corresponded with Fantin for years, until they drifted apart. In London he stayed with Deborah at first and then lived with a painter friend, continuing to lead a bohemian life. The fol-

Arrangement in Grey: Portrait of the Painter, a self-portrait of Whistler painted around 1872. *The Detroit Institute of Arts, Bequest of Henry Glover Stevens in memory of Ellen P. Stevens and Mary M. Stevens.*

Whistler's *Nocturne in Blue and Gold: Old Battersea Bridge,* painted between 1872 and 1875. *Art Resource/Tate Gallery, London.*

lowing year, *At the Piano* was exhibited at the Royal Academy in London and was bought by an English artist.

Whistler was fascinated by the scenes of life on the waterfront of the Thames River, which runs through London. He loved the river and found poetic beauty in the boats on the water, the great bridges, and the dingy warehouses lining the shore. To be near his subject he often stayed at an inn on the Thames below London Bridge, in the Wapping district. He painted pictures with misty outlines, capturing the atmosphere, and created some of his works in only two color tones. He was giving up the realistic style he had admired in Courbet and was developing simplicity and directness in his work.

This was the Victorian period in England, named after the long-reigning queen, when most painters created works that had a moral or told a story. Whistler, however, did not want his pictures to present a moral or tell a story. He wanted them to be admired for their beauty alone, strongly believing in art for art's sake. In time he influenced what came to be called the Aesthetic movement in art and literature, a trend that stressed pure beauty.

Whistler's paintings of the Thames were well received in London, and his work was admired by artists in Paris. In the summer of 1861 he went to France accompanied by Joanna Hiffernan, a redheaded Irish woman who was intelligent, loyal, and beautiful. Jo, as she was called, was his model and became his mistress for a period of ten years. She posed for his startling painting *The White Girl,* which was later called *Symphony in White No. 1,* in which she stands on a bearskin rug in a flowing white gown, holding a white flower against a white background, her long red hair hanging over her shoulder. (See reproduction in the color section of this book.) While in France she and the artist spent some time on the seacoast in Brittany and then went to the south of France and on to Spain.

Back in England Whistler submitted *The White Girl* to the Royal Academy in 1862, but it was rejected, so he exhibited it in a gallery. It received a bad notice in a publication and the artist wrote a letter of protest to the editor. This was the beginning of a lifelong habit of replying publicly to bad reviews and feuding with critics.

In London Whistler lived in rented rooms in the Chelsea district and enjoyed the company of a number of bohemian friends who often gathered at his home. Among them were young Englishmen whom he had met in Paris and several poet friends, including the painter Dante Gabriel Rossetti, who lived nearby. Rossetti was leader of the group known as the pre-Raphaelites, who were devoted to medieval culture. They expressed sentimental themes of life around them with the aim of creating pure beauty. Another friend was the poet Algernon Charles Swinburne, who was fascinated by *The White Girl*, especially the sad dreamy quality of the model, and wrote a lovely poem about it.

Whistler again submitted this painting to the Salon in 1863, and again it was turned down. However, an exhibi-tion called the Salon des Refusés had been established for works not accepted by the official Salon. When *The White Girl* was shown there in 1863 it was admired by artists, who found it exciting. The general public, however, laughed at it because it was so very different.

Rossetti and Whistler shared a passion for Oriental art, and they both collected blue-and-white porcelain plates, bowls, and other vessels. Whistler had been introduced to Oriental art in Paris where Japanese works displayed at the Universal Exposition made a great hit with French painters. On a trip to Amsterdam that he took with Haden in 1863, the year Whistler's etchings received a gold medal in The Hague, he bought blue-and-white porcelain imported by the Dutch. After their return from Holland both men produced etchings with views of Amsterdam.

In 1863 America was in the midst of the Civil War, and the artist's mother came to London to live. At first she stayed with the Hadens, but then her son took a house so they could live together. The arrangement would last for twelve years, until her health began failing.

Whistler decorated their home with Japanese prints and screens and Chinese porcelains. He was so enthusiastic about things Japanese that he posed for a picture wearing a kimono and shaped his initials into the form of a butterfly, using this symbol as his signature. He began to paint pictures with a Japanese theme, dressing his models in Japanese costumes and including screens, fans, and porcelains in the compositions. At the same time, he was developing a rapid, flowing manner of painting, applying the colors in broad sweeps with swift strokes. He wanted to create a quickly passing impression with changing effects of light and atmosphere. One of his finest works from this period is *Rose and Silver: The Princess from the Land of Porcelain,* a portrait of the daughter of the Greek consul general in London. The consul general, however, did not like it and refused to pay for it.

In 1865, when the Civil War was coming to an end, Whistler's brother William, who had become a physician and served as a medical officer in Lee's Confederate army, arrived in England. Their mother was having serious problems with her eyesight so the brothers took her to Koblenz, Germany, to see a doctor. Afterward the artist traveled around France.

Just after he returned to London, early in 1866, he unexpectedly left for South America. The people of Chile were struggling for independence from Spain, and Whistler, like some other young men in England, wanted to help them. He stayed for nine months in Valparaiso, and while aboard a ship in the harbor, he got the idea of painting night scenes.

In 1867 he and Haden were in Paris at the same time. The brothers-in-law had been working together over the years, but professional rivalry was developing because Haden's etchings were highly praised by critics and Whistler's were not always noticed. Also, Haden did not approve of Whistler's life-style and forbade his wife to visit his home. The rivalry grew so bitter that a fight broke out between the two men in a Paris restaurant. Whistler pushed Haden through the glass window of the restaurant and they never spoke again.

In London the artist had begun creating views of the Thames at sunset, dusk, and night. At first he called them *Moonlights;* but later, for an 1872 exhibition, he gave them the title *Nocturnes,* a musical term used for a dreamy piano composition. He also renamed some of his pictures *Symphonies, Harmonies, Arrangements,* and with other musical terms. He felt that his pictures should harmonize with their surroundings and that they were meant to appeal to the eye as music appeals to the ear. He wanted them to be decorative and said his aim was to produce "an arrangement of line, form and color."

Arrangement in Grey and Black, No. 1: Portrait of the Painter's Mother, Whistler's famous portrait of his mother in 1872. *Giraudon/Art Resource/The Louvre, Paris.*

This was true even of his portraits. The most famous of these is *Arrangement in Grey and Black, No. 1, a Portrait of the Painter's Mother.* The artist had a great gift for choosing a pose that suited the sitter and for arranging the clothing and background into a decorative scheme. He tried to create a total image, linking the sitter with the outside world and at the same time reflecting the subject's inner life. In the portrait his mother looks solid and per-

manent, and her purity as well as her son's tenderness toward her are revealed. Whistler sent the picture to the Royal Academy in 1872. At first it was refused for exhibition then accepted only after pressure was exerted. That was the last time he sent anything to the Royal Academy, and he was never invited to become a member.

In June 1874 he had his first one-man exhibition, in London. Whistler was a decorator as well as an artist, and to show his works at their best and connect them with their setting in a harmonious arrangement, he designed the interior of the galleries himself. After he had painted portraits of Frederick R. Leyland, a wealthy Englishman who owned a steamship line, his wife, and his four children, Leyland asked the artist to help decorate the family's home near Liverpool.

In 1876 Leyland bought an elegant new house in the Prince's Gate in London and hired Thomas Jeckyll to design and decorate the dining room to display his collection of blue-and-white porcelain. Leyland now owned Whistler's portrait *Rose and Silver: The Princess from the Land of Porcelain,* and he wanted it to hang over the marble fireplace. He called in Whistler for his advice in the design, and when the artist examined the room, he decided that the red flowers on the Spanish leather walls and the red border on the rug did not harmonize with his painting. Leyland gave him permission to paint the flowers on the wall yellow and gold, and Whistler proceeded with the work while the Leylands were traveling.

Whistler completely changed the interior, however, without the owner's consent, painting over the precious leather walls in shades of turquoise and adding large gold and blue peacocks. He went so far as to hold a reception in the room, in February 1877. He invited the press, and even issued a pamphlet entitled *Harmony in Blue and Gold: The Peacock Room.* The decoration was highly publicized, and rumors spread that the artist had done the work with a paintbrush fastened to a fishing rod as he lay in a hammock.

Leyland was furious and offended by the publicity over "The Peacock Room." The artist had charged the cost of gold leaf to Leyland and run up a large bill. Matters got worse when Whistler demanded four times as much money as had been agreed on. The two men quarreled, Whistler was forbidden to enter the house, and their friendship ended. Jeckyll, who suffered from a mental illness, was so disappointed over the change in his design that he had a nervous breakdown and was confined to an institution.

Whistler also quarreled with the respected art critic John Ruskin. That same year some of the artist's paintings were exhibited at the opening of the Grosvenor Gallery and Ruskin gave them a bad review, accusing the artist of "flinging a pot of paint in the face of the public," referring to the painting *The Falling Rocket.* Whistler was angry and sued Ruskin for libel. Ruskin lost the case when it was tried in 1878, but the judges made him pay only a single farthing (less than a penny). Instead of spending the coin Whistler wore it on a watch chain for the rest of his life as a symbol of his victory.

Unfortunately the artist had to pay half the court costs and ended up bankrupt after the trial. He had to sell his house that the architect E. W. Godwin had designed for him and auction off some of his blue-and-white porcelains, and he went to stay with his brother William.

Whistler had always wanted to go to Venice and was able to do so in 1879 by getting a commission to make some etchings there. He was joined in Italy by a young Englishwoman named Maud Franklin, who had replaced Jo as his model and mistress in 1870. Maud had a baby girl by Whistler, who already had another child, a little boy whom Jo took care of even though she was not the mother. The artist did not treat either woman well, nor did he pay much attention to his children.

Whistler stayed fourteen months in Venice, making friends with some American artists, borrowing money to survive. He studied paintings by Venetian masters and produced numerous scenes of the city in various media. Even though he was poor, he returned to London in style, sporting his long cane and holding a little white dog on a ribbon leash. At first he stayed with his brother, who was newly married. A dozen Venice etchings appeared in a series *First Venice Set* exhibited at the Fine Arts Society in London in December 1880.

The following year Whistler's mother died; it was a great loss to him. The artist sent her portrait to the United States for exhibition at the Pennsylvania Academy of Art in Philadelphia. He had hoped that it would be sold and remain in America. However, even though Americans had begun taking notice of his works, they never sold well in exhibitions. He also sent the portrait of his mother to the Salon in Paris in 1883. It won a medal and in time was bought by the French government. It is now in the Musée du Louvre in Paris.

Whistler liked to have total control over the way a viewer saw his works. He selected special frames for the pictures, controlled the source of light, and used other techniques of exhibition design that were far ahead of their time. He even designed the posters and labels for the pictures, prepared the catalogs for exhibitions, and sent out invitations decorated with a butterfly. For an exhibition at the Fine Arts Society, mostly of Venetian scenes, the galleries were decorated in yellow and white, including the walls, floors, and seats. Yellow flowers were displayed in yellow pots. The doormen were dressed in yellow and white uniforms and the artist wore yellow socks. He even suggested to some of the guests that they dress in harmony with the color scheme, and he gave away yellow and white silk butterflies to certain guests.

Whistler also liked to decorate his home splendidly and give fine parties for prominent guests. His Sunday breakfasts were attended by the Boston art collector Isabella Stewart Gardner when she was in London and the brilliant, witty playwright Oscar Wilde, who shared an interest in Oriental art. Wilde, whom Whistler called Oscarino, was a generous and loyal friend, but the artist fell out with him. Although Whistler moved in a fashionable world he was not entirely accepted in society because of the way he lived.

And most of his relationships ended in disagreement. The Society of British Artists elected him a member in 1884 and president two years later, but by 1888 he had resigned because of what he felt was the Society's old-fashioned way of exhibiting pictures.

He liked to make his ideas about art known to all, and on the night of February 20, 1885, dressed in elegant evening clothes, he delivered a lecture at Prince's Hall. He called it the Ten O'clock Lecture, named for the hour, and had it published. His good friend the poet Stephane Mallarmé, whom the artist met in Paris through the Impressionist painter Claude Monet, translated it into French so it could be read in France as well as in England.

The artist's wide circle of friends included Beatrix Godwin, wife of the architect who designed Whistler's White House. Trixie, as she was called, was the daughter of an artist, and herself an amateur artist. Two years after her husband's death in 1886, Whistler, then fifty-four years old, married Trixie Godwin.

That summer the newlyweds went to France. Whistler had now won an international reputation and his paintings and etchings were generally selling well. The next year he had a one-man show in America and was knighted in France, receiving a medal of the Legion of Honor. His works won gold medals in Munich and at the World's Columbian Exhibition in Chicago. Still, he continued to quarrel with people. In 1890 he published *The Gentle Art of Making Enemies,* a collection of his letters to the press, and this led to further lawsuits.

One of the few friendships in the painter's life that lasted was formed in 1890 when he met Charles L. Freer, an American businessman. Freer already owned dozens of Whistler's prints and watercolors. He began visiting the artist's studio to see works in progress and get advice on his art collection.

Freer amassed the largest collection of Whistler's works in America, even acquiring the Leyland Peacock Room for his home in Detroit. Whistler encouraged Freer to buy Oriental art, saying the treasures would go well with his paintings.

Whistler and Trixie moved to Paris in 1892. Two years later Sir William Eden commissioned him to paint a small portrait of Lady Eden, but there was disagreement over the price and the artist refused to give up the picture. Sir William sued Whistler, and the case took three years to settle. Whistler was the winner. He published the incident in another of his books in 1899, calling it *Eden vs. Whistler: The Baronet and the Butterfly*. He designed the book himself using the simplest brown paper for binding and the butterfly emblem as a decorative motif.

Trixie fell ill with cancer in 1894, after only eight years of marriage, and the couple returned to London for medical help. During this painful period Whistler quarreled with his brother William over Trixie's illness and they broke off. The estrangement upset William for the rest of his life. When Trixie died in 1896 Whistler could not bear the anguish of losing her and he never recovered from the loss. He drifted about until two years later when he founded an art school in Paris to teach his ideas of creating perfect harmony through the form and arrangement of a picture. His own health was failing, however, and three years later he had to close the school.

The artist continued to receive honors. In 1898 he was elected president of a new group, the International Society of Sculptors, Painters, and Gravers, which showed the works of several French Impressionists when they held their first exhibition in London. In 1900 he was awarded a gold medal at the Universal Exposition in Paris.

That year he decided to go to a warm climate. He went to Algiers and Corsica, but he fell ill along the way. Then, in 1902, he sold his house in Paris and took one in London. His mother-in-law, Birnie Philip, and her daughter Rosalind came to look after him. That summer his friend Charles Freer traveled to Holland with him, but Whistler was so ill that a newspaper published his obituary. Of course, the painter replied with a letter.

He lived long enough to receive an honorary doctorate of law degree from Glasgow University in 1903, although he was unable to receive it in person. He died of a heart attack that year, on July 17. Ignoring his own children, he named Rosalind Philip his heir.

A memorial exhibition of Whistler's works was held in London, and he was acknowledged as a remarkable talent. Joseph and Elizabeth Pennell, whom the artist had chosen to write his biography, spent some time with him the last three years of his life, so he continued to receive publicity after his death just as he had in life.

Further Reading

History of Art for Young People by H. W. Janson and Anthony F. Janson (Harry N. Abrams, fourth edition 1992) gives an overall view of the history of art and helps to put each painter in context. *The Pantheon Story of American Art for Young People* by Arianne Ruskin Batterberry (Pantheon Books, 1976) and my own books *The Art of America in the Gilded Age* (1974), *The Art of America in the Early Twentieth Century* (1974), and *The Art of the Old West* (1971) all published by Macmillan, provide an overview of American painters.

For books on individual artists there are a number published by Abrams in their First Impressions series: *Mary Cassat* by Susan E. Meyer (1990), *Marc Chagall* (1990) and *Paul Gauguin* by Howard Greenfeld (1990), *Leonardo da Vinci* (1990) and *Michelanglo* (1993) by Richard McLanathan, *Claude Monet* by Susan E. Meyer (1991), *Pablo Picasso* by John Beardsley (1991), *Rembrandt* by Gary Schwartz (1992), and *James McNeill Whistler* by Avis Berman (1993). Another series, *Portraits of Women Artists* published by Little, Brown and Company, includes *Georgia O'Keeffe* (1991) and *Mary Cassatt* (1992) by Robyn Turner. *What Makes a Degas a Degas?* and *What Makes a Monet a Monet?* are two of the titles in the series by Richard Mühlberger (Metropolitan Museum of Art/Viking, 1993). *Inspirations: Stories about Women Artists* by Leslie Sills (Albert Whitman, 1989) has sections on O'Keeffe and Frida Kahlo, who was married to Diego Rivera.

A Weekend With series, published by Rizzoli International Publications, New York, offers *Rembrandt* by Pascal Bonafoux (1992), *Degas* by Rosabianca Skira-Venturi (1992), and *Picasso* by Florian Rodari (1991). But the young reader must be aware that these are fictional treatments of the subject, as is *I, Juan de Pareja* about Diego Velázquez's assistant by Elizabeth Borton de Treviño (Farrar, Straus and Giroux, 1965) and *Meet Edgar Degas* by Anne Newlands (Kids Can Press, Toronto, 1988) which describes a selection of his works.

Finally, there are two quite different books about Rivera: *Diego* by Jeanette Winter (Alfred A. Knopf, 1991) and *Diego Rivera, Artist of the People* by Anne E. Neimark (HarperCollins, New York, 1992).

Additional titles on individual artists include *Marc Chagall, Painter of Dreams* by Natalie S. Bober (The Jewish Publication Society, 1991), *Vincent van Gogh* by Eileen Lucus (Franklin Watts, 1991), *Introducing Picasso* by Juliet Heslewood (Little, Brown, 1993), and *The Princess and the Peacocks* (about James McNeill Whistler) by Linda Merrill and Sarah Ridley (Hyperion/Freer Gallery of Art, 1993).

It is my hope that reading this book and others will encourage young readers to look at original works of art whenever possible.

Index